Fatima's Good Fortune

JOANNE AND GERRY DRYANSKY

LARGE PRINT

Oxford

First published in Great Britain 2003
by
Hutchinson,
The Random House Group Ltd, 2004

Published in Large Print 2004 by ISIS Publishing Ltd,
7 Centremead, Osney Mead, Oxford OX2 0ES
by arrangement with
Hutchinson,
The Random House Group Ltd, 2004

Joanne and Gerry Dryansky have asserted their right
to be identified as the authors of this work

British Library Cataloguing in Publication Data
Dryansky, Joanne
    Fatima's good fortune. – Large print ed.
    1. Women domestics – France – Paris – Fiction
    2. Paris (France) – Fiction
    3. Large type books
    I. Title II. Dryansky, Gerry
    823.9'2 [F]

ISBN 0–7531–7181–3 (hb)
ISBN 0–7531–7182–1 (pb)

Printed and bound by Antony Rowe, Chippenham

For André and Larisa Dryansky,
our other creations

With special thanks to Lynn Nesbit and Cecile Barendsma, wavers of magic wands; and to Youssef ben Amara, Lucienne Blanchard, Nicole and Michel Robert, Isabelle Pierre, and Yann Chichizola, for their hospitality.

In the same rivers we step and do not step.
We are and we are not.

—Heraclitus

Prologue

It was the twenty-seventh of August, and rain had been falling on Paris for several days on end. As if in winter, the Eiffel Tower was amputated above the hips by fog. The swollen Seine was splashing the boots of the stone Zouave below le Pont de l'Alma and covering the gangways of the rising houseboats. In the blurred city, on streets that smelled of wood fires lit in yellow-windowed living rooms, the cobbles were all that glistened. But if you looked out of a maid's room, on the sixth floor somewhere, you could see fading perspectives of tin roofs slick as glass, mottled where water overflowed their gutters. Below, drainpipe caps leaked in bursts and splashed the shoes of passersby, hunched under umbrellas.

An attractive young person in a light summer dress stood now holding a furled umbrella in the doorway of the Café Jean Valjean, staring at the downpour. She was Rachida, a dark, Tunisian-born woman in her mid-thirties with quick, fine hands and long limbs. She had walked in from 34bis avenue Victor-Hugo, right next door, to deposit the empty cup and saucer of the espresso she'd earlier taken out for her employer, the Countess Poulais du Roc. There was no sign now of a letup in the rain and she had the rest of her errand to accomplish. With a faint sigh of resignation, she stepped out of the protection of the doorway, seized the wicker shopping basket she'd parked there, unfurled her umbrella and set forth.

The traffic was horrendous. Somehow, rain in the city is the only thing that will slow a French driver; he or she will blithely, blindly drive at 180 kilometers an hour on a super-highway through impenetrable fog, but a touch of heavy rain can bring Paris traffic to a near standstill. You might say that this does not correspond to the French attachment to what is reasonable. It is simply the case.

The cars crawled and stalled along the avenue Victor-Hugo. Horns were blowing loudly, as if making noise could bully out of your way not only the cars in front of you but also the rain itself. Water pulsed through Rachida's sandals, conceived for walking on sand, as she strode in her elegantly rhythmic way. She held high the wide golfer's umbrella, a useful gift to the Countess Poulais du Roc from the middle-aged bachelor who was the Countess's nephew, Didi. Didi golfed a lot and also sailed, shot animals and chased them on horseback in the woods of Rambouillet. These were the things he was brought up to do. Rachida recalled that Didi had once glanced at her, as she'd stooped to pour tea, with eyes that shone as if he'd spied a deer bolting out of underbrush. But when she'd looked back at him directly, assuming the compliment — a reflex of her vigorous character — he turned away and reached for a slice of the butter cake she'd laid out. He and she were in the same place physically, perhaps in more than one sense, but they were also socially on separate planets. Rachida was the Countess's maid.

Rain dripped from her umbrella as she made her way back from the covered market in the rue Saint-Didier. Behind her she trailed the shopping wagon, whose canvas top now sheltered a dressed rabbit, a small jar of rabbit blood and a plastic jug full of water. She had gotten the rabbit and its blood from Monsieur Vermeersch, the farmer who had just reopened his stall in the marketplace after his six-week summer absence. And she had gone on to fill the jug at the artesian well that stood, since time immemorial, in the Square Lamartine nearby. The Countess had drunk the water from that famous *pompe* as a child, and like other stalwarts of *Seizième Arrondissement* traditions, she would continue to drink it despite all the money huge international corporations spent on advertising the bottled waters other people drank. The Countess detested advertising. It was, she said, like strangers coming up and speaking to you in a public place. Thoughts of the old woman's varied intolerance made Rachida look at her wristwatch. She hurried her step.

At that moment, Monsieur Robert, a small, fragile man in his sixties, petulantly opened his umbrella onto the rain from the doorway of 34bis avenue Victor-Hugo, on his way to give a piano lesson to a lycée student in the rue de la Tour. As he stepped onto the sidewalk, he was disturbed. The drainpipe of the building was not gurgling. Which meant that rain was accumulating on the roof.

Monsieur Robert, during a routine inspection, had discovered that a portion of the drainpipe was cracked near the skylight that illuminated the main hall. He had put off dealing with the problem until the September meeting of the co-owners rather than repairing it immediately. Monsieur Robert had told himself that there was no reason to expect heavy rain at the end of August. Moreover, every tradition-honoring artisan — and everyone knew that conservatism was a guarantee of honesty in an artisan — was away for the annual August locking-up of small businesses. What chance would there be of having a decent repair job done without getting scalped? Monsieur Robert would not take the responsibility. Monsieur Robert was the chairman of the co-owners' association of 34bis avenue Victor-Hugo, a post to which he was elected because, being more or less retired from teaching music, he was the one who had the time for it. His proactive thriftiness fitted him equally for the role. For example, Monsieur Robert had recorded in three trials that it took only thirty-five seconds to walk from the front door to the elevator, ride it to the fifth floor and arrive at the door of the highest apartment in the building, that of Countess Poulais du Roc. Consequently, he was able to propose a motion to the co-owners that the timing of the *minuterie* — the hall light people pressed when entering the building at night — be reduced to fifty-two seconds, instead of the eponymous minute. This would give the Countess seventeen seconds to

4

turn her key before the hall returned to darkness, which, notwithstanding her age, was a reasonable delay. In an emergency, she could always press the fifty-two-second *minuterie* again. The savings in electricity had been voted by the co-owners, with only the Countess opposed.

As for the roof problem, Monsieur Robert was convinced that his decision to put off repairs for a vote based on three competitive estimates rather than handle it under his emergency powers was prudent and based on sound reasoning.

Monsieur Robert had no exceptional accomplishments to boast of in a life that no longer held out any possibility of inspiring events, but he was proud of being French. His people had given the world the Age of Reason three centuries earlier, and in the face of all of history's tumult ever since, they had assumed the duty to civilization of trying to perpetuate it. One of the worst admonishments a mother may give a child in France is "you are not *raisonnable*."

When it came to weather, God appeared to have indeed given France, which the Germans consider His Secondary Residence, a reasonable climate. After a few torrid afternoons at the beginning of the month, known as *un temps orageux* because of the refreshing short downpours they provoke at evening, August in Paris is expected to move in a suave, imperceptible pace toward fall.

Reason should tell us, however, that between what is expected and what will happen, there often falls a shadow, as it fell now on Paris.

Rachida had only to get a cake, and then she could hurry out of the downpour to 34bis avenue Victor-Hugo. Béchu, the bakery the Countess favored when she was not making her own cakes, was, of course, still closed for the month. There was no other *boulangerie* or *patisserie* in walking distance. Suddenly Rachida remembered that a couple of women who were fashionable residents of the quarter had just opened an English-style tearoom and pie shop in the rue Mesnil. The tarts they put in their windows looked heavy and crude, perhaps deliberately so, to argue for being home-baked. The Countess might not go for that sort of argument. She preferred honest professionalism. But it seemed to Rachida that there was no choice.

She stepped off the curb near the kiosk opposite Béchu, about to head for the rue Mesnil. The light had turned red, but just then a woman in a little Smart, fed up with the traffic and with whomever was annoying her in her mobile phone conversation, swung out from behind the car ahead of her at the light and sped through the intersection.

Rachida shrieked, as the car seemed to head right for her, as if only killing her could bring some relief to the woman's frustration. The woman braked. Just short of Rachida's feet, the short Smart, a high ostrich of a car, began to tremble.

"*Connasse!*" screamed the woman with streaked blonde hair. Rachida heard her mutter as well: "*Y'en a marre de ces arabes!*" And then the woman rolled her window up and began shouting into the mobile phone that had not left her hand during the whole event.

Rachida knocked on the window. The woman bolted her door. "*Raciste!*" said Rachida. And then, as the woman stepped on the gas: "*Salope du quartier!*" Which meant that the woman in the Smart was a typical spoiled young bitch of the privileged neighborhood, which she obviously was.

Cars honked, then twisted around Rachida. Rachida shuddered and walked away. In the rue Mesnil at La Tarte de Mamie she bought an apricot pie and headed quickly home. The woman who sold her the pie had the same carefully streaked blonde hair as the woman in the Smart.

The incident came back to Rachida and wounded her again. "*Y'en a marre de ces arabes!*" Enough of these Arabs. As she stood shaking the umbrella in the stairwell of 34bis avenue Victor-Hugo, waiting for the elevator, it seemed to her that her whole life here had been a mistake. In bed at night, she would soothe herself with images of her bright, sultry native land to drive away all the frustration of a day in this stone city. She missed home — not in a reasoned way but because of the visceral compass that told everyone where home was. And hers was, in any case, regrettably beautiful. Thinking rationally and bottling emotion into determination, she had left Tunisia a year ago to remake her life as much in a new era as a new place. She'd seized whatever job she could, but now the job had become an emotional relationship that could never be a friendship. She'd been seduced by that highborn old Frenchwoman into an affectionate loyalty, a quality that helped her to value herself but kept her forever subjugated. She was in another way reliving everything she had hated between her and the husband she'd abandoned in Tunis. She had let herself fall into a trap. Yet her means to do otherwise had been so slender.

Rachida bit her lip.

On an upper floor, the elevator door clanged. Someone got out. She thought she recognized the stiletto heels of Madame Marchand, whom Hadley, Rachida's young American neighbor among the sixth-floor rooms, had nicknamed "the Romantic Pharmacist." She watched the old wooden-sided cage slide down on its cable. It looked, she realized, like a literal trap, even though the co-owners adored it and treated it like a pet, doing everything to make it appear the way it did the day the Société Roux Combaluzier installed it, in 1896.

The pet elevator came down. She could smell the turpentine in the wax that Carmen the concierge lavished weekly on the paneling. Carmen. *Another trapped woman.* Now there was nothing else to do but go inside and press "5." She turned her thoughts to the Countess's lunch. The shallots were peeled and sitting on the kitchen table, alongside the opened wine, waiting for the rabbit. *These people eat rabbits.*

The Countess, who loved to cook, would soon begin the *civet*, which she would finish by adding the blood. *And they consume blood.* Cooking was the one form of physical exercise the Countess's condition allowed her. She, who had ridden to hounds, had maintained a single-digit golf handicap into her fifties and had played tennis well enough to have once been an acceptable partner for René Lacoste in a sociable game of doubles. That was, as the Countess always put it, "in another era." Before the dashing Monsieur Lacoste became vastly rich, thanks to a crocodile, and the Countess became arthritic.

The thought crossed Rachida's mind now that the Countess's treacherous affection for her was based, perhaps more than a little, on a fellow feeling of disappointment. But then the harder thought to assume came to her: The Countess might surmise what disappointments Rachida felt, but they mattered little to her except as they might affect her work. They had not. The Countess enjoyed liking her, but that didn't mean she wanted to know all about her and in particular about her problems.

Rachida had a strong will and an independent temperament, which her will had deliberately bent to create Rachida the dependable. But Rachida the rebellious, who had run away from a disappointing husband, told herself that, all things said, she was better off now than she was before, and her story wasn't over yet. And so she slipped into her necessary persona of the moment once more, and worried again whether the phony "homemade" apricot pie would affront the Countess's taste and her sensibility.

But the quality of the pie would soon be irrelevant and the rabbit would never be stewed, because just then, after a rush of water as if a dam had burst, the skylight fell on Rachida's head.

ONE

CHAPTER
ONE

The sun shone intensely on the island of Djerba in Tunisia. The beige earth refracted heat with the dry odor of ripe fennel and thyme. Fatima slid open the window of a bedroom in the Club Rêve holiday camp, let out the stale overnight air tinged with the irrepressible, bitter, funereal presence of new concrete, and breathed in the spice of the waning season. Beyond the empty beach, the sea off the peninsula of El Oudiane still had the indigo hue of summer, but there were waves far out like patches of cotton that signified a change in nature. Fatima felt the gentle shift coming on as she looked out the window at the sea, for just a brief moment, before continuing with her work. Fatima, for all her sturdy build, her arms and hands that spoke of down-to-earth capabilities, was a person prone to vague dreams, someone who sensed things better than she could articulate them. If you took the time to look past her plainness, you'd note the quick response of her eyes — one green, one brown. The way worry, fear, delight, but never resentment could reveal themselves in such sharp focus. And you'd conclude that there was something in this simple presence that was what the French — in her second language — call *fin*. Fine. Her unusually smooth skin, her good white teeth, seemed a confirmation of that.

Nonetheless, there was no way to ignore that she was on first sight quite plain, had just turned forty, and had neither children nor a husband. So there was no question but that Fatima was the unluckiest woman in her village of Batouine.

She tugged the top sheet off the bed. A prophylactic fell onto the imitation Spanish-Arab tile floor. French people had made love in that bed.

A blurred recollection of lovemaking came over her. Her imagination protectively censored the crude, mechanical details she'd experienced, but now she could not, would not push back a memory of her husband, as once they held hands looking out at that sea together, before he boarded the ferry to get a cheaper flight in Tunis than the direct flight from Djerba to Paris. A short man like herself, small and hard: the arranged husband. Her cousin. Mahmoud the adventurer. Who pushed beyond the lot birth had assigned him. Not even his betrayal of her could keep her from admiring that in him. Not even his insensitivity to a woman's intimate nature — a way of being that was also part of what he'd been born into. That bright day at the pier was ten years ago. He was forty-five, half-bald, and she was thirty, already a bit plump, already resigned to the shameful lot of spinsterhood, having a widowed mother, no brothers, and no fortune to assure her a husband. He'd just lost his wife, her cousin, to a slow cancer, during which the wife, Nour, had made him vow to do something good

14

by marrying Fatima after she was gone. Her motivations were unclear to Fatima. The thought occurred to Fatima at times that Nour did not want Mahmoud to have a second wife more appealing than herself. Such was the self-esteem in which Fatima held herself. It was that lack of a sense of her worth that made her step docilely, led by her mother, into the marriage with Mahmoud, whom, she felt, was fundamentally a gentle and kind soul. She liked him. Loved? She had no clear notion of romantic love. In Batouine, a woman who rejected a marriage would be an outcast, if ever any woman of Batouine showed the courage to do so.

She would think of that moment in the port — the warm abrasiveness of his thick, callused hand holding hers, the very differentness of his hand perhaps already foreboding a gap between them — she would think of that moment uncontrollably, in all the time since he'd divorced her, whenever she envisaged the confrontation that she still resolutely planned. And she could not help but think of all that with regret, because it amounted to the one thing she had to be fond of. Belonging to someone. Which meant belonging in her world. In the world she'd lived in, a grown woman without a husband was more unfortunate even than a woman without a child. And she was both. The life she'd had being married to him was no idyll. But it had had stasis if nothing better. The world had not been swirling under her feet. She had her fixed place. Her arranged marriage was no less romantic than all the others in Batouine. Mahmoud's leaving and then divorcing her had knocked her all off-balance. And she'd lived in that precarious state of mind until her mother died.

Weeks after she'd buried her mother, when she had the courage to put away the old woman's belongings, she scrubbed the house clean. It did not mitigate her grief to realize that death had freed her of a charge, but the realization came over her all the same. She no longer had her mother to help support nor her mother's honor to care for in the eyes of the village. Her loss brought her an emptiness that was also an opening. It was at that moment that she'd run the whole brief life she'd had with Mahmoud over and over in her mind and concluded that for her, there was no closure: She was going to confront him. She would not let herself go on forever as someone dismissed by a divorce in the mail, no matter what a conniving holy man might have worked out for her husband. Fatima of Batouine would go all the way to Sheboygan, Wisconsin, just as Mahmoud of Batouine had, to confront him. Face him. Let him know that she wasn't chattel you could buy and get rid of at will. And the upshot of that confrontation? She honestly couldn't say what she wanted of him beyond that satisfaction. She would have to see him to know for sure.

She began saving money daily to do so, what little she could save. He was an adventurer, that was his nature, she could understand that about him. But her nature was determination. She remembered her co-worker Ahmed reading her his last letter:

"Alison and I have not married. We are living in a free country and each of us wishes to be totally free. I do not think I shall marry again. What need is there?"

She wondered whether this free Alison had changed Mahmoud's intimate ways. And whether she meant to bear his child.

So long as he was not married to her, Fatima felt she still had the perfect right to confront him. Sometimes she told herself that her object had to be to bring him back, that the repudiation he'd sent by mail from Morocco meant nothing. She would bring him back. They would have a child. He could find work now with all the building on the island. All this seemed possible for a woman of her determination. It was also possible that deep in her determined heart the one thing she really wanted unequivocally was simply to confront the man who had knocked her life off-balance.

That day in the port was this time of year, the end of what was known then as the second "season of the men." Men. The "season of the men." For a long time, there had been only one season of the men, when the husbands came back after Ramadan from their grocery shops in Tunis to be with their wives for a few weeks of the year. This was a practice that went back as far as anyone could remember, as far back as men of Djerba owned and ran the grocery stores of Tunis. They would go off as clerks and eventually become partners in their stores. Partners could spend a whole year at home, alternating these sabbaticals, year by year, with their other partner, who would come home only for the post-Ramadan break. The second season of the men came about when other men of the island began emigrating to France, to work in construction. They would come home for August, when building stopped in France for the great French holiday hiatus.

Between the seasons of the men, the women lived among themselves and with the children conceived during those annual renewed honeymoons. Weeks before, they would groom themselves for the homecoming. They would henna their hair and palms, spend hours in the *hamman* scraping and massaging one another's bodies over and over, rubbing in oil of jasmine and essence of orange flowers. They would splash their faces with rose water and make each other's eyes up with kohl. Among the women of Djerba, the weeks before the season of the men were a time of stomach-fluttering excitement and optimism about life.

Fatima had known one season when Mahmoud came back for the month of August, home from his job on a building site at the Charles de Gaulle Airport. The season had not given her a child. Mahmoud had prepared himself by eating dozens of oysters. He came home with hepatitis and was sick for the whole month.

There was no way for Fatima to deny that in the village of Batouine on the lovely island of Djerba, she passed for the unluckiest person. A childless woman born on a Friday. "An empty nut." The child of a mother who herself had had the ill luck of bearing only two daughters. She had one green eye and one brown eye and she was plump and short. And poor, poor even by comparison with others in a poor village. Fatima was unlucky, but she bore her singular misfortune with such equanimity that people finally came to believe that somehow she was blessed. Women came to her for advice in domestic matters. Which she gave quite naturally, without undue reflection on her role, as if they were strangers asking for directions on the road. In Europe, people once believed that touching the deformation of a hunchback brought good luck. So it was, in a way, with Fatima, as if she were a magnet for ill fortune that could draw it away from others. She told storekeepers in distress what people wanted to buy, what brand of tomato paste, what make of television set would leave the shelves while other models would gather dust. She told mothers whose children seemed to have been born angry how to reason with them. She would draw a hairdo on a piece of paper that would regain the lust of a listless husband. She also had a certain understanding of herbs, knew which infusion would bring the milk back to nursing breasts that had gone dry, which eased swollen joints. She acquired the reputation of a sage, but no one saw fit to pay her for her services. Nothing had come of them to improve her own lot — nothing except for the ten-speed mountain bicycle that had added a rub-off of stardom to her reputation.

The bicycle had arrived one day at the club when a FedEx delivery truck pulled up. There were "oohs" and "ahs" as the driver opened a great box addressed to "Fatima, the maid." Inside was a bright blue Gary Fisher Big Sur model bicycle and a photograph signed "Love, Dawn, Rudolph and little Fatima." It was a picture of Dawn McConnor, the Hollywood actress, her husband, the director Rudolph van Leiden, and their newborn daughter. Fatima admired her plump, rosy namesake and smiled when she noticed that where there had been traces of a chicken neck on Dawn there was instead the gentle, faint beginning of a double chin.

Nine months earlier, when the cast and crew that was filming *Galactic Warfare* on Djerba had taken over the Club Rêve, Fatima had come upon the female lead, Dawn McConnor, weeping in her room. Her husband had sent an assistant to drive her to the set, but she would not go out the door.

Fatima had only to touch Dawn's pulsating shoulder as she wept to know what to tell her.

"Dawn," Fatima said, "you are too hard."

"What?" asked the actress, looking up at the cleaning woman, bright-eyed with curiosity through her tears. Nature had not made Dawn hard. She was a slight, fragile-featured, red-haired woman on the hazardous cusp of thirty-five.

The way Dawn would tell it later to her New Age friends in Los Angeles was "like suddenly I felt this warmth, engulfing me. Like these waves." Whatever she felt drove her into Fatima's arms. Fatima held her as if the world-renowned star was a child who'd had a bad dream.

Dawn McConnor had arrived at the Club Rêve with a truckload of equipment a generation ahead of the exercise machines in the club's gym. In charge of all the weights and machinery was one Juan, Ms. McConnor's personal trainer. His mission was to keep the star convincingly muscular as the field marshal of the army of Planet Zircon. Her career, as well as that of her husband the director, depended on their getting this movie right.

The trouble was that the more convincing Dawn was in the role of feisty Field Marshal Xuka, the further she changed physically from the woman Rudolph had married. As the filming progressed, their love affair, their marriage, began to shrivel.

The next day Juan's gym equipment went back into the truck. Juan fumed in impolite Mexican-Spanish until he was put on a plane. The filming went forward. Some earlier scenes were reshot. The critics who would love *Galactic Warfare* praised Dawn McConnor for what *Time* called the "tender subtlety" she brought to a role that other actors and another director would have turned into a stereotype.

At the time of the filming, Fatima had been content to get back and forth from Batouine to the Club Rêve on an old bike left behind by Mahmoud whose wheels wobbled as she pedaled. But there was no denying that once Ahmed, the eighteen-year-old handyman at the club, had taught her how to work the gears, "the Hollywood bike" — as it was known thereafter to all — improved her life.

Now she gingerly wrapped the condom in toilet paper and flushed it away in the toilet. She finished changing the sheets, vacuumed the bedroom, and scrubbed and mopped the bathroom, then put out new wrapped soap. She restored someone else's temporary environment of pleasure to an appropriate state of virginity, and now it was time for her to go home to her house in the village.

As she pointed her glamorous bicycle off the highway into the sand and gravel lanes of Batouine, Fatima could already see another bike leaning against the whitewashed wall of the house. A man was standing near the door. Now, closer, she recognized Ali the postman with a yellow paper in his hand. She let her famous bike fall to the ground and ran up to him.

Before she even asked Ali to read the telegram to her, she had already divined that in it was a confirmation that she was the unluckiest woman in Batouine.

The man whom Didi brought with him from the Préfecture de Police was not the sort of person the Countess Poulais du Roc would normally be thinking of receiving at her home. He had on one of the politicians' suits, with shoulders twice the size of his own, a little man in a cloth box that had the same blatantly false effect on the allure of his physique as a hairpiece would have had on his balding head. The Countess noticed that the trousers of Didi's Prince of Wales plaid suit were worn to a lighter color than his jacket. But who these days could spend respectable money at the rate that good tailors were asking? She herself had not been back to Givenchy in years, long before that billionaire new owner had brought in the clowns for designers. Her wardrobe closet, however, was still full of ball gowns cloaked in tissue paper.

"Everything is in order, *Madame la Comtesse*," the man assured, straightaway, as if he sensed her distrust or even her disdain.

"Would you like a whisky, Monsieur Durand? I always have one this time of day. In any case, I can use one."

Didi was already pouring drinks.

"A woman with a Tunisian passport and no French papers was unexplainably in the hallway at the time —" He took the glass from Didi and drank in the middle of his sentence, as if to demonstrate that he could use it — which is to say he merited it — as much as anyone could. This was not a particularly pleasant matter, but it was his duty to be here, where he knew he normally would not fit in. There is a principle in the conduct of affairs in France known as "sending back the elevator." The metaphor dates to the days when elevators in France could not be called down from where they'd been halted but had to be sent to the ground floor again by pushing a button outside the elevator door. French technology. Not long ago, an old schoolmate of Didi's had done an important favor for Monsieur Durand. His daughter had been slipped into the Lycée Henri Quatre to take the preparatory course for the Ecole Normale Supérieure. It would be fair to say that her entire future took an immensely favorable turn with that admission. He was sending back the elevator for Didi, returning a favor to the friend of his benefactor.

"I never thought about her having papers," the Countess said.

"Be of good conscience, Madame, social security payments are a scandal in this country. You would have had to add on nearly half her salary," Durand said. "And she would not at all have liked paying her share, as well as taxes."

Didi kept silent. He was doing what he had to do. Beyond family loyalty, which of course mattered to him immensely, he loved his old aunt. Finally he said, "You can't bring her back again. And it was in no way your fault."

"It was just an accident. No one's fault," Durand added.

"All the same, I have to do *something*," the Countess said. She knocked back her supermarket-brand scotch with determination.

"Everything is settled. You needn't worry," Durand said.

"Would you like a refill?" Didi asked him amiably. Durand shook his head. He drank pure malt at home. He was becoming very knowledgeable about spirits and wine. He presumed that for the Countess, scotch was scotch, it was something British and what could they know about nuances of taste? *These nobles in their narrow world. Their unpredictable snobbisms.* In addition, these people, not understanding money, when it came right down to it, liked to reassure themselves with quirky little economies. His uncle had been an accountant for a woman whose family had owned a sugar plantation in Martinique since the eighteenth century and a foundry in Lorraine. She would steam open the envelopes that came in the mail, turn them

24

inside out and reuse them, and she made her woman use the washing machine after eleven at night, when electricity rates went down. All this, while what she spent on just the hounds for the pack she ran at Rambouillet could have fed several families. Durand looked around the room, which seemed shabby to him, with its conglomeration of old pieces. He noticed a canvas strap sagging under the seat of a Louis Seize armchair covered with dog hair. As if Durand's glance had cued her, the dog, the Countess's ancient Labrador, Emma, strolled in from the hallway, rolling her hips, and began to sniff suspiciously at Monsieur Durand's zippered half-boots. The dog trailed a faintly unpleasant smell, resembling the odor of a cellar.

Durand hiked his trouser leg nervously and Emma's saliva wet his hairless leg above a low sock. Her teeth grazed his skin. Time, he thought, to get back in the literal elevator.

Durand slipped away from the dog gingerly and voiced a floral expression of good-bye to the Countess. Didi saw him to the door.

"*Merci, Durand,*" he said, making the man a gift of complicity, of the fraternal tinge of *entre-nous* in his calling him just by his last name. Didi had been in government, too, in the Ministry of Foreign Affairs on the Middle Eastern Desk, before he'd been encouraged to retire at fifty.

"No. I have to do *something*," the Countess insisted, the moment the door had closed on the stranger. "I don't feel it, but I know it. Brought up the way you were, you know it, too."

25

Didi put his hand on hers, reassuringly. It was settled.

She pulled her hand away. It was not. "There is a sister," she said.

The backpacks and valises with wheels of the departing members of the Club Rêve were piled neatly outside the doorway of the low reception building. Each item had a tag with the logo of the club on it, a mermaid holding a parasol. The voyagers were still inside, buying last-minute souvenirs with what was left of their beads, the monetary standard of the club, useless in the real world. They began to straggle out, keyed-up, chattering agitatedly in little groups. Fatima couldn't say whether they sounded happy to go home or distressed to end their holiday. This batch was composed of "seniors" from Dijon, as the one senior who'd tipped her, a gray, jovial restaurateur, had told her. He was the one who'd come with a young woman — one of his waitresses? The one who'd had use of the condom. They had all come to profit from the end-of-season rates and were quite different from the sleek, sporty, high-summer crowd.

Fatima stood alone near the luggage. Nervous. In a little while the bus to the airport drew up. As he tossed the bags into the compartment below the seats, Ahmed, the young handyman, looked her way a few times with regret. She was well liked by everyone at the club, she knew that. Monsieur Choukroun, the manager, had told her "we will miss you very much." He'd even given her a member's mermaid T-shirt, extra-large, which she'd politely tucked in her shoulder bag, even though she knew she'd never wear it.

"Three-eleven is still undone, Monsieur Choukroun. I'm very sorry. They're still asleep. I'm sorry to leave it."

"Mouna will see to it."

"She is very capable, Mouna," Fatima had said, with a tinge of guilt.

He'd reassured her again. "It's not your worry anymore."

"She's from Batouine. I know her parents."

Monsieur Choukroun had taken Fatima's hands in his. They'd looked into each other's eyes, and the loss that had provoked her leaving had seemed to express itself again in each of their looks. Monsieur Choukroun had wiped his eyes.

"You will make more money in Paris," he'd said. "What will you do," he'd joked, "with all the money you're going to make?"

"I intend to make a trip."

"To Mecca?" he'd bantered again.

She hadn't answered. It was not for him to know that the more money she made in Paris, the sooner she would get to Sheboygan, Wisconsin.

The members' luggage was all in place in the baggage compartment of the bus. Ahmed took Fatima's two loose, cheap bags of multicolored plastic and squeezed them in. He slammed the hatch shut and reached into the belt below his shirt where he'd been hiding something. He held out a package of *haloua*. She had a

27

lump in her throat as she thanked him in Arabic. And then he put his right hand on his heart as he looked at her.

"*Salaam aleichum, Fat'ma.*"

"Wait," she said.

She, too, had a surprise. She hurried to the other end of the parking lot and came back wheeling her bicycle.

"For you," she said.

"The Hollywood bike?"

His eyes shone. He swallowed hard.

"When I come back, you will let me ride it again."

"Come back, Fat'ma." He swallowed again and lowered his head.

"*Inshallah*, Ahmed, as God will have it," she said, and boarded the bus before he looked up.

As the bus pulled away, she could see from the window of her rear seat the amiable Monsieur Choukroun, his scalp shining in the sunlight from under the black hair he combed across it. Standing next to Ahmed, who had the bike already between his legs, Monsieur Choukroun waved professionally at the French and then gave a serious look in her direction. The bus turned out of the compound. Fatima reached in her shoulder bag for the sweet *haloua*, but then something told her to save it for when it would mean more to her.

"*Olé Olé Claude-Clo-Clo-Clo!*"

The old departing holiday-makers were singing children's songs about each other. They had arrived at the Club Rêve calling each other "*Monsieur*" and

28

"*Madame*," and now it was nicknames and "*tu*" instead of "*vous*." As promised in the club brochure, Djerba had rejuvenated them a little, loosened up their tight, urban lives. But they were no longer taking notice of the island as they sang and joked among themselves. Home seemed to be what was on their minds now.

At the back of the bus, Fatima took notice of her native island. She had lived on Djerba all her life, but in point of fact, she had rarely seen much of it beyond the village of Batouine and the Club Rêve. She had only gone places she needed to. And she'd never felt a need that was not banally practical. A few years ago, she had contracted conjunctivitis and that had brought her to the town of Sedouikech for several visits to an ophthalmologist. She was easily cured. *Hamdou'lah*, thank the Lord, a proclivity to illness was not, at least yet, part of her ill fortune.

Djerba la belle! How could anyone ever cease to thrill to the beauty of her island, despite all the clubs and hotels that had invaded the countryside since she'd driven in a taxi to the ferry with Mahmoud her husband. The regretful thought crossed her mind again that had he stayed on a few years more, he would have found the same work for those hands, so capable of constructing things, that he found in France.

As she sat apart, in her long, saffron-colored djellaba, a few rows back from the French, Fatima's eyes tasted the bright landscape that had defined her life as much as her dress. There was something that seemed elegantly ceremonious in the way the rows of palms, aligned like guardians, cast shade onto the thick, feathery barley at their feet. Something in the rhythmic twists of the old olive trees that complemented, like refrains in a song, the low roll of the tan fields. A woman dressed like her, but wearing a straw hat, crossed a field on a thin dirt path. The tall new buildings here and there notwithstanding, the lanes of Djerba could still bring to mind Bible days. The woman looked as right as a tree on the landscape.

Over there, in a gray country, Fatima might have to dress differently. Or not. She was not ready to squeeze into a pair of blue jeans like the young girls of Batouine these days. Monsieur Choukroun, however, had given her a nylon parka he wore when he went to France, along with the T-shirt.

At length the airport bus stopped in the fishing port of Aghir to pick up a handful of other French who'd been staying in hotels. Young people, traveling cheaply with heavy backpacks but unburdened by much else in life. A girl with a shaved head and hooped earrings had long, well-shaped legs protruding from her shorts. A good body is a blessing, no doubt about it. Rachida, Fatima recalled, had had a lovely body, good legs she may have shown too much.

The bus was stopped in front of the eighteenth-century Turkish fort. Black smoke. An old man was grilling sardines beside a table on the pier where nets were sprawled, and beyond, small felouks, their sails furled, were bobbing in the water. The wind was up. A change was coming on with the new moon.

The bus continued through Midoun, past the ancient olive groves and the oil factories imparting a thickness to the air. Past the bright poppies on the terraced gardens of the *menzels*, the white-walled plantations of Mahboubine. Past fig trees that sent their powdery sweet odor through the open windows of the bus. Orange, lemon, and apple trees with reddening fruit.

Tall hotels and apartment dwellings, built and partly built, announced the suburbs of El May. The driver kept looking at his watch as the traffic crawled in El May. The French began anxiously consulting their watches, too. Fatima did not have a watch. But there was nothing that looking at a watch could do about their arriving on time. She sat there, giving herself over to what time would create, now and later.

There was no one waiting at the El May bus stop. The driver was finally able to make up time outside the city. The road took them along the edge of the Jewish village of El Houani: a cluster of low houses around the walls of the tall, cream-colored synagogue with its twelve narrow windows representing the twelve tribes of its people. It had all been quickly repaired, so it was hard to imagine the horror that had taken place there not long ago when the bomb had killed those tourists. Fatima could not fathom how anyone could throw away his own life so as to destroy the lives of others and the way other people live peacefully. The Jews who worshiped there were people of the Book. She knew that, although, other than Monsieur Choukroun, she'd never known any of them personally. They believed in the same God, one and indivisible, that she believed in.

Believed in but did not understand. She could not understand the reason for so many heartrending events in the world and in her own life. What she had felt and those she loved had felt. And yet there were so many things to lift your heart in the world God had made. The beauty and the abundance. The bus passed the huge marketplace of Houmt Souk before the last leg of its trip. Fruits, vegetables, flowers, fabrics, shining pots, carpets, caged animals — God had provided that so many things would exist.

On the low, long road to the airport outside Houmt Souk, Fatima's spirits lifted. An undeniably pleasant excitement came over her. There was a reason for everything, and we all fitted into the reason. There was a reason for each thing. A reason that Mahmoud and Rachida were gone and a reason that she was going to board an airplane for the first time in her life.

CHAPTER
TWO

She hadn't counted on so many choices. After the train from the airport had dropped Fatima at the Gare du Nord she found herself in an anguishing labyrinth. Tunnels led in all directions. People hurried by, sometimes casting denigrating glances at her saffron djellaba and at her North African thin plastic luggage before ducking into stairwells. They all knew where they were going. This *métro*, this underground realm, was a casual part of their lives, and she was as lost and alien in it as if she'd been shipwrecked on some savage shore. The challenge kept her from feeling as tired as she ought to have felt, but she was definitely out of sorts. The charter plane had been delayed arriving and didn't leave until four in the morning at the Mellita airport, and she'd arrived when the sun was just dissolving the mist over Charles de Gaulle. The young customs guard had turned her bags inside out and kept her waiting a long time as he went through her belongings piece by piece. Now, she told herself, as she often had need to in the past, that she would survive, get where she had to go, do what she had to do. But she didn't yet know how. Suddenly she heard soothing music. A waltz prevailed over the clatter of a train. Farther down in the long tunnel, a man with rouged cheeks in a worn evening suit was playing a violin. Her mood sank again. He had something written on a piece of cardboard near his torn sneakers, and there were coins scattered in his violin case. He looked at her absently as he played, until he noticed that she gave him back a look of sympathy. His eyes became pathetic. She reached into the pocket of her djellaba, where the euros she'd bought were pinned into a handkerchief. His look became very hungry. As she unpinned the handkerchief she realized that she had no coins. Now the man would not leave off looking at her. She took out a five-euro note, threw it into his case and hurried on, so as to make the pain of separation from that money go by quickly. A lot of money, she thought, but maybe making her first expenditure in Paris that way would bring her good luck. Behind her back, the old violinist played more resolutely.

With her purse slung over her shoulder and a bag stuffed with her belongings in each hand, she kept walking — but where? Her face showed confusion as she halted where stairwells descended on each side. Below one stairwell, a train had stopped and a horde of people rushed up while others ran down to catch it before it moved on. A teenage girl with a backpack brushed past her. The crowd dissolved. She put down her luggage and sighed. Just as she heard the arrival of another train below, she felt a tap on her shoulder. She squeezed her purse close to her side and wheeled around. A very tall black woman, as stout as she was, blocked her passage. She was wearing a dress as strange here as hers — a boubou with huge palm leaves printed on it. Another bright cloth was wrapped around her head. Fatima looked up, confused, into the woman's face.

"*Qu'est-ce tu cherches, chérie?*" What are you looking for, dear?

Fatima hesitated, then handed the woman her little paper. The woman shook as she burst into a high-pitched laugh. "You're far, dear," she said. "Avenue Victor-Hugo?" And she laughed some more, a deeper, rich, hearty, good-natured laugh, regarding which the Parisians passing in the tunnel didn't even bother to show curiosity.

The woman rattled off directions, names of stations, a *correspondance*, whatever that was. She smiled, showing gold teeth, when she noticed, in Fatima's distressed face, that what she was saying was of no help to Fatima.

"You truly have come upon good fortune," she said, speaking in the beautiful nineteenth-century French that Africans are still taught in the former colonies.

Fatima saw no solution in all of this. She smiled thanks and began to head toward a stairwell. Any one would do. *Inshallah.* As God will have it. Somehow she'd end up in the right place.

"Your right path is on the opposite side, but it is your good fortune that I am employed in that same quarter, so that if you are in agreement you can conveniently come with me."

And so the two of them, the eloquent black woman in the boldly printed boubou and the shy, tan woman in the orange djellaba, rode side by side through the gray bowels of Paris. One outlandishly tall and the other quite short, and both very round. Some people smiled at the bizarre image they created together. Some white people, standing above them, showed tribal resentment, but most people deep in their own existence outside this temporary burial didn't even look at them, even when Victorine — for that, Fatima soon learned, was her name — a housemaid from Senegal, began to laugh again, spontaneously.

They came to the stop at Etoile and got out. This is where we part, Victorine said to Fatima, pointing her way into a tunnel different from the one she herself would head into. "Victor Hugo," she said. "It's the name of the stop."

Fatima looked at her plaintively. And Victorine sensed what was wrong. "Come with me to my stop," she said, "it's approximately the same thing for you."

They rode further on the number 6 line for two stops and stepped out together at Boissière, through a wind that made the stairwell doors flap back at them. They were on the avenue Kléber.

Leaves were blowing off the chestnut trees that lined the wide avenue. Cars passed in a thick stream. Looking left, Fatima could see the Eiffel Tower peering over the buildings. She had seen it before on postcards from former clients at the Club Rêve. And on one she had received herself, just one, years ago, from Mahmoud. The avenue went on in a straight line clogged with more traffic to where the cars were creeping in a circle, the Place du Trocadéro. Fatima looked at the gray buildings that lined each side alley. High walls of stone, high windows where, inside, people lived one above the other. Paris.

Victorine walked with Fatima across the street to the opposite corner of the rue Boissière and pointed her toward the Place Victor-Hugo at the end of the street, a few blocks down.

"I am obliged to direct myself the other way," she said. "Good luck."

Fatima put her right hand on her heart. When she turned a moment later, she heard Victorine giggle once again, across the avenue. A boy on rollerblades speeding out of the side alley of the avenue nearly hit Victorine just then. He swerved around her and kept skating, and she kept walking as if he didn't exist. All this was Paris, Fatima noted. And in Paris, this busy cosmopolis, she sensed it was possible to feel, during a twenty-minute *métro* trip, that the exotic person with whom she was sharing the ride was like someone she'd known all her life and at the same time someone she'd never see again. She felt a strange attractiveness in that. Something about that realization gave her a feeling or an illusion of freedom that she'd never known before.

At that moment, the Café Jean Valjean on the avenue Victor-Hugo had resumed its function as a cocoon for the handful of regulars. The peak time had passed, when the shrill radio proclamations would resonate over the promiscuous bustle at the zinc bar — that time of the street sweepers and businessmen and the office workers who, after their crushed rides on suburban trains, would reward themselves with an espresso and a croissant, smoke a cigarette, and hurry off to the computer. It had all ended as it did every weekday morning, in a quick dissolve. In a few hours would come the occasion for the noisy elbow-to-elbow lunches of various salads, *le plat du jour* of the Portuguese chef, Nelson, or *steak-frites*. Now, as always, during the muffled hours in between these crowded moments and afterward, the Café Jean Valjean seemed to exist out of time.

The Jean Valjean drew people who felt at home there, and there were not many of those in the quarter of the avenue Victor-Hugo. Its luxurious buildings were either inhabited by the wealthy or occupied by companies profiting from the neighborhood's prestige. Neither the business crowd nor the residents would see fit to hang out an entire morning or afternoon in a café.

Paris's cafés had become less and less the living rooms of the idle, the artistically removed, or the socially disconnected. But people like that continue to exist, and the few left in the neighborhood were able to gravitate toward an implicit welcome at the Jean Valjean. Monsieur and Madame Richard, who ran the place, were old-fashioned. They had come up from their native village in the Aveyron in 1962, right after their honeymoon, to take over the café, and they had kept it as it was ever since. Their conservatism, equally apparent in Monsieur Richard's daily white shirt and necktie and Madame Richard's knit suits, was something innate that they shared. They hadn't touched the plastic décor and its elements of neon that had been installed right before they took over. It looked, for café people, reassuringly like a real café. Cafés all over Paris were being *relookés* — given new, upscale, hard-edge restaurant images, but not the Jean Valjean. Monsieur and Madame Richard had lost a lot of their lunch business when L'Ecrivain, directly across the avenue, had been *relooké* in minimalist gray and black, but the Jean Valjean still had an important commercial advantage: the local license for selling tobacco and lottery tickets. And those among the young office people who could tell the difference between the prepared food that arrived vacuum-wrapped in plastic across the street, as it did in so many cafés these days, and Nelson's sincere cooking, still kept eating at the Jean Valjean.

At the bar now, Hippolyte Suget, the night clerk at the Villa Saint Valentin, a small hotel specializing in discreet encounters, serenely sipped his morning glass of Côte du Rhone. He was a man in his forties, slender, but well built thanks to the weight set that occupied a good part of the room he lived in across the Seine in the Fifteenth Arrondissement, with his parrot Cacahouète. He had a narrow, sensitive but sad face crowned with a thick, romantic mane of pepper-and-salt hair. He took good care of his appearance, wore neat trousers and always a blazer, because there was an indelible history of elegance in his past. And because his appearance, he knew, was important in holding down his job. For a man in need of mending another part of his past, a job was in no way to be taken for granted. Hippolyte Suget had just accomplished another night-through of being diligently awake at the Villa Saint Valentin, during which nothing particular had happened, which is to say nothing had gone wrong, except, perhaps, for the immodest amount of intimate noises escaping from the room named "*Eglantine*." (At the Villa Saint Valentin, the rooms were not numbered but bore, instead, the names of flowers.) Management would be happy to know that he had sold "*Eglantine*" a tray of champagne and cod's eggs dubbed caviar and two other trays to the rooms "*Chèvrefeuille*" and "*Pivoine*." He sipped his wine with faint satisfaction.

Behind him, Clément, a corpulent computer engineer of forty, whose former employer's Internet business had failed, was shaking the pinball machine with his belly, his arms, and hips, creating the only bit of agitation in the room. The young man whose name no one knew lifted one eyebrow in mild irritation. He was some kind of scholar or poet who had drifted into the Jean Valjean about a year ago, and although he spoke to no one and no one spoke to him, he had become a regular by the sheer dint of his daily presence. He was an unkempt, dark-haired person still in his twenties, frail under the stained U.S. Army raincoat he wore in all weather. Sometimes while he scribbled notes over his *grand'crème*, coffee with milk, his hand would shake, and he would sometimes scatter crumbs eating his chocolate bun. Madame Richard had concluded, with sympathy, that he was probably on some kind of neuroleptic medicine that gave him these side effects. But he was never a problem, never unpleasant to anyone. He just kept to his coffee, his

40

bun, and his notes, and maybe after all, as Monsieur Richard once speculated, his thick green notebook was being filled with reflections of genius.

Two other regulars, not quite part of the intimate circle, were seated at the bar. Known to the others by their first names only — Louis-Paul and Thibault — they were real estate brokers in their forties from the agency down the avenue, two fashion plates. In tweeds in the winter, gabardine in the summer, they each seemed rarely to wear the same suit twice, each a paragon of what the French call "*bon chic bon genre*" and what in the United States is called "preppy." Louis-Paul was short and balding and Thibault tall and angular, but they both carried themselves with the same easy, loose *démarche*. In their dress, they were in competition, or in complicity, it was hard to say which, because they were ever so amiable toward each other as they consumed their croissants and coffee before strolling back to the agency. They might well have belonged to the same club — the Racing or the Polo de Paris — but they did not scorn joining in the conversation at the Jean Valjean when a topic was launched for all to consider. Their sporting republican attitude was evident in the very gallant tone in which they said a general good-bye after they finished their coffee breaks. They were up on athletic events and news about automobiles. They each made it a point to address Elodie Couteau, the retired chambermaid of the Hotel Ritz who sat, as always, deferentially a few empty stools away from them, as "*Madame*." She knew their genre from her experience at the Ritz and had been the first in the café to notice that each wore a signet ring.

Now Nelson, the cook, a stocky young man nearing thirty, came out from his kitchen behind the bar, flicked a crumb off his white jacket, wiped his hands on a napkin and poured himself a glass of water, to which he added a shot of mint syrup. He sipped, taking a breather. The winy-spicy, garlicky odor of the *boeuf bourguignon* he'd prepared wafted into the room. Nelson had been born in Lisbon, but like many Portuguese of his age in France, he'd assumed a Frenchness, made the choice between the culture of his future and the melancholy, dated one of his past. He was quick and deft in the little kitchen and quite proud of having assimilated French bourgeois cooking. He had a French girlfriend with whom he lived in *concubinage*. Nelson dreamed often of opening his own restaurant, with his girlfriend, Béatrice, receiving their guests instead of answering a phone for a dentist. He might have been imagining that future just then, or remembering Lisbon with a trace of remnant *saudade* in the way he inhaled his cigarette.

Ginette, the red-haired waitress in her forties, straightened up and rubbed her troublesome back. She had just bent over to serve Monsieur and Madame Strasbourg, sitting diagonally across from each other over a *café allongé* — an espresso with extra water for the sake of their hearts. Ginette's back and what might be the best thing for it were an occasional topic of Jean Valjean conversation. Ginette also liked to keep everyone abreast of the evolution of the plants in her garden, which belonged to the *pavillon* she shared with her husband, a long-haul truck driver, in the suburb of Rosny-sous-Bois. Sometimes she also shared events in the life of her tiny fox terrier, who was, notwithstanding his size, the Don Juan among dogs of her neighborhood.

Monsieur Strasbourg, the retired haberdasher who had sold his lease on the avenue to the Gap, was explaining the weather to his wife, Vivianne. Monsieur Strasbourg read and annotated the news to his wife every morning, with great detail and formal authority, as if this woman he had lived with for more than half a century was each day someone new, and a potential protégée. He was a dapper man in his seventies, always in a recent suit. He favored white shirts with gold "MS" cuff links and sported a clipped mustache. His wife, too, was always well groomed in the Chanel-type suits she had accumulated over the years of prosperity that had followed their move from a shirt shop in the working-class Tenth Arrondissement. Madame Strasbourg kept her silver-gray hair carefully coiffed at Jacky Internationale, the hairdresser at the end of the avenue, while Monsieur Strasbourg's pate and mustache were of a shoe-polish color that betrayed administrations of youthfulness in the privacy of his own bathroom, which he gallantly might have concealed even from his wife.

Looking up from his *Figaro*, Monsieur Strasbourg had told Vivianne Strasbourg that the rare, unseasonable floods had subsided in Burgundy.

"We had plenty here for our money, as well," recalled Madame Strasbourg. "It's those scientists."

Madame Strasbourg was still one of those people who blamed crazy weather on atomic explosions, even though no country had openly detonated a bomb in years.

The rain had finally ceased, and now the regulars of the Jean Valjean could talk about it not so much as an annoyance but as an extraordinary experience, and extraordinary experiences, all things said, always have some element of subliminal delectation.

"There were deaths," Pedro said, with a thick accent that best accommodated Spanish morbidity. Pedro, who had left behind him a village in the Estremadura, was the concierge of the building that housed the *relooké café* across the street, L'Ecrivain. He tapped the long nail of his pinky on his empty little coffee cup to signal, with acquired French savoir faire, to Madame Richard. It was a way of asking her to fill it with calvados apple brandy while the cup was still warm, a rite she performed for him every day at this time.

"One can never live too carefully," said Hippolyte Suget, stopping himself from finishing his wine. What remained in the glass was an analog of how much time he had to relax before catching the 82 bus home. He decided to use the time to concentrate on the last two numbers to choose on the Lotto ticket he'd bought from Madame Richard the day before.

Just then, Monsieur Richard, who had been resting his eyes, put on the glasses that were hanging from a string around his neck. He'd noticed, myopically, that something wide and orange was moving back and forth outside the terrace of the Jean Valjean.

A dark woman in a bright robe came into focus. And now she walked hesitantly through the door.

Fatima didn't know whether she had gone into the right street among the nine that gave into the Place Victor-Hugo. Now she rushed up to the bar, beside Suget, where Monsieur Richard was peering at her through his thick glasses and handed him her little piece of notepaper.

"Thirty-four bis avenue Victor-Hugo," read Monsieur Richard.

"It's just next door," mumbled Suget, without looking up.

Did she have to order something here in exchange for the information? Desperation had finally driven Fatima into a café, after she had seen that there were other members of her sex inside. She had never in her life on Djerba been in a café — and now she faltered over the protocol. Better to pay for something than not:

"A coffee, please," she asked Monsieur Richard. He slapped a measure of grinds into the base of the espresso machine.

She looked at the little cup in front of her on the counter. A good, nutty smell was coming up from it, and it had an appealing, creamy, tan head. But suddenly she lost the courage to be there, even though out of the corner of her eye she could make out the presence at the end of the bar of another woman, Elodie Couteau, drinking coffee. Fatima put down a five-euro note and hoped that coffee in Paris would not cost more than that. When Monsieur Richard came back from the cash register with a plastic coaster containing her change, she was gone.

In the mirror behind the bar, Suget saw her ample form hurrying under the bright djellaba as she stepped into the street. He looked at her cup of coffee going cold and scratched his head.

"*Bizarre*," said Monsieur Strasbourg to Madame Strasbourg, who simply nodded over her *Figaro Madame* magazine, her cup of *café allongé* in hand. Monsieur Strasbourg felt almost an offense to his values in that someone who was on the avenue Victor-Hugo did not know where precisely he or she was.

Hippolyte Suget stared into his glass. He reminded himself that it was the day to clean the cage of his fussy parrot, Cacahouète. He drained the *ballon* of wine. Before he paid and headed for the 82 bus stop, he crossed out three and four in their slots of the lottery card and handed it to Madame Richard.

Emma was barking in the entrance hall of the Countess's fifth-floor apartment at 34bis avenue Victor-Hugo as if the old dog were expecting someone she knew in the elevator that was cranking its way up. In the hallway, there was the clatter of metal as someone got out. The Countess had just gotten her egg whites into high peaks for the chocolate mousse she was preparing when she heard the front doorbell from the kitchen. The Countess got particular pleasure out of using her arms and hands, because the arthritis that had attacked her knees had spared her upper body.

There was another short and timid sound of the bell. She put down her big copper basin and her whisk, worried that those lovely peaks, which always recalled the Alps she'd loved to ski down years ago, would sink. Nothing stays, she told herself philosophically. But without regret, thinking about both the egg whites and the bright white days at St. Moritz, Gstaad, and Cortina. She had, all things said, wonderful memories. The Countess was never of a morbid turn of mind.

She shuffled in her fat felt slippers through the long hallway from the kitchen to the front door and said, "*Qu'est-ce que c'est?*" Emma, beside her, was barking again.

She heard Carmen, the concierge, say something in her heavy mix of French and Spanish, rendered even harder to understand by the separation between them of the door. The Countess opened the door and there was Fatima, shy and nervous, with Carmen a little apprehensive, standing a half step behind, in disassociation from the stranger.

The Countess had flecks of egg white on her thick glasses. She cleaned them on her cashmere cardigan, put them on again and squinted at Fatima.

"You don't have any bags?" she asked.

Carmen felt somehow challenged. She interjected: "They are *abajo chez moi, a la conserjeria* Madame la Contessa, I wanted to be sure that *la señora* had business with you."

The Countess looked at the round woman in orange on her doorstep and a flash of disappointment came over her. "You're not at all like your sister," she said. It was not yet a reproach, but her voice carried suspicion.

Fatima didn't know how to answer, and before anyone could say another word, Emma charged through the doorway and ran up to her and began to lick her hand. It was as if the dog in any case had retrieved something of its beloved Rachida in Fatima. Fatima didn't know why the old dog was licking her, but it did make her feel better.

Angel, Carmen's husband, was bent over the two plastic plaid traveling bags with a suspicious air when Fatima returned with Carmen to the concierge's *loge*. He had been about to leave for his daily visit to his friend, Francisco the shoemaker, in the rue des Sablons, with whom he never tired of reminiscing over Franco days. Now he had to stay and find out what these bags, blatantly, suspiciously North African, were all about. His immediate reaction on seeing Fatima come in behind his wife was a scowl.

Angel, who'd been a street paver, had taken early retirement at fifty after he'd suffered a hernia, and despite his still burly physique, he'd accumulated ten more years doing almost nothing while his wife cleaned the hallways, lavished much wax on the elevator walls, polished all visible brass and delivered the mail at 34bis. He had claimed for himself the passive part of a concierge's charge, which was to guard against intruders. Angel had also evolved into a sort of general policeman for the building, and his surprise raids among the maid's-room dwellers of the sixth floor, to be sure no one had taken in cohabitants, had become notorious among the maids and students who lived up there.

"What is it?" he asked Carmen, with irritated suspicion, as if he knew his wife was a soft touch for anyone pleading distress.

"*La Señora* is the new maid of *Madame la Contessa*," she said. Her voice was matter-of-fact, unemotional. She was used to his irritations.

"Another Arab," he muttered in Spanish, as he looked Fatima straight in the eye.

Carmen made a sour face at him and grabbed Fatima's bags in a gesture of innocent hospitality. Fatima, of course, insisted that she would carry her own bags. Finally, they turned their backs on Angel, each carrying a bag.

Fatima could not keep herself from giving Angel a polite nod of good-bye over her shoulder.

"The back stairway!" he called after them. But they were already in the garden on their way to the service stairwell. Fatima's mouth opened in awe and something like relief as she looked around at the garden. It was nothing short of an oasis in this gray city. Ferns, a fig tree, grass, rose trees still in bloom, and peony bushes, which, though they had lost their flowers in the recent rainstorms, had rich, glistening leaves. Fatima looked down and saw tiny strawberries, *fraises des bois*, turning bright red under a pine tree. Carmen, who had worn a sober look until now, brightened. She smiled, and her strong-featured face turned pretty.

"How beautiful!" Fatima said, as the smell of the roses evoked vague memories. Carmen flushed and lowered her head, wearing a bigger smile. Fatima touched the long, mottled leaf of a sapling.

"Avocado," Fatima said.

Carmen gave her a look of complicity.

"It was once an avocado stone," she said. "This," she said, pointing to the pine tree, "was thrown out by Madame Denis-Rabotin of the ground floor. After Christmas, five years ago."

"You take wonderful care . . . You have a gift."

"I do what I can." Now Carmen felt comfortable enough with Fatima to share a seditious opinion: "They don't give me much to work with, the co-owners." Her voice lowered. "They don't like to spend. Monsieur Robert —"

She broke off her indiscretion, as she looked toward the third-floor balcony to see if Monsieur Robert might happen to be looking down on them.

"The year after I planted it, Madame Denis-Rabotin insisted on having her tree back for Christmas. Luckily the co-owners voted that since she'd thrown it out, it was no longer legally hers. *Porque* it was planted in the ground, it belonged to the co-owners of the ground.

"Madame Denis-Rabotin's husband is in charge of the yoghurt division of an international food company. *Muy importante.* All the co-owners are very important people."

She sighed. Fatima surmised that Carmen kept a lot of things bottled up within her. She felt that what people in Batouine had sometimes called her "magic"

50

was working. People automatically confided in her. Uncorked their problems. She had never considered that faculty for hearing and advising a blessing, but now it gave her a certain vague feeling of reassurance — to know that it worked even in this strange place. It was a grain of confidence she sorely needed.

"But sometimes," Carmen added cautiously, "some of them can also be very nice."

As they trudged up the six flights of the narrow, winding service stairway, Fatima concluded that Carmen was a good person. She felt a flash of concern as she watched Carmen halt at the third floor and hold the rail as she panted to catch her breath. She worked hard.

Fatima's heart went out to her immediately. The poor woman's husband was patently a mean fellow. Fatima reminded herself that she missed being married, but a marriage such as the one she had quickly surmised to be a tragedy for that poor woman was surely even worse than being alone. There were women, she assured herself, even less fortunate than she was.

The stairway ended on a long narrow hall with a glistening red tile floor and beige walls in which there was an identical door every few feet. As Fatima and Carmen caught their breaths from the climb before going on, they could hear a low medley of radios. Breathing deeply, Fatima inhaled strange spices. Carmen noticed her nose puckering.

"Sri Lankis," she said. "They do their food. Sri Lankis, Africanos, Filipinos, Arabs" — she pronounced the last word gingerly, avoiding any suggestion of offense — *"Aqui c'est les Nations-Unis."*

They walked down the long hall, which came to a right angle and went on for just as long again. Before they reached another turn, Carmen stopped and knocked on a door numbered 14.

"El señor Americano, Hadley *tres,"* she said. "He was given the key. His name is Hadley Three Times."

The door opened and a very tall, thin, boyish blond man bent his head through the doorway and straightened himself in the hallway in front of them. He was wearing an old tweed jacket with sleeves that were considerably too short, and in his hand he had an open paperback book.

"Fatima!" he exclaimed and hugged her as if she were a long-lost relative.

Carmen dropped the bag she was carrying beside the neighboring door and gave Fatima a gentle, encouraging tap on the back while she was still, stunned, in Hadley's grasp. And then she even bent her head round to wink at Fatima before she shuffled away toward the stairwell.

Fatima let the man's grasp loosen. Now she couldn't hold back laughing inside at the strange name she'd been told: *Hadley three times.* Rachida had referred to him, in the letters Ahmed had read to her, only as Hadley.

"Hadley?" she asked.

"Hadley Hadley the third," he said, with nothing short of generous self-mockery.

★ ★ ★

52

Hadley Hadley III, originally of Beaufort, North Carolina, Ph.D. UNC, was a gentleman just the far side of thirty who had left his job as an instructor in French literature at his alma mater seven years ago to be a writer living in Paris. He had had reason to believe in his ability to fulfill the role, since he was already being published in little magazines and was also very much a Francophile. Hadley Hadley II, the young man's last living tie to the United States, had just died then, leaving his second wife, a young former Miss Mississippi, the fortune he himself had inherited in the chicken processing business. But well before he died he had also made a gift to his artistic only son of a small income and some cash. The summer before the old man's death, Hadley three had invested some of the cash to buy a maid's room at 34bis avenue Victor-Hugo in Paris.

Hadley two had been hypocritically happy that his son had a good address for his pied à terre in Paris — he'd even boasted about it at the Beaufort Forest Country Club, though he knew he'd given him no better possibility than a walk-up room on a sixth floor. As soon as the old man was no longer around to cast his shadow over the "artistic decisions" in his life, Hadley Hadley III gave up his teaching post and moved to Paris for good. Some time later, with his books overflowing his little room, he was able to buy the room next door. It was clear that Hadley three did not share Hadley two's need for luxury. What he simply needed — which was no easy goal — was to blossom as a writer.

Fatima held her breath with apprehension as Hadley unlocked the door of room 15. Sunlight blinded her and made her head spin as it poured through the big slanted window built into a gable of the roof. When she breathed normally again her nostrils were pricked by the smell of fresh paint. She went in. Under the bitterness of the paint, she thought she could smell the spirit of her sister — her scent, the lusty patchouli. Hadley was worried that Fatima might break down. But now she sighed with something unforeseeably like relief. The room had been stripped of everything of Rachida's except a mirror that, with its bright floral-painted, oriental frame, spoke of home. The walls, the bed, the low chest and the wardrobe had all been painted white. But the scent persisted, like a message left behind. She sat down on the stripped mattress, where the scent was stronger now. There was no logical way to explain why it heartened her, as if it were a benevolent living presence. Fatima looked into her sister's mirror as if she expected the face she'd see to be Rachida's. For a moment memory brought it to her, bright, provocatively cheerful. The real image in the mirror was of course her own, but the memory had made her unknit her brow and smile. And under that smile was the perseverance that she and her sister had shared in different ways.

Hadley handed her the key Didi's painter had left with him and tactfully slipped out the door with a smile as well, a discreet adjunct of the generous American enthusiasm he'd shown for the sake of her sister when he first laid eyes on her. She nodded politely.

In room 14, Hadley turned on his little electric hot plate and began to boil water in a teapot. Through the thin wall, he could hear Fatima installing herself, drawers opening and closing. Hadley had heard a lot about her good sister Fatima from Rachida. Rachida had said that in their village, Fatima was known to have a magic way. Not witch magic, she'd insisted, not miracle magic, but a way of beaming through people's dilemmas and surmising solutions. Yet knowing Rachida — her intuitive urbanity, her will to be a contemporary woman in a modern city, in defiance of the necessary part of her life that was a menial job — Hadley could not help but notice immediately a difference between the two sisters. Fatima, in her orange djellaba on the avenue Victor-Hugo was definitely a fish out of water. He didn't think like a snob, but he could not help but perceive of her as, well, third world. And because he had been so fond of Rachida, of the evenings when they used to confide their aspirations and share their perceptions of the world, he felt a worry for Fatima. Would she work out here? With that grouchy old Countess? And if not?

There was a knock on his door. He opened it and she was standing there. Short — and monumental, it seemed now — under her wide native dress. In her hand she held out a tissue paper on which there was a mound of halvah. She was smiling again, but her eyes went beyond polite amiability now. He sensed that in the time he'd spent on his impression of her she had

55

figured *him* out, *essentially*, and those eyes were looking not at him but right into him, and the look itself was a compliment, an approval.

And while she marveled at the vast accumulation of books — on shelves, on the floor and even bulging from the wardrobe in Hadley's disordered room — he took another cup from the pre-World War II colorful Japanese tea set above his sink. They drank flowery Earl Grey tea together and ate the sweet, crunchy halvah without exchanging a word. She simply chuckled when he passed her a paper napkin to wipe her awkwardly sticky fingers, and he chuckled back.

"*Salaam aleichum, Fatima*," he finally said, with his right hand on his heart, the way Rachida used to do it.

And that was how Fatima's friendship began with Hadley Hadley III.

Fatima spent an uneasy night in her late sister's narrow bed. When her alarm went off at six-thirty, she was already long awake. She put on a robe and slippers, and closed the door behind her gently, so as not to disturb the other tenants of the floor, but when she got to the WC around the bend in the hallway, there was already a line of people waiting to use it.

Waiting first in line, with a dignified distant air, was a tall woman who was definitely North African by the blue tattoo on her forehead and the can of water for intimate hygiene, like Fatima's, in her hand. She was Selma, who cleaned for Madame Finkiel, of the fourth floor. Behind her, two little young women, very, very short, were chattering in a language Fatima couldn't

56

place. In fact, they were Maria Luisa, who worked for Madame Paumier d'Aurange of the second floor, and her sister, Imelda, whom Madame Paumier d'Aurange allowed to share Maria Luisa's room while she tried to find her own job as a maid somewhere.

Behind them Eugène, a black African from the Côte d'Ivoire, who rented his room from Monsieur Robert, was reading his book of economics with a yellow marker in his hand. Eugène was a graduate student at the University of Paris, Jussieu Division.

The toilet flushed and out came Helga, a pretty young woman from Stuttgart, who was the au pair for Madame Denis-Rabotin while learning French at the Alliance Française. She was wearing her polite "Germans are nice now" smile and bestowed on everyone, in her well-accented French, a *bonjour*. She got back her good morning in sleepy murmurs.

Fatima headed back to her room. She washed herself carefully at the cold-water sink, hoping that the line would subside by the time she headed back down the hall. As she brushed her teeth, she looked out the window filling her room with sunlight again. At the end of the avenue, she could see automobiles already thick around the Arc de Triomphe.

As was her nature, she drew — from that swarm of efficient chaos, from all those cars each going somewhere with deliberation — a feeling of optimism. When she was ready, the WC was free.

"In the morning there are two things of prime importance," the Countess told Fatima, "my espresso and the dog, or rather the other way 'round, *n'est-ce pas*, Emma?"

The dog looked up with what could have passed for an expression of agreement, already frisking in anticipation of her important moment.

"Today you were three minutes late. That's not a good way to start off." The Countess tightened the belt of her orchid Porthault robe, like a British officer squaring away his uniform.

Fatima withdrew her eyes from the Countess's blue gaze and swept the elegant, faded salon with them. There was no point in explaining that she'd had to wait to use a toilet.

"Let me explain about the *espresso*." The Countess seemed to enjoy pronouncing the word in Italian, rolling her *r*'s with relish, in a way that conveyed the coffee's appealing singularity.

"Anyone can make coffee. I don't want you to make coffee. No doubt in your country you have your own cherished way with coffee. Coffee for me is *espresso*, drawn by a professional on professional equipment. I learned that in Rome when I was an adolescent, and ever since the Italian machines came to France, which was in 1962, I've never settled for any other version. Downstairs at the café what's-it-called, they do not make a coffee in any way comparable to what is common all over Italy and reaches its apotheosis at the Caffè San Marco in Trieste, but it is an *espresso* all the same. Rachida tried several in the neighborhood and there's none better, and anyhow it's right downstairs so my coffee will be hot. And that, in short, is what I take

58

every morning, except on Sunday when they're closed downstairs, on which day I make my own tea, since that will also be your day off.

"You know you get a day off," the Countess added, her voice secreting generosity.

"As for Emma, she is, I was told, always quick and obliging about her business, but you get the coffee afterward, in any case, so that it will be hot. They know about my coffee down there and they take care with it."

Emma, who had retired from the scene, was back now holding an expensive leash in her mouth. The dog nudged Fatima's calf.

The Countess went into the entrance hall with Emma at her heels. She fastened the dog's leash and held it out to Fatima.

"It will take the time it takes me to bathe nicely and dress," she said.

Emma came through as quick and obliging as the Countess had said. Fatima had barely walked with the dog half a block when Emma just slowly bent her hind legs and left behind what she'd come to leave behind. Right in the middle of the sidewalk of the elegant avenue, before Fatima, taken by surprise, could steer her to the curb.

There were no sidewalks back home in Batouine, but Fatima knew that where civilization reached the extent of having them, they were not meant to be soiled by dogs. She looked around furtively to see if someone had noticed what happened. There seemed to be no one on the street that early in the morning.

Hippolyte Suget was perched over his glass of red wine, striking poses in the bar mirror to judge whether he needed a haircut, when he noticed the return of the stout Arab woman in orange. She slipped through the line of people at the cash register for cigarettes and lottery tickets. In a moment she was right beside him at the bar. Intent on her coffee mission, she didn't even notice him. Fatima cast a look over her shoulder to be sure that Emma was all right tied to the lamppost outside before she told Monsieur Richard:

"For *Madame la Comtesse.*"

Monsieur Richard loaded the tap of his espresso machine with extra care, tamping down the ground beans with a spoon. He sniffed the grinds to be reasssured of the freshness before he clamped the tap back into the machine. The Countess missed no flaws in her coffee.

Suget eyed Fatima, putting two and two together. The coffee, the dog. So this was the new maid from up there. The unfortunate other one, he recalled, had been very good-looking.

"*Voilà,*" said Monsieur Richard, handing Fatima the coffee with the saucer over it to keep it hot. She paid and hurried away from the counter. Everything, Fatima felt, was going as it should. She walked holding the coffee gingerly, past the table where Monsieur Strasbourg, in a new double-breasted pinstripe suit, was reading to his wife from the pink financial pages of *Le Figaro*.

"Orgatron has cash-flow problems," he told Vivianne.

"You didn't listen to me, Maurice," she answered, then she kicked him gently under the table and turned her face toward where Fatima was leaving the café. He followed her gaze with his own. Yesterday the woman was a passing curiosity; now that she was back again, they might actually be adding something new to their lives.

"She found her way," joked Madame Strasbourg, with all the same a touch of endorsement for the newcomer in her voice. Something about Fatima's mien, or in Vivianne Strasbourg's own good nature or both, made her feel indulgent toward the exotic woman. Monsieur Strasbourg replied with a nod of approval. Truth to tell, although it was his role to keep her informed about what went on in the world, he almost always took his cues from his wife about how they had to respond to it. His buying Orgatron had been an exception that proved the wisdom of the rule.

Unfortunately for Fatima, just as she was untying Emma's leash from the lamppost with one hand, while she kept the Countess's coffee aloft in the other, the dog saw what might have been a friend, an Irish setter loping without a leash, farther down the avenue. As soon as she was loose, Emma bolted away, and before Fatima knew what happened, the two dogs had taken off around a corner. Fatima stood there, with the cup and saucer dashed to the ground, and then she hiked up her djellaba and with her sandals flapping she started to run.

In the side street, the rue Camille Lafarge, there were no dogs to be seen. Fatima was in a panic. She hurried to the next corner, turned into the next small street and still no Emma. Fatima wandered from street to street.

At length, she turned into the avenue Foch. Oblivious to the speeding traffic, people were jogging and walking dogs on the islands. Cars whizzed by. Fatima's head swam. None of the dogs were Emma or the friend that had lured her away. The very scale of the avenue Foch with its pompous buildings intimidated her. It was wider and grander than any street she'd seen before. She looked up and made out the Arc de Triomphe to the right, at the end of the avenue. It was familiar; she had seen it from her maid's-room window. She thought she could find her way home from there. Her only hope was that the dog would be waiting. In strange contrast to the luxury of the surroundings, mannish-looking young prostitutes were standing near the curb, heavily made up, wearing high boots and the shortest of skirts, their bosoms bulging from their blouses.

She walked past a group of them with her eyes to the ground and was gratified that they took no notice of her. Farther ahead was another group, and now she could make out a man sitting on a bench in front of them with his two hands in his trouser pockets. It was Angel, the husband of Carmen. The concierge of 34bis. As he rose, without yet noticing her, she darted behind a tree. He started to walk. She waited for him to get well ahead and decided to follow him. She was lucky, she thought, to come upon him to trace a shorter way home than from the Etoile, but she knew, by his affectedly nonchalant stroll, that he would not respond well to having been seen where he'd been loitering, by anyone he knew.

Fatima kept her distance while she watched him finally slip into their building. What to do now? She saw herself on an airplane again. But now, as she approached the Café Jean Valjean, she could make out a leash on the sidewalk near where someone had put out an old TV for the garbage men. Behind the TV, at the lamppost, Emma was sitting on her hindquarters, drooling and panting from her excursion. She gave Fatima a shy look, as if to pretend that nothing had happened. And then she rose and licked Fatima's hand so gently that it seemed an expression of apology.

Fatima let out a long sigh of relief and picked up the leash and started toward their building.

"*Attendez!*" she heard, behind her.

Ginette, the waitress of the Jean Valjean, was in the street with a cup of coffee covered with a saucer. Fatima realized in distress that she'd forgotten all about the coffee. She looked where she had dropped the cup. It was gone, the sidewalk was clean.

The new cup was warm as Fatima took it, mumbling thanks and reaching with her other hand toward her pocket.

"*Non, non,*" said Ginette, refusing the money. "Don't worry. It was just a tiny misfortune." But as she looked through the terrace of the Jean Valjean at the gaily colored plastic electric clock, Fatima already knew that the Countess would not be of the same mind.

Monsieur Robert came out of the elevator, round-shouldered, head down, in the posture his body had unrelentingly assumed for the past decade, since he'd turned fifty and his wife had died. He looked up when he saw Fatima's sandals. A flash of memory caused him to turn white, and he quickly shut the grill of the elevator behind him before she had the chance to say excuse me and step in.

"Strictly forbidden," he said. Emma twitched her nose without getting any closer to the man in front of her, as if she knew and did not like Monsieur Robert's odor.

"You are not supposed to use the elevator," he said gently now — a tone that gave the flavor of both logic and moral rightness to what he was saying. "There is a service staircase."

"It's through the garden," he added, and his voice now had the obliging tone of someone polite who is happy to give directions to a fellow mortal lost on the street.

Fatima actually thanked him for the information.

Monsieur Robert watched to make sure that she was heading for the right place before he hurried to give his piano lesson to his student in the rue de la Tour.

Monsieur Robert knew that dog — knew her for stupid because she hadn't once shown him a sign of recognition since she was a puppy. And by the coffee cup in Fatima's hand as well, Monsieur Robert knew who she was and where she was going and that she had to mount five floors on foot to get there. But a rule was meant to be obeyed, unless it was revoked. The rule forbidding domestics to use the elevator had been passed in a co-owners' meeting of January 12, 1942, and no one had seen fit to contest it since. Anyway, the old elevator, to which all the co-owners were sentimentally attached, would fare better without burdening it with any more traffic. And — the thought came to him bathed in irrepressible regret, despite all reason on his side — if the other one had not been cheating, as he knew she always did, the proud other one, if she had not been standing there waiting for the elevator, she would not have had the accident.

Monsieur Robert was distracted by the memory of that unfortunate event as he stepped into the street, and so he walked right in front of Madame Marchand's Porsche, just as she was parking it on the sidewalk. She jammed on the brakes. She rushed out of the car, wearing a jeans suit molded to her lithe figure, and although he would not admit it to himself, Monsieur Robert became suddenly, totally vulnerable to her profuse apologies. They exchanged a pitter-patter of concern and embarrassment, with a politeness only the French language can achieve.

Looking back at her figure from down the street, as she passed through the building doorway, Monsieur Robert felt cowardly relief that Madame Marchand remained civil to him, despite his protests against her music at the last co-owners' meeting. He was in his right, and perhaps she'd recognized that. In point of fact, however, Madame Marchand — "the Romantic Pharmacist" as Hadley had accurately dubbed her — was a woman of great heart incapable of any grudge.

Madame Marchand, a divorcée, was very active in a friendship club. Monsieur Robert's objection had to do with the fact that whenever she fell in love with a gentleman from the club she would play soundtracks from current movies on her CD player, loud enough for the entire building to hear. The music would last for days and nights on end, while the gentleman and Madame Marchand would stay cocooned in her apartment, accessible to few but the delivery boy from Speed Rabbit Pizza. Invariably, the music would stop after several days, and there would be a big bouquet of flowers at Madame Marchand's door. Perhaps the parting bouquet was a rule of the club, a rule more poetic than any the co-owners had conceived. It meant the end of a romance, and Madame Marchand's tender heart would have to subsist on the impulses of its mere kindness, until the next episode of the real thing.

Monsieur Robert had politely protested against the loud music without making any indiscreet reference to the circumstances (of which everyone was aware) at the co-owners' meeting of April 23, 2002. But there was nothing in the bylaws that allowed any specific action against her, other than a reprimand. The music still went on, intermittently.

While Monsieur Robert recalled all this, the latest victim of his fastidiousness, Fatima, was struggling to get Emma up the winding, narrow back stairs. She realized for the first time just how old the poor dog must be. Emma's hindquarters trembled as she scaled each step, slowly, painfully, stopping every few steps in an awkward effort at repose, panting and drooling. By the third floor, Emma's life seemed seriously challenged. And so Fatima wrapped her arm around the old Labrador's belly. Stopping to gain her strength about as often as the dog had, she gently dragged her up the other two flights while balancing a cup and saucer in her free hand. She wondered how she was going to manage to ring the rear doorbell when Emma jumped out of her grasp and began to bark triumphantly. There was a rattling of bolts on the steel-reinforced kitchen door.

The door swung open.

Fatima timidly held out the coffee as if she were making an offering to a reigning potentate. The Countess snatched it from her hand, held it just long enough to feel the cup was cold, before she spilt the coffee into the sink. Fatima, who had no trouble reading time, could see from the kitchen clock over the Countess's shoulder that she had been gone an hour and a half.

"This is not a good start, Fatima," the Countess said unemotionally as she let the dog in. Then she almost closed the door in Fatima's face.

Hadley was scratching his head for a fresh rhyme for *désir* when he heard Fatima's footsteps begin to resonate against the tiles of the long sixth-floor hallway. He opened his door to find her pacing from one end of the hall to the other, with a wrinkled letter in her hand.

"Hadley," she said, as he sat her down once more to tea in his room, "I want to hear this again." Her voice dropped shyly. "Will you kindly read it?"

He looked at her perplexed for a moment.

"I'm not good at opinions," he warned, "the last person on earth for advice. Fatima, I am a poet and a storyteller. My father told me the day I was first published in my high school magazine that my head was in the clouds. I'm afraid he was right. Is there a good rhyme for *désir* in French?"

"*Plaisir*," she said. She handed him the letter.

He took it. Then a realization clicked in his head.

"How do you spell '*plaisir*'?" he asked, although he knew how to spell it.

She blushed and didn't answer.

"So you want me to read the letter *for* you?" he said.

She lowered her head and nodded.

Without waiting to prolong her embarrassment, he began to read:

Dear Fatima,

I write to you as if on the recommendation of your late sister, my much-missed employee, with all my sympathies. She had mentioned your existence to me more than once, and each time in endearing terms.

Rachida was an ideal aide to me whose qualities I know would be difficult to find again in another person. The thought came to me that she might have wished for you to improve your own station in life by taking her place and that it would be a great service both to her memory and to me if I could offer you the opportunity of doing yourself that service.

Voilà! I have made up my mind. You will find a check to cover an aeroplane ticket to Paris enclosed. The money is a gauge of my conviction in the appropriateness of what I am proposing. Room, board and a salary that will be increased to the level of Rachida's if, after a determined amount of time, you fulfill my expectations.

I look forward very much to your arrival.

Please accept, Fatima, the expression of my consideration.

Monique Poulais du Roc.

"The old witch," said Hadley, when he finished reading the letter.

"I have not fulfilled her expectations," said Fatima objectively, in a voice that did not sound like she was feeling sorry for herself. But her eyes were moist.

Suddenly Hadley spread his arms like a performer on stage. "Rock of Ages, cleft for me!" he began to sing in English, off-key and mockingly. "Not the labor of my hands! Can fulfill Thy law's demands!"

Fatima had no idea what Hadley was singing, as he deformed the hymn now into a rock 'n' roll beat, but he succeeded in making her laugh so hard that she cried.

In Hadley's lexicon of English nicknames he'd created for some of the people of 34bis avenue Victor-Hugo, the old Countess Poulais du Roc figured as "Rock of Ages." Her daughter, Séverine, who had long since fled the Poulais roost, was "Rockababy," a title that suited her doubly, because she'd quit the prestigious Ecole des

Sciences Politiques, where her cousin Didi had hoped she'd prepare to be a diplomat like himself, to become a backup singer for an Icelandic group come to Paris called the Rotten Rockers, to which she'd attached herself as a teenage fan. That was years ago, and now at the age of fifty, Séverine was vice president of a recording company. She'd survived the drugs that had killed two of the Rotten Rockers, including the one she'd married. (A union that had not lasted long enough for her to have learned to spell Reykjavík.) She was a turbulent person with some deep antagonism toward her noble upbringing, and she'd turned her back on all of it, including her mother. There had been a quarrel between the two women that had never been mended.

Hadley had heard about Séverine Poulais, as she was now known, from a friend who was a guitarist and had done recordings with her company. The friend's description of her was "crooked, ugly bitch." The rest of what he knew about her came from Rachida, whom the Countess would sometimes make the slip of calling "*ma fille*" — my daughter — in what might have been the only sign that she felt something missing in her life with Séverine's estrangement. Hadley's estimation of the Countess's hauteur was not ill-placed, but Fatima had already divined that the old woman's petulance covered over important wounds.

The tea finished, Fatima cleared the dishes for Hadley and put them in the sink where she noticed a pile of dirty plates already accumulated. Hadley protested, but she washed all of them faster than he could get her to stop. That night, as if his mind had been rinsed fresh, lines came to him easily for a sonnet he'd been stumbling through for weeks.

Near eight o'clock the next morning Angel charged along the hallway of the sixth floor, pounding on all the doors. A disaster had occurred in the ground-floor apartment of the Denis-Rabotins and Angel was out to find the responsible party. Hugues, the eldest of the Denis-Rabotins' five tow-headed children, had been showering as he prepared to go off to classes at Saint-Louis de Gonzague, the private lycée of the quarter, when suddenly he found himself ankle-deep in foul water. He was a meticulous young man by nature, always having his hair cut twice a month like clockwork, always in freshly pressed chinos and well-polished loafers and Oxford button-down shirts. In the world of brands, he owed his allegiance to Lacoste, Façonnable, and Ralph Lauren, even though many of his equally privileged schoolmates were affecting a homeboy look and a cool, syncopated walk. Imagine, then, the shock that drove him running naked out of the bathroom, staining Madame Denis-Rabotin's oriental hall rug with his befouled feet.

His mother drove him back into the bathroom, where she was able to throw his Polo robe over him, concealing a maturity that she had never before had the opportunity to gauge. She by then was in a state of shock equal to his, and soon all the family was standing paralyzed outside the bathroom where the floor was now well flooded. It took the presence of mind of

71

Helga, the au pair for the young Denis-Rabotin twins, to go out and get Angel to call the plumbers.

In Hadley's lexicon, the Denis-Rabotins were the "*Figaro* family" — so perfectly did they match the profile of the ideal readership of France's most conservative newspaper. They were a large, blonde family, faithful attendants of the Eglise Saint-Honoré d'Eylau at the Place Victor-Hugo. In France, the middle class has three castes: *la petite bourgeoisie, la bonne bourgeoisie*, and *la grande bourgeoisie*. The Denis-Rabotins were of the highest category. Thierry Denis-Rabotin, forty-five, was a descendent of Denis Rabotin, a nineteenth-century pharmacist in Quimper, Brittany, who had invented a highly effective, inexpensive shampoo that destroyed the lice and nits that plagued the children of the Breton peasantry. His progeniture, enriched by what would become a prosperous pharmaceutical company bought out by the international giant LaRouche in 1960, honored his memory and drew attention to their own exceptional lineage by changing their family name to Denis-Rabotin. The Denis-Rabotins were now so numerous that Thierry could not count on his share of their fortune alone to keep his head up in life, but the prestige of his name was seasoned enough for Thierry's wife, Chantal, now forty, to have had the blessings of her family when they fell in love while he was a twenty-six-year-old real estate agent and she a teacher at the private school Lübeck, now attended by her youngest children. She was a La Source. The La Source were members of the *petite noblesse* who raised sugar beets for a difficult living on their seat in the sad north of France. Through a friend at the Jockey Club, however, Chantal's father, Amory, found Thierry a job, right after the wedding, in an international food company where his good sense and good manners had propelled him to the head of public relations for the yoghurt division, worldwide. Hence Hadley's other English nickname for Madame Denis-Rabotin: "the Dairy Queen."

Who was directly responsible for the flood? Angel, who fancied he had a keen aptitude for police work, thought he'd figured out the case. He was sure that someone on the sixth floor had thrown garbage into the WC, too lazy to walk down with it and walk back up the six flights of stairs. The garbage had blocked the sewer pipe, causing it to back up on the innocent Hugues Denis-Rabotin.

Angel interrogated everyone in sight upstairs. There were vociferous protests of innocence and no confessions. The WC showed no telltale trace of garbage. As Angel headed back toward the staircase he realized he had one more person to question, the new Arab woman, but Fatima did not respond to his pounding on her door.

She had already gone out to do the Countess's shopping. She was passing through the garden, wheeling a shopping cart, when she heard the Denis-Rabotins' maid, Josette, screaming at Carmen inside the Denis-Rabotin apartment. The event was a problem for which the building was responsible, she insisted, not a problem that developed in the

Denis-Rabotins' apartment. Consequently, she proclaimed, it was Carmen's job to clean the mess and not hers. Carmen, who had been screamed at too often in her job, was in tears.

Fatima saw the two of them through the open window of the ground-floor apartment, from which a sulphury smell was announcing the disaster. As she peered in she spied the flood around their feet. In an instant she was inside the apartment with a mop and pail from the utility closet beside the concierge's *loge*. In fifteen minutes, the Versailles-pattern parquet floors of the Denis-Rabotins' were gleaming with clean water, the air smelled of chlorine and the long oriental rug that had once graced the hallways of the crumbling La Source manor in the north of France was hanging, sudsed and sparkling, from a branch of Carmen's fig tree.

Madame Denis-Rabotin offered Fatima a euro, which she declined to accept. What could be more obvious to Fatima than that an apartment building was basically a vertical village, and that in a village when fire, an accident, a childbirth or whatever other exceptional event might occur, it was anyone and everyone's natural role to lend a hand immediately?

Carmen was still upset. She had a feeling that the upshot of all this was that Fatima's spontaneous good citizenship in some way humiliated Madame Denis-Rabotin — never mind her own humiliation. "Do a French person a favor," Angel had once warned her, "and you have an enemy for life." Before Carmen could show her own innocent gratitude to Fatima, Angel stormed up from the cellar with a plumber in a blue worksuit at his heels.

Angel barely glanced at Fatima before he announced: "It's the Russians!"

The plumber was maliciously holding out the little painted, wooden matryoshka doll he had retrieved from the drainpipe, with filthy paper wound all around it. He had the look of a man who'd caught a nice carp, but when he pulled a dusty-smelling yellow-paper cigarette from his lower lip and spoke, his words sounded like a reprimand to all the carelessly rich of the city.

"*Voilà votre petit problème.*"

This, *monsieur-'dame*, was what he'd been put upon to deal with. The further subtext was that his bill would be spicy, as the French say.

Madame Denis-Rabotin gasped and turned her face away from the wet blob. The question of the unruly children of those Russians who had recently bought the apartment across from Monsieur Robert — with what was rumored to have been a valise bulging with dollars — would have to be placed on the agenda of the next co-owners' meeting. The older brats had already been using the elevator with their roller-blades on. They had, as Madame Denis-Rabotin put it, "no upbringing at all." She had asked Carmen to raise the question of the rollerblades with the Russians when she delivered their mail. The muscular young man in black with a stubble beard and sunglasses, who was always on the other side of the Russians' door, had slammed it in Carmen's face.

Fatima still had her shopping to do and didn't linger to hear whatever else might be said about the inhabitants of the apartment Hadley had dubbed "the valley of the dolls," not because of any matryoshkas, but because of the Russians' garishly conspicuous way of overdressing, both the parents and the children.

Having done a perfect job with Emma and the cup of espresso earlier that morning, Fatima was on her second mission of the day. She had a shopping list now in her hand as she headed in her wet sandals for the supermarket whose whereabouts she'd fixed in her mind during yesterday morning's wandering-about. On the list, beside each name, was a picture Hadley had drawn to save her.

At the Espace Bonprix *hypermarché*, Hippolyte Suget, having finished work and his *ballon de rouge* at the Jean Valjean, was putting a box of birdseed in his cart loaded with packaged dinners when he spied Fatima moving down the aisle looking at the paper in her hand and then left and right at everything on the shelves. He hadn't noticed her from afar, because she was no longer in orange. She wore a brown version of those long Arab dresses, the kind the other one, the thin one, had never seen fit to wear.

She passed looking very preoccupied, as her eyes swept the shelves, left and right, left and right, without noticing him.

Later she turned up on the checkout line beside his. When she got to the cashier, she began to fumble with the euros, confused, and people behind her went "tsk" and "*alors!*" and advised her to go back to her own country. Suddenly Suget stepped out of his line, went up to her and sorted out her money without a word. She beamed at him with gratitude and he noticed what he hadn't noticed in the Jean Valjean: the unmatched colors of her pupils. She had, he noticed as well, an agreeable smile and bright, even teeth.

She thanked him.

He didn't know why he was moved to say something for the sheer sake of talking to her, nor did he know what to say. Finally he blurted what came into his head.

"Three and four," he said, "didn't work out."

She didn't know what he was talking about.

"The Lotto," he said. She still didn't understand.

Behind, on Fatima's line, a woman with a leathery tan face — proof of her August on the Côte d'Azur — became indignant that the line was being held up by their conversation. "*C'est pas possible!*" she shouted in her cigarette-roughened voice. "*Ils nous font chier.*"

Faire chier means to cause one to defecate. In French, the commonest way to say that someone or something greatly annoys you is to say that he, she or it makes you defecate. It is a curious expression, whose explanation may stem from the very early and perhaps traumatic toilet training of French infants.

Suget, who could never adjust to that kind of language, turned red and mute. He hurried Fatima's groceries out of the way, on the other side of the checkout counter, rapidly packed her shopping cart and made her a faint bow and a gesture that would have been a tip of his hat had he been wearing one. Once again she smiled at him as she went off. It was an embarrassed smile. In Batouine, strange men do not come up and speak to women, but given his politeness, she was willing to believe that it was a harmless custom in Paris.

When Suget went back to his own line, the people behind him had moved ahead, pushing his cart out of the way. There was no use trying to edge himself back in. And he had time on his hands. All his knightly gesture had cost him was his place in line. Up six floors, in a worn building across the river, Cacahouète might be impatient for his birdseed, but not many occasions presented themselves any longer in Hippolyte Suget's checkered life to practice the gallant manners instilled in him in those days he'd lived in this luxurious neighborhood, when it was dominated by a better-mannered sort of people, back in his childhood.

Fatima looked back once again. The emotion that had finally distilled in her was gratitude. By then Suget was emptying his cart onto the cashier's belt. It was then that she noticed that in his hand he had a Pokémon doll. A child's stuffed toy. Amid the birdseed, there was also a package of lollipops.

"I've misplaced my glasses, Fatima," the Countess said. "I want to know the headlines." She reached for the newspaper Fatima had placed on top of the groceries piled on the kitchen table.

And then she said what Fatima already dreaded: "Read them to me."

Fatima lowered her eyes and kept silent.

The Countess looked at her curiously just before she spied her spectacles on top of the refrigerator. She seized them and put them on.

"What is this?" she cried. "*L'Equipe?* Do you think I read *L'Equipe?*"

L'Equipe was a newspaper devoted entirely to sports.

"Maybe you see me at the Stade de France, throwing beer bottles from the crowd. I asked for the *Figaro*. Why did you buy this?" And she threw the paper back onto the table.

Now her eye was drawn to the groceries. She pulled a plastic bottle from the pile. "This is what?" she asked, accusingly.

Fatima didn't answer.

"This is dish soap. I didn't ask for dish soap. But where is the cooking oil? Where is the oil?"

A light went on in the Countess's mind as she realized that a bottle of dish soap looked like a bottle of cooking oil.

She snatched the shopping list Fatima was still clutching. She looked at the pictures Hadley had drawn and let out nothing short of a wail.

"This won't do, Fatima," she said. Her voice was not angry, not indignant, but pathetic, as if her life were suddenly seriously affected by some bad mistake she'd made and saw no way to repair.

The Countess sent Fatima up to her room while she pondered what next would have to happen between them. Hadley, who had heard Fatima opening her door, asked her how the shopping expedition went, and she could not hold back the tears that said everything.

"Things will work out," he said, trying to comfort her, although at the moment he didn't know how.

Hadley had told Fatima that his drawing pictures would not save her for long. Right now, though, there was nothing else he or anyone could do.

"How can that be?" he'd asked, when she'd shown him the shopping list in desperation, confessing her shortcoming.

Compulsory grade school education had become law in Tunisia since the new government came to power in 1956. But between the law and the enforcement of the law there is often a cleavage, sometimes a chasm, in her country, and Fatima had fallen into one such cleavage as a child. Djerba was a much more primitive island in those days, the tourists hadn't yet introduced a cosmopolitan strain. Fatima's widowed mother had no sons to support her, and as soon as Fatima had been old enough to wield a broom or a mop, she'd been working full-time cleaning at l'Impérial, the one hotel there since colonial days, outside Batouine. At the time, working at that big white establishment seemed prestigious, both to her mother and to the young Fatima. In their eyes it seemed she'd embarked on a career. Rachida, five years younger than Fatima, had been a strong-willed, bright child. With Fatima bringing in money, Rachida was able to go to school. Between the two sisters there was, from the beginning, that portentous generation gap.

She dried her eyes and got out the remains of the halvah Ahmed had given her, and Hadley made tea once again. As she held out the candy to him, the tissue paper seemed to communicate something to her hand like the warmth of an active presence. The feeling seemed natural to her; she knew it right away to be an emanation of the power of friendship Ahmed had imparted to his gift. Fatima considered herself a good Muslim, but for centuries before the warriors of the Prophet had swept across the north of Africa and proselytized its people, her ancestors had been animists, believing that life and also the spirit of immortals were everywhere, inhabiting everything moving or still. Some of that old emotion, that faith in the omnipresence of spirits good or bad, survived among her people, even after they were colonized, even after the cultural shifts inspired by television and tourists, even after almost all of them knew how to read.

Fatima was not yet sure what kind of spirits inhabited the patinaed walls and faded furniture of the Countess's apartment. But whether she herself would be among them for long was a sore question.

CHAPTER
THREE

"Well it's a delicate dilemma. You've reaped what you sowed," Didi told the Countess.

"I did what my conscience told me to. I don't regret that."

"And what does your conscience say now?"

"My conscience is clearing her throat."

And then the Countess sighed into the phone. "Enough badinage," she said, "we're not in an eighteenth-century novel of manners. We're not figures in one of your engravings. I have a little problem and I don't know what to do about it."

Didi didn't answer. The accusation about his engravings was a storm warning. The Countess, when something troubled her, would start out with a little dig like that and wind up exploding at the person she was with, regardless of his lack of relation to her problem. In this case, he had indeed been involved, beneficially, he thought. He had brought in Monsieur Durand, and that should have settled the whole unfortunate Rachida matter right then and there. It was the Countess who had the misguided conscience. The only thing she could have been faulted for was the woman's irregular immigration situation, a detail she'd never thought of addressing. And now she'd got involved with the illiterate sister. More complications. Anyway, what would happen now would be what she decided. All advice notwithstanding, *Tantine* Monique always made up her own mind.

"My eyes are getting worse," she said. And then there was a long silence at her end. She opened a door in her mind and slammed it shut, speechless with fear.

He could hear her breathe a little more heavily.

Still holding the phone, waiting for her to take the lead again in their conversation, Didi cast a self-reassuring glance at the walls of his living room, covered with eighteen-century engravings of historical events and scenes from the life of his own class, before the catastrophe of 1789. Did she seriously fault his collecting them? His engravings were his preoccupation, ever since he'd left the Quai d'Orsay. He was known among the *commissaires-priseurs*, the men who ran the auctions, as a "talented connoisseur." His preoccupation and his fortune. Over the years, he'd sunk a lot of money into those pictures, scrimping on other things, living in this tiny two-room apartment, giving his little dinner parties in his kitchen — a practice that was soon taken up by well-heeled hostesses, inspired by the iconoclastic reverse snobbery to which his great family name gave a guarantee of chic. Through those treacherously fashionable acquaintances, *Architectural Digest* had found out about his two rooms with a view of the Seine, a short walk from the ministry that had provided him with a superficial raison d'être — for he'd never risen, having never striven — much of his life. Naturally, he'd refused to have the place photographed.

"Are you still there?" the Countess asked, on the other end of the phone. Her voice was bright and feisty again.

Didi didn't know what to say. As he often did when he didn't know what else to do, he reached for something to eat: a slice of the *quatre-quarts* butter cake the Countess had baked that morning, keeping herself busy as a way to bury her dilemma.

She'd pressed the cake on him, almost as if she were buying his counsel. (He knew she would in any case eventually ignore it. What she needed was a sounding board for her anxiety.) He'd left her with no advice, and now she'd rung him up, still perplexed.

On her end of the phone, she could hear him chewing.

"You're putting weight on again," she said.

He swallowed the cake before he'd chewed it properly.

"Well," he snapped, "you can just buy her a ticket home *e bastà*."

"Stop talking like a waiter."

He hadn't got the reference for a moment, until he remembered that the last time they had had lunch out together it was at Il Conte, and the headwaiter kept insisting on dealing with them in Italian.

"I'm so tired of that man and his comic opera," she'd said when they'd sat down. "After all the years I've known him to be here, you'd have thought he'd learn how to say hello properly to a client, in French."

"I have eaten in Italian restaurants in various parts of the world," Didi had answered, "and that is their manner everywhere. They like the sound of their language; they want to make you a little gift of it, like a song."

"*Commedia dell'Arte*," she'd sniffed, but her own pronunciation was generously musical.

"So what is the answer," she said now, "that I send her right back to Tunisia, like that?"

Just as she listened for Didi to answer, Fatima walked into the Countess's living room with a vacuum cleaner.

The Countess nodded, as if Didi could see her assenting to what he was saying in the phone.

"You understand I will not see anything at all before long . . . You're no help!" She listened. "Yes," she said. "Well, yes, Carmen. The concierge. She might have someone for me. In the servant milieu."

The Countess listened on the phone for a long time to something Fatima could not overhear.

The Countess sighed. "All right," she said. "Tomorrow is her day off, at least I won't have to face her."

Fatima waited for the Countess to hang up before she turned on the vacuum. Startled, the old woman wheeled painfully around in her chair when she heard the roar behind her, and there was Fatima, stooped conscientiously — with an air that seemed almost pious — like some humble figure tending a field in a painting by Millet or Pissarro, as she vacuumed the parquet floor with the loud machine.

★　★　★

Sunday, her first day off, was a beautiful, warm autumn day in Paris. A bright Fragonard sky. A breeze bearing just the faint flavor of a coming winter stirred the clear air. The grainy pollution of weekday traffic was gone, and with the streets nearly empty of cars, the physique of the city seemed to come into sharper focus.

Fatima was consoled by the good weather — she had a difficult excursion to make. And she was even more grateful for Hadley's kind gesture to accompany her.

They walked to the Champ de Mars station of the RER suburban line C. It was a longish walk, but a lovely one, and Hadley wanted to help Fatima take her mind off her thoughts — the sad reason for the trip as well as her anxiety over her job. They walked down to the Seine through the Trocadéro Gardens, where the green husks on the chestnut trees were already bulging with brown kernels. A bright merry-go-round was spinning at the far edge of the basin, whose cannon-like fountains projected streams of water. Children went round and round, shrieking with delight. Hadley and Fatima passed through the throng of tourists being solicited by a row of Sri Lankis, each selling the same miniature version of the Eiffel Tower. None of them took someone looking like her for a tourist, so she had to ask to buy one. Hadley seemed to want to tell her she was doing something wrong for a Parisian, but she ignored his urging her to move on and not get ripped off.

She bargained for a gilt model tower and got it at her price.

"It will be a little gift, for when I go . . . home," she said. "When I go to Djerba," she said. "The nice young man at the Club Rêve named Ahmed. He gave me the halvah."

When I go home, she'd heard herself say. Soon? Defeated?

The Eiffel Tower itself stood ahead of them. Fatima touched Hadley's arm for them to stop as she peered at the tower from bottom to top. She was reminded that her former husband, Mahmoud, had worked on high constructions. They moved on to the underground station.

The RER line C followed the Seine east, but the river was invisible as the train traveled through tunnels and then out into a vast expanse of rails bordered by warehouses. It made its way south through suburbs that were a jumble of flat, high, rectangular public housing, low factories, and empty lots. Fatima and Hadley sat in the upstairs part of their car and looked out without speaking at this gray landscape brightened by only the big, bold, fat-lettered taggings wherever there was a concrete wall beside the tracks. Groups of teenage boys got on and off at various stations, all of them dressed in baggy shiny sweatpants and sweatshirts, wearing caps with their brims turned back. Fatima marveled at their elaborate sneakers. A handful of Arab boys who were settled across the aisle from Fatima and Hadley tussled with each other for fun, and then glared at Fatima. Because she was bareheaded and with a blond young man? Hadley didn't notice. He seemed inspired by this exotic little journey. He scribbled notes, or lines, on a well-worn little pocket pad. Neither he nor Fatima were moved to make conversation for the sake of conversation.

Finally there was the Seine again, wide and fast-flowing. A barge rushed downriver. Fatima saw a red-haired woman on it, hanging cartoon-printed children's bedsheets on a line that ran from the cabin to the rear. Another life so different from her own.

An old-fashioned railroad station with a new extension had a decorative tile fringe on its brow, on which, in turn-of-twentieth-century lettering, was written CHOISY-LE-ROI. Here the two of them got off. They walked down to where the bus they were to take was already at its stop, with the motor running. Hadley grabbed Fatima's hand and they ran for it.

Panting for breath while she popped her *métro* ticket into the ticket machine, Fatima noticed, sitting with his face toward the window, someone she'd never thought she'd run across all the way out here. It was Hippolyte Suget.

"*Hippolyte, te voilà!*" Hadley said, punching his ticket after Fatima. Suget turned away from the window, startled, and then he got up and accomplished a formal, flustered handshake with the two of them.

"I am going to visit a friend," Suget said, almost as if it were an alibi.

"I don't see you very often," said Hadley.

"Changed my hours," Suget said. "I work at night now."

"Ah . . ."

Neither knew what to say next. It was not a meeting of long-lost friends. More like an exchange of *politesse*, or a bit of bar talk without the crutch of a bar in front of them. Fatima had nothing to say other than "*Bonjour, Monsieur.*"

A moment of awkward silence and then Hadley led her to a seat comfortably far from Suget, who quickly turned his face back toward the window.

"He is your friend?" Fatima whispered to Hadley.

"I would always see him around five o'clock at the Jean Valjean," he answered lowly, "when I'd go for my afternoon pick-me-up. You know him?"

"I go there for the Countess's morning pick-her-up."

The bus passed through a landscape of tall public tenements interspersed with little stucco private houses, the *pavillons* that are the pride of clean-poor French stubbornly hanging on against the incursions of state-sponsored slums. In a while it approached what looked from afar like incongruous meadowland. Hadley rang for the bus to stop. Across the road there was a grimy concrete wall with a sign that read CIMETIÈRE PARISIEN DE THIAIS.

Suget saw fit to make a formal wave of the hand good-bye to Hadley and Fatima, from the bus window.

"A polite man," Hadley said, "and he's gone through a lot."

Fatima looked at him with curiosity.

"Well, it wouldn't be indiscreet to tell you the first part of his story. He was a child ballet dancer, a *petit rat* at the Opéra —"

Fatima took a bouquet of dried jasmine from Djerba out of the little plastic sack she'd been carrying.

"Please," Fatima interjected. "Let's go in."

She wasn't of a mind for hearing anyone's story. The cemetery loomed ahead. They had to find Rachida.

"*La Fosse Commune?*" Hadley asked. The porter at the side gate where the bus had left them didn't respond with any emotion to the term. It was, he said politely, down near the middle of the cemetery, lots 48, 49, and 50.

La fosse commune. The common ditch. Fatima felt her stomach flutter with nausea as she heard it again in her mind, while they walked on the long, wide central avenue of the graveyard. They passed an area with a soiled French flag drooping on a pole over rows of concrete crosses with porcelain name tags on them, some of them chipped, rust obliterating the names. The defeated, humiliated dead of the Algerian conflict.

Fatima tripped on a pebble in the road. Hadley took her arm as if he feared she was in danger of fainting.

"*Merci,*" she said. She was all right.

Where was the ditch?

They came to lot 49. There was no ditch. Instead, unlike the other lots, the whole space was paved with brick-colored cement, implanted in which were rows of concrete slabs. Some of them had names on brass plaques, some of them just little black letters and numbers on their sides. The names were mostly foreign — Arabic, Armenian, Polish . . . Some of the slabs had plastic flowers and little stone decorations placed on them.

La Fosse Commune was still the word for the place paupers were buried, but its literal meaning had become an anachronism. As Fatima looked around, it seemed to her that these poor were better off, in their neatly sealed area, than many of the dead in the untidy graves with rotting stones nearby.

"I think we can find which one," Hadley said gently. "They're identified."

The porter they'd spoken to earlier told them that if they went to the main entrance they could consult the records kept there.

It was a long walk again to the other end of the cemetery. Overhead, planes roared incessantly, people heading for more fortunate destinations. Orly Airport, Hadley noted, was nearby.

The main gate was quite lovely — Modernist architecture of faintly Egyptian inspiration — and near it was a matching, well-proportioned little building inscribed CONSERVATION. The records were in there, but the porter had forgotten to tell them that it was closed on Sunday. They peered in through the window at a stone counter, behind which there were canvas boxes of the kind where files are stored in French offices.

A guard came up to them, wearing the same uniform as the porter, looking like a soldier in blue with his overseas cap.

"Is it recent?" he asked. "If it's recent, I have the sheet in my office. The admissions sheet."

And so they got the letter and the number for Rachida.

"Why do some have names and some not?" Hadley asked. He would insist that Rachida get a plaque with her name.

"Every name we know gets a plaque," the guard said defensively. "We just can't do them one by one. They make up a batch of plaques as soon as there are enough to make it worthwhile."

Fatima and Hadley were finally at Rachida's slab. Fatima bent and gently placed the jasmine on it, just a little spot of pink compared with the pot of red plastic roses on the slab to the right, which already had a plaque.

Hadley brushed away a tear.

"You knew Rachida well?"

"Lovely," Hadley said, "such a lovely person."

Fatima was silent. Hadley thought it best to leave her there alone a moment. He walked back toward the gate they'd come through, while Fatima felt that her feet were cemented to the pavement in front of her sister's slab.

Why? Rachida dead at the prime of her life encased in cement in a strange place. All the big "why's" never get answered on earth, and you could waste your life asking.

She remembered all the bright letters that Ahmed would read to her on their lunch hour. "I intend to take an evening course in stenography, if I can manage it . . . The Countess has made me a gift of a dress designed by one of our own whose name is Azzadine Alaia. He would sew things for her himself, before he became famous. I look very Parisian, don't laugh at me, sister, and don't laugh again, I am buying a lottery ticket every week, and when I win, I'll bring you over to France and get you a good job too."

Fatima wiped her eyes with a Kleenex. How much she wished that Rachida were alive and on her way to fulfilling herself in an exciting life. As for herself, she was born unlucky, but she had no choice but to put that out of mind. She didn't know what would become of her future in general, but she could not be at rest until she'd somehow repaired the great hole that had been torn in her life. She had no choice but to put one foot in front of the other and keep going. For a moment, standing at that graveside, she was standing in her mind at the ferry pier on Djerba.

Hadley had paused at a shelter like a bus stop, where a sign listed the "celebrities" residing in the Cimetière Parisien de Thiais:

"Serge Orloff, descendent of Catherine the Great of Russia," "Lèon Sedoff, son of Nathalie Sedova and Lèon Trotsky," "Ahmed Zog I, King of Albania," . . . the list went on.

Hadley saw "Joseph Roth, Austrian writer" just as Fatima came up beside him. She looked composed. Enough for him to ask a favor.

"Do you mind? There's a grave near the gate," he said.

She walked with him while he counted the rows until he came to the granite slab with fading gilt letters that marked the tomb of Joseph Roth, novelist, author of *The Radetzky March*, chronicler of the decadent and absurd. Someone had planted hyacinths in the slot of earth at the foot of the slab, over which there was also a wilted rose on a long stem.

The stone noted that he'd died exiled in Paris, in 1939. Hadley bent and put his palm down on the flat stone. Fatima knew he was seeking an emanation.

"He had a great sense of humor," Hadley said.

He looked up at her. For now, there was nothing more to be done here.

She had the same thought.

"You must be hungry," she said.

At the main gate, they'd seen the colored plastic figure of Ronald McDonald over a Ronaldland, across the busy highway. Behind it was a restaurant with the famous golden arches. Because they didn't expect to find any place better out near a graveyard and open on Sunday, they began to walk, reconciling themselves with the prospect of eating hamburgers to stanch the hollow each felt in the stomach.

The 396 bus had hurried ahead after leaving Fatima and Hadley off at the cemetery. Hippolyte Suget watched the streets with their little *pavillons* peel back into the immediate past. There was no one at any of the stops and the driver sped through Thiais, and from there he crossed over a highway and entered the empty food depots of Rungis. Spic and span on a Sunday, empty, locked up. A lonely landscape. Suget was a connoisseur of the signs and symptoms of loneliness.

94

He had had few friends since his adolescence. That was clearly in another life. After the Opéra. The Lycée Janson de Sailly. The golden youth of the Sixteenth Arrondissement. Another life, before which there had been another and after which there was another, and now this one. He had not one life, he realized, but a series of lives.

His thoughts turned for a moment to the two who had gotten off at the cemetery. So Hadley had befriended the Arab woman. She had something. Appealing eyes.

Bobby was *his* platonic friend. Bobby had protected Suget, taught him what he had to do and know in his second life. Bobby had buoyed his faith that yet another life was possible. That's why he was bringing Bobby marrons glacés, expensive candied chestnuts.

The bus let him off at the Mairie de Fresnes. From there it was a short walk downhill to the highway he used to see from his window.

Down at the *Carrefour de la Déportation*, everything looked the same: the roadway with speeding cars, the *Intermarché* he used to stare at, wondering what was in the shopping bags of people coming out and what delicacies he'd buy if he could just cross the bridge on the highway and go into a supermarket, just like that, come and go. The ochre-walled apartment building still had writing on it calling it LA PEUPLERAIE, though there were no poplars in sight.

The elegant, tall pine, however, still stood beside the main gate of the prison. Beyond, the same yellow, brick buildings, the same clock on the turret of the main cell block.

It was getting late. Suget went over to the side gate. He had hoped he'd never have to spend a moment within those walls again, but a friend was a friend.

The traffic sped by at a breakneck pace on the National Route 7 that bordered the main gate of the cemetery. Fatima could feel the pavement vibrate under her feet. No provisions seemed to have been made for pedestrians, although there was a traffic light a little farther south. The whoosh of the traffic, the roar of planes overhead, and the empty feeling in her chest combined to make Fatima light-headed. Hadley hurried across a grass island, assuming she was beside him. He dashed across the highway through a hole in the traffic, and when he turned to where he thought she'd be, he discovered she was still on the side of the cemetery. She stood there looking at the road like a swimmer afraid to try deep water.

Behind him, she saw the McDonald's with its parking lot, the Ronaldland, bright and busy on the other side of its glass walls.

"I'll come get you!" Hadley yelled. She'd have none of that, though. My luck to die here, she thought, a fat Arab woman splattered by a car bearing a French family home from Sunday lunch with granny, and papa at the wheel, who'd had too much bordeaux. *No!*

Another hole developed between the speeding cars, and in one swoop, she lifted her long djellaba, closed

96

her eyes and raced across, taking the island in a few leaps, her sandals flapping.

Hadley could not help but laugh. Breathless, she landed beside him. She burst out laughing herself, finally. It felt good to laugh.

The air in the McDonald's was saturated with canned music and the smell of cooking oil. The tables were crowded with families wearing sports clothes with brand names all over them.

Hadley sniffed and sighed.

"It's everything I left behind in my life."

The smell was making Fatima nauseated.

"I bet you've never before set foot in a McDonald's," Hadley said. "No reason why you should have." Her face looked truly ill.

"Let's go," he said. "There's got to be something else somewhere."

They walked south along the highway, each getting hungrier and hungrier, and then, lo, at a bend in their path a micro-miracle stood before them. An oasis. Three Moroccan restaurants in a row, side by side. "La Palmeraie de Ouarzazate, le Marrakech and Les Délices de Maroc." Hadley rolled the names on his tongue, with a hungry gleam in his eye. The modest-looking tile-faced Délices de Maroc was closed. But through the windows of each of the other two they could see walls inspired by an Alhambra, shining brass tables with bright vegetables and roast meat in clay pots. Contented-looking people were spooning couscous onto their plates or pouring mint tea from silver pots while they nibbled at rose-colored *loukoum* and smoked langorously.

Fatima's face beamed as if the bend in the highway, by some magic, had led her home. Was this not, in any case, at least a little stroke of luck?

Which? Although they knew they'd be delighted with either.

"La Palmeraie," Fatima said. The palm tree grove. "It's a more *poetic* name." She gave a smile of complicity to remind him that he was a poet.

"Couscous," Hadley said. "Never mind the poetry. Couscous." He actually rubbed his hands the way Frenchmen do, at the prospect of a good meal.

They ordered a *couscous royal*. Out came a brightly decorated clay bowl of vegetables in aromatic broth — zucchini, carrots and turnips, and beside it a platter of chickpeas dotted with plump raisins. Then the grain, steaming in a clay platter, redolent of the grassy sweetness of butter. Finally, with an understated *voilà*, the waiter set down the meat: chicken and boiled lamb and lamb skewers and meatballs and spicy *merguez* sausage, all in a great heap.

Hadley had ordered a bottle of Mascara. The waiter hesitated after Hadley tasted the purple wine and nodded with a look that was nothing short of eager. The waiter held off pouring for the Arab woman, waiting for a signal from either her or Hadley.

"You take wine?" Hadley asked. He didn't know how strictly religious she was.

She didn't answer.

98

"Well, the Koran . . . ," he cleared his throat, "is a little ambiguous, isn't it?"

She nodded.

"Actually, it forbids intoxication. But it promises wine in heaven to the deserving."

The waiter stood over her with the bottle.

"Rachida liked wine," Hadley said softly.

She looked up at the waiter, who took it for a signal for him to pour.

"A drop of wine will be all right," she said to Hadley.

And she lifted her glass, stared into the dark, shimmering liquid, inhaled its heady bouquet, a little like a diver high above water. She plunged. Drank wine for her deserving sister's sake and for the first time in her life.

She stayed with that single glass, feeling a warmth but not quite a light-headedness, while Hadley made his way without thinking about it through the rest of the bottle. They ate and ate.

By the time the waiter brought out a tray of stuffed dates, *loukoum*, and pastries and poured mint tea into their glasses from high above the table, they were both as if cleansed of the touch of death they'd felt across the highway.

Hadley looked across the table at the heavy woman from a continent, a culture, and a history so different from his own — as different as their personal journeys — and he marveled that life was such, the currents that ran under it were such, that the two of them could be sitting, mellow after a feast together, like old friends. Of course, he had, in a sense, known her before he'd ever seen her, because of Rachida, whom living side by side had made a true friend, a *confidante*. Rachida had spoken often of her luckless sister Fatima. That she was very "special." He told her that now, to assure her of a touch of confidence in herself.

"Specially unfortunate," she answered, "but then she was more unfortunate than me."

Hadley was silent a moment. "She told me about her husband," he said. "I think it was extraordinary of her, I mean, a Tunisian woman. I mean, just getting up and leaving him."

"She always wanted everything to be better than it was. Bakir was no good. He was running a grocery in Tunis and left her in Batouine. My sister was too bright for Batouine. The best student always. She went to Tunis and surprised him with another woman. Another wife. Children running around. She walked right out and kept going. She took whatever job she could get in Paris."

"It was strange between her and the Countess," Hadley said. "The old woman seemed to show her real affection. But it was also a way of keeping her down."

Fatima fell silent.

"Well, here I am," she finally said.

She shrugged. "I do what I can. I had a husband too, but he left me. He went to France and lived in a room like ours, and next door there was a pale American au pair. Mahmoud was a man who worked on tall buildings." She smiled. "He liked to see far. The two of them own a restaurant like this one, in Sheboygan."

"Sheboygan, *Wisconsin?*"

"That's it . . . And you . . . Hadley?"

Hadley felt a low coming over him. He was coming down from the rush of euphoria brought on by the wine, the food, the sweets.

"The person I wanted," he blurted, "he wouldn't have me. That's my misfortune." He looked at Fatima to see if he'd shocked her, to see whether he should have regretted his confession. Her eyes were narrowed with concern.

"Alexandre." He gave her the name. "He came from this old-old-old family. Saint Cyr — the military school, you know. Army in the family way back. Cavalry. He was terrified that his father would find out. He only wanted to see me in secret. When we got close to being inseparable, he bolted. Got scared off. I see him in the neighborhood sometimes now, when he takes his kids to school, the Cours Madeleine. He noticed me once and pulled his daughters' hands to hurry away. They ran, actually. Two little twin girls in school uniforms, a father in *his* uniform, running a little delicately."

Fatima saw that there was wine still in her glass and she drank it down in a gulp. She reached across the table and took Hadley's hand, not knowing what to say and not having to say anything by the way she looked compassionately into his eyes.

She looked now at his long hand. "You touched the writer's stone for luck?"

"I'm going to start a novel."

She nodded as if she knew he was up to something like that, had made some resolution. She had actually sensed that something had passed into his hand from the stone, but she didn't see fit to tell him that.

"Hadley," she said, "your rooms are a mess, you know that. I will clean them for you."

He started to protest.

"If you teach me to read."

She held out her hand now the way people do to shake on a bargain. He took it, took it in both his hands. Her grasp felt remarkably strong for a small woman. But there was something more than strength he seemed to feel, something active, a strange energy.

When they left the restaurant it was raining. The barometer had fallen and Fatima felt her spirits begin to fall too, as if the rain were flooding into a hole in her heart. But she steeled her will against the weather, both within her and in the outside world. Steeled it against whatever it had to encounter. She was going *home* to the avenue Victor-Hugo. All things said, she had come too far simply to give in and let herself be chased off.

"Hadley," she confided, when they reached the shelter of the bus stop, "after I learn to read. After I have the money I need, I am going to your country."

"What?"

"To Sheboygan, Wisconsin."

"Of course you will, Fatima. Because you're you. But, Fatima, I don't know what you'll get out of it."

"When he sees me, face-to-face —"

"What do you really think?" He tried to be gentle about her fantasy of reconciliation.

She didn't answer for a long moment as she watched the bus approach, swirling water off its tires. Then she said, "Maybe he is waiting for me."

Hadley looked at her keen eyes and thought best to leave it at that. He grabbed her waist and pulled her back, as the bus drew up splashing them, and that was enough to break off the conversation.

On Monday, there was a long line of people buying lottery tickets from Madame Richard at the cashier's counter of the Café Jean Valjean. Coming back from a walk with Emma that had presented her with a new concern, Fatima got on line and bought a four-euro-twenty ticket. Not because she believed that her ill luck was in any way over with, but because, even if it would always be with her, she would defy it — and not let it run her life. She asked Madame Richard to check off whatever numbers she wished.

TWO

CHAPTER
ONE

Days passed before Fatima would have to undergo the
trial of the supermarket again — several days while the
Countess deliberated over the situation Fatima had put
her into. One morning, the sun had just begun to peer
through Fatima's maid's-room window when she was
awakened by a pounding on her door. Disobliging
words concerning Angel came immediately to her
mind, and she was even capable of shouting them out
loud, but when she unlocked the door, she was
astonished to see the Countess. Half-awake, she
wondered for an instant whether she was being visited
by a nightmare.

The Countess stood there with her hair in curlers,
wearing a bathrobe. Her face was stricken.

"It's Emma!" the old woman said.

There was a rattle of a lock in the next room, and
Hadley, in just an oversize University of North Carolina
T-shirt, peered through his partly opened door, blearily.

"It's Emma!" the Countess insisted to him, although
she'd never spoken to Hadley before — as if she needed
help from anyone she could get it from. "She hasn't
slept all night. She's been making the most pitiful
sounds!"

Hadley shut his door quickly and began to dress.

"*Tout de suite, Madame la Comtesse*," said Fatima.

Fewer than ten minutes afterward, Angel, on his way home from his early-morning session of voyeurism on the avenue Foch, spotted the odd trio: The Countess, Fatima, and Hadley were walking toward the rue Spontini, with Emma wrapped in a merino wool blanket like a stretcher, while Fatima held one end and Hadley the other. The Countess walked behind them, encouraging them to hurry and moving her creaky joints as fast as she could. She had managed to dress quickly, but her curlers still poked out from under a Hermès scarf.

Angel muttered an opinion about the sanity of the three of them in Spanish, to himself, as he turned the corner to avoid creating suspicion about his own odd ways. Too late. Hadley spied him and whispered to Fatima, with a wink:

"*Voilà Señor Corazon*, who makes the hearts of all the girls on the avenue Foch beat faster."

Señor Corazon, Mister Big Heart, was Hadley's term for the black-hearted Angel. The thought crossed his mind that it was just possible that Angel, for some devious reason, had tried to poison Emma.

The brass plaque on the former townhouse in the rue Spontini said that the hours of consultation of Georges Cheval, veterinarian, were between 10h and 12h, and 15h and 19h. However, the Countess knew that Cheval lived above his practice, and she began stabbing at his buzzer repeatedly. From the other side of the thick black doors came the bleating, meowing, barking, and wailing of the many animals who were Dr. Cheval's temporary boarders: some recovering from operations, some under medical observation, and those left behind by vacationing owners, all sharing their misery in a cell block Dr. Cheval referred to as his *pension*.

In a minute, the good doctor appeared at a second-floor window in black silk pajamas. The silhouette of an old woman in a fussy bathrobe could be seen behind him. His mother.

"*Qu'est-ce que c'est!*" A protest not a question.

"Open immediately!" shouted back the Countess. "Open the Goddamn doors!"

Emma lay moaning on her side on Dr. Cheval's white examination table, while, in his bathrobe, he poked at her stomach with his index finger. He had taken her blood pressure and checked her heartbeat, and now his poking had a redundant air to it, a little like someone playing with food after he was full. The doctor had already made up his mind.

The Countess had noticed his hair implants as he'd bent over Emma. Could someone who went to such trouble to practice dissimulation in his private affairs be trusted professionally?

"When did she last —?" he asked.

The Countess looked at Fatima. Her eyes showed a faint accusation.

"What was she doing all these mornings?" she said.

"Very little, *Madame la Comtesse*. Nothing yesterday or the day before."

109

"You didn't tell me!"

"It is not abnormal," Fatima said, "for dogs of a certain age. I thought the problem would go away."

There was an old yellowed card that was Emma's medical record on the table. Cheval picked it up and looked at it with the air of a man who had proof that he was right in the face of obtuse opinion to the contrary.

"She is twelve years old," he said. And then, with a more congenial voice: "She has obviously had a good life, apart from never having given a litter. When they're that old and stop ... eliminating, *Madame la Comtesse*, that's the last sign they're ready to go."

The Countess held her breath.

"I can make an appointment for this week." He looked at the Countess's stricken face. There was silence between them for a moment while a sick cat, foreboding its destiny, cried from the cell block.

"Or we could do it now, if you are ready. It will be painless."

His eyes asked for an answer.

"Never! Never on your little life!" the Countess said. "Fatima," she shouted. "And what's your name?"

"Hadley," Hadley said.

"Fatima, where's the blanket? Hadj-li, pick up Emma!"

Fatima and Hadley swept Emma off the table and back into her merino wool blanket. The Countess stormed out behind them without looking back at Dr. Cheval. To make matters worse for him, his bathrobe belt had become undone. The three of them were gone

110

before he could make himself decent and show them to the door.

"Hadj-li?" the Countess said in the street. She was a little hard of hearing and thought she had understood the name Muslims give to someone who has made his pilgrimage to Mecca. "Where does someone with a name like that get blond hair?"

"We get what Allah gives us, Madame," Hadley replied mischievously, with a faint, oriental bow of his head.

The Countess's thoughts turned to God, and they were rebellious. Why was He torturing poor Emma? "That might be the trouble with this world," she said.

At this point Fatima spoke up. Not with the deference of a maid to her mistress. For it was as if a current of complicity, something like an esprit de corps, had passed between the three of them. At that rare moment they were no longer mistress, maid, and dubious foreigner, but three heroes accomplishing an urgent, humanitarian mission together.

"Everything has a reason," Fatima heard herself saying, without inhibition. "It's not because we don't understand the reason that there is none."

The Countess looked at Fatima with raised eyebrows.

Meanwhile Emma moaned in the blanket. The old Labrador sounded awful, but her voice seemed to show appreciation for having been rescued from the examination table.

★　★　★

At this point Victorine came back into Fatima's life, and it would prove a good thing. They met again in a local pharmacy, which is where Parisians meet often, because, with the exception of cafés, restaurants, and bakeries, more Parisians congregate in pharmacies than in any other public place. The French, though no more sickly than other ethnic groups and probably less so, given their privileged lives, consume great quantities of medicine. Why is a subject that takes us far from our story. In any case, the Countess had explicitly sent Fatima to another pharmacy from the one Madame Marchand owned at the far end of the avenue Victor-Hugo, because: "We don't need our neighbors knowing our insides."

Fatima's business that morning was to buy babies' suppositories in the hope they would relieve Emma of her crisis. Victorine had been commissioned by her Madame, a distinguished middle-aged Paris lawyer by the name of Odile Benamou-Kahn, to get a month's supply of face treatment to take with her on her yearly concert cruise, which was scheduled this year for the Aegean islands.

As Fatima stood first in line at a counter among serious souls of the neighborhood, she heard a laugh whose rich, generous tone she remembered immediately. It was Victorine's way of noting the coincidence of their meeting again, and of saying a pleasant hello. The others on line, perhaps faintly suspicious that they were the object of some jest, as rightly they appeared to be with their absurd gray faces and conspicuous clothes of privilege, seemed to try cowardly to make themselves smaller as they stood pretending they hadn't heard anything.

Victorine stepped out of her place in line and embraced Fatima like an old friend.

"*Ma soeur*," she said, "how has one's acclimatization progressed?"

Before Fatima could answer, the pharmacy clerk put a box of the laxative suppositories on the counter in front of her.

Victorine looked at Fatima mischievously and burst out laughing again. Soon, to the displeasure of all around, they were both laughing at the French way of administering medicine while the little prematurely bald clerk stood there with the box in his hand as if he'd offered a treat and if they kept laughing he'd take it back.

Fatima told Victorine the medicine was for an old Labrador named Emma, and that it was a matter of life or death.

"On Djerba there were herbs," she said with regret.

"In the City of Light, *ma soeur*," said Victorine, "there is everything. Meet me at the corner of the avenue Kléber and the Place du Trocadéro tomorrow evening."

Emma expelled the medicine as soon as the Countess applied it. And nothing else. The old woman looked at Fatima, who was holding the poor, wailing dog's paws during the administration, as if everything were Fatima's fault. Nothing like this had happened to Emma during the time of Rachida.

Fatima thought only of her appointment the next evening.

There was still the clear blue-gray light of an early fall Paris dusk as Fatima and Victorine boarded the 30 bus at the first stop on the avenue Kléber near the Place du Trocadéro. After the Etoile, they drove past the luxurious apartment buildings, ornate bulwarks of Belle Epoque wealth, in the Plaine Monceau, and came to Villiers, where there was another of those colorful French merry-go-rounds that could be out of a picture book for children. Now the boulevard became more commercial, a mosaic of storefronts of all sorts. At the Place de Clichy, on the face of a huge movie theater, there were enormous signs advertising films. The street was a hive of traffic and the sidewalks were crowded with people far less well-dressed than in the neighborhoods they had passed. At the Place Blanche, the row on row of sex shops and peep shows began. Opposite a red-browed building with a windmill on top, a store window was full of strange underclothes with cutouts and leather masks and whips. CUIR, LATEX, LINGERIE read the sign in the window. Fatima sucked her breath in as she noticed the rows of life-size photographs on the walls of theaters across the boulevard. They showed people in the throes of lovemaking, with just black rectangles at strategic points to cover their shame. But their faces were all visible. What must those women's neighbors think when they recognize them, and when they see them again in real life? None of these photographs stirred

114

Fatima erotically. There was a sort of short circuit, a downed bridge, in her association with them. What she'd known of lovemaking had been clumsy and disappointing.

Soon they were at the Place Pigalle. Fatima noticed more and more black people and North Africans in the street.

In the City of Light, we have everything, she heard again in her mind. So much for her to assemble and assimilate in one bus ride. Victorine had said *we*. Her city. Fatima wondered if she could ever feel that this varied city, swarming with both suave beauty and raw physical life, was *hers*.

Victorine seemed hardly to be taking notice of it. She sat with a certain almost monumental serenity, her thoughts elsewhere, Fatima sensed. Someplace perhaps immaterial.

Now the shops literally overflowed with people grabbing at fabric and clothes piled on stands. A *métro* train clattered out of a tunnel in the middle of the boulevard and raced up onto elevated tracks. The bus stopped below the tracks.

"Barbès," said Victorine, nudging Fatima to get up.

Black men and North Africans stood around, each apparently on his own, yet grouped together under the *métro* station, all with vacant looks. Perhaps they were each waiting for someone. Perhaps, Fatima thought, this was a meeting place. Men alone. Waiting for their families to arrive — that sentimental thought, tinged with old regrets of her own, came into her mind even though there was no logic in their waiting here, in the middle of the city. No logic in her feeling sentimental about those memories either.

"*La drogue*," Victorine whispered. "Dealers."

They crossed the boulevard.

They entered La rue des Poissonniers. La Goutte d'Or: the drop of gold. Could a neighborhood have a lovelier, more evocative name?

They started to walk uphill on the rue des Poissonniers, long ago the fishmongers' street. They passed fabric shops piled with *waxes*, bright African prints, and with diaphanous embroideries threaded with gilt. A disheveled travel office had a big photo of Mecca in the window. Beside it, another storefront was full of brightly colored sandals and gold chains. They passed rows of greengrocery stores, one after another, with roots and vegetables and fruit such as Fatima had never seen before. Across the street, a store was selling wigs beside a butcher shop hung with sides of lamb, and beyond it a bazaar that could have been in Tunis overflowed onto the sidewalk with plastic kitchen dishes, bright aluminum couscous pots and wooden salad bowls.

Victorine stopped to catch her breath.

"First we must visit Samuel," she said. "He would take umbrage were he informed I made the journey to the quarter without learning his news."

"Samuel?"

"My true cousin, *ma soeur*."

Victorine pushed open a doorway in the rue de la Goutte d'Or and Fatima saw a different world. It was a mews of poor but not ugly nineteenth-century houses

116

with little front yards planted with flowers and in one case with tomatoes and corn. Samuel's workshop was at the bottom of this *hameau*. A worn sign in early-twentieth-century lettering that surely predated his presence hung above the wired glass front of the shop. It read: COUVERTURE. PLOMBERIE. Roofing and Plumbing. To which had been added in red paint: ELECTRICITÉ ET TOUS TRAVAUX DE RÉNOVATION. SAMUEL DIOP. If you believed the sign, Samuel, in short, could do anything with his hands.

Somewhere, among the backyards nearby, chickens were clucking and a rooster crowed. Fatima even heard the quack of a duck.

Samuel was a strapping, very dark African of about forty. His grip, as he took Fatima's hand and without any hesitation kissed her on each cheek like an old friend, was the grip of a man who made daily use of his strength.

"*Bienvenue à la Goutte d'Or*," he said. And he repeated "*la Goutte d'Or*," as if he had not yet come to take the poetry of the name, that came from a once-precious vineyard, for granted.

Victorine and Samuel exchanged news. Victorine's Madame had been photographed leaving the Tribunal de Grande Instance with an Air France pilot wrongly accused of murdering his wife, whom Madame Benamou-Khan had successfully defended. Victorine had a copy of the clipping from *France Soir*, which she unfolded for Samuel, who clucked with appreciation as if a touch of glory had rubbed off on his cousin and was in turn now rubbing off on him. Samuel's plumbing and electricity business was doing well. He had acquired clients beyond the quarter, and his wife was pregnant with their fifth child.

"What stimulates your visit, dear cousin?" Samuel finally asked.

"Fatima is in need of medication."

Samuel shot Fatima a concerned look.

"For a dog," said Fatima, causing Samuel to smile spontaneously with relief.

"Hmm," said Samuel.

"Farida Bounajem," said Victorine.

"Precisely," said Samuel. "Exactly. You stole the name from my lips."

Fatima brightened. Perhaps Farida was Tunisian.

She was Algerian. From far south near the desert, a Berber of eighty with a tattoo on her pale forehead. Her hair was covered with a chador, but her face was fully exposed, a big-browed, wrinkled face with high cheekbones. Farida looked the way women did in what might have been another, heroic age for her people.

She stood erect behind an old wooden counter in her shop. The shop had served another purpose — the wooden counter, the woodwork of the walls full of little drawers were the trappings of a *mercerie*, of which few still survive in Paris. Shops where people sold loose buttons and needles and laces, in quantities no longer efficient to sell. Farida had kept the long mirror behind the counter. Mottled now, with chipped gilt, it still read GRYNZSPAN ET FILS.

Once perhaps the shop had the sulphury smell of new cloth and dyes. Now it was redolent of a medley of herbs. Farida was an *herboriste*. On their way over from Samuel's, Victorine had explained that she was *très forte et pas chère*. A trickle of people, advised by word of mouth among domestics, came to her from every nook and class of the city.

"What sort of dog?" asked Farida of Fatima, addressing her directly in Arabic.

"A Labrador."

Farida knit her brow. What could she possibly have learned about Labradors near the Sahara? Emma was the first Labrador Fatima had ever seen.

"A large dog," Fatima said, "a large cold-weather dog."

"What does she complain of?"

"She's thirsty, she won't eat, she sleeps and sleeps and she whimpers. She won't move. In Tunisia we have —"

"And she does her *besoins* —?"

"Not at all. I should have said that first. Not for days. Do you have —"

"I choose the remedy. We are not in Tunisia."

Fatima chose not to take offense, nor to press her own knowledge on the woman. It was Emma's survival that was at stake here. All during their exchange, Farida had not looked up from staring into her old hands. Big, well-shaped hands. Fatima noted that Farida had the hands of a midwife. She'd yield to their care. Finally Farida clapped her hands together.

She walked off into the back of her store without saying another word. Fatima and Victorine could hear her shuffling things around back there, moving boxes. Farida came out with some dark roots in one hand and a handful of seeds in the other. The roots were still damp.

"These were just harvested," she said of the roots. "Dandelions. Two-year-old plants."

She held the roots out for Fatima to smell. They gave off a bitter, clay-like odor.

"The seeds are psyllium. Old, very old. Their use is ancient. In your home and in mine."

"Thank you," Fatima heard herself saying. She would have asked for psyllium, but she said no more.

"What do you do?" Farida asked.

"Madame is a lady's helper," Victorine broke in. "She is with a countess of historical importance."

Farida went "Pfff." She said: "They have titles and money and *la science* and they hand their bodies over to doctors and surgeons and we have to pay for all that with the social security. They think the world began with the Age of Reason. Pff.

"I leave you the choice," Farida added, "the seeds or the roots. I'm not certain. I've never dealt with a 'Labrador' before."

"I think that I'll have trouble getting her to absorb either one," said Fatima.

"The animal is thirsty? Boil the roots and leave them in water overnight. Don't give her any other liquids."

As Fatima and Victorine left, having paid Farida a small sum, the old Berber called after them:

120

"If it doesn't work, come back for the seeds . . . or I have something Chinese.

"'Globalization,'" she clucked with irony, "Chinese rhubarb. But I can give no guarantees regarding 'Labradors.'"

Emma stared at the leash in Fatima's hand. The old dog's eyes shone, as if full of fond memories. She blinked and then she shifted a little on the Louis Seize armchair in the Countess's living room — *her* chair, Emma's — before she closed her eyes again and lay her head on her side. Fatima exhaled a long, sorrowful sigh. Not yet ready to give in, she waved the leash in front of the dog's face. The clasp rattled. Emma opened her eyes again. For a moment, Emma and Fatima looked into each other's eyes.

"If you lie here like that you will die," Fatima said gravely in Arabic. After a moment of silence, Emma replied with something between a whimper and a bark.

"Do you want more?" Fatima asked. Cagily threatened, actually. But before she could try to drag the dog back to the kitchen for more of the root decoction, the dog stirred her hind legs and gave a real bark.

"Emma!" shouted the Countess anxiously from her bedroom, where Monsieur Li, Paris's high-society acupuncturist, was administering to the Countess's knees.

"She's all right, *Madame la Comtesse*," Fatima said. And as she said that, Emma jumped off the chair and began to bark repeatedly.

121

"What?" came the Countess's voice again.

But Fatima was so excited that she didn't wait to answer. Emma had her leash on, and they were out the kitchen door.

Emma made her way down the backstairs as slowly as ever, but Fatima resisted an impulse to try to pick the dog up in her arms. Emma would not be an invalid. By the time they reached the ground floor, Monsieur Li was coming out of the elevator. He looked like his entire face was false, a rubber mask. His wig looked like straw. When he smiled at Emma, his teeth were bigger and more even than real teeth. Monsieur Li was known in the *Tout Paris* as a man who often worked miracles, but Fatima could look at him now without being at all intimidated. She remembered that she'd had no need of Chinese rhubarb and that, anyway, the Chinese ate dogs.

Hippolyte Suget was furious. He'd been taking a reservation on the phone, at the desk of the Villa Saint Valentin, when a couple walked in, bringing with them a smell quite different from the heady perfumes the women of these couples liked to wear for the occasion of their trysts. It was unmistakedly *la crotte de chien*. No sooner had Suget identified the odor than he saw the gentleman of the couple tracking the dog excrement on the red welcome carpet of the Villa.

"*La Rose*," the man had said impatiently. He was a middle-aged heavy man, and his face was red, his brow faintly sweating in anticipation of the business of his rendezvous. Suget had remembered him as a regular client. Something in his mien made Suget sense, as someone with his experience could sense, that the man might be a plainclothesman. Come for a break in his duties. The woman, with dyed blonde hair and rose red lips, Suget had never seen before.

"Monsieur," Suget had begun, pointing to the maculated shoe. Then he looked up, and through the window he could see a Labrador resisting being pulled on a leash. By that woman.

Fatima had tugged. She'd been torn between joy and mortification. There was nothing to do but get away from there. She'd tugged, and God only knew why, the leash slipped through her fingers. And she'd had to race after Emma, frisking like a puppy.

The man had presented his Visa card. Suget didn't finish his sentence. He popped the card into the card reader on the desk. The odor rose again. Suddenly Suget, furious, was out the door. He saw where the man had stepped and then he turned to see the Labrador racing free of its leash. Behind it was the heavy Arab woman, holding the edge of her djellaba and running quite fast. They looked like they were shamelessly running away from the scene of the transgression. When he'd gone back inside, the couple was looking dour, as if the interruption had cast a shade of doubt onto their tryst. The man's face was no longer flushed but pale. Slips of paper had come out of the card reader. As far as Visa was concerned, the deal was on. The man ripped away his copy and grabbed the key to *La Rose* that Suget handed him. Suget was too challenged now to remind the man about the stuff on his shoe.

Suget had spent the hour that the couple spent in *La Rose* on his hands and knees in the lobby, with rug shampoo.

Emma had bolted away, and Fatima had had to run as fast as she could to catch her. That Emma could run now, and pull at her leash, like a young dog, was a miraculous stroke of grace. And the Countess would have to be grateful. Fatima's heart had quickened at the possibility of what might even somehow be a happy future in Paris. And Emma had at last done her business. Unfortunately, right at the steps of the Villa Saint Valentin. There had been a reason for it to happen, but if there was a reason for everything, what valid reason could there be that it did not happen at the curb?

"On the other hand," said Monsieur Strasbourg, "one should not exaggerate."

"What is this but exaggeration?" insisted Hippolyte Suget from his barstool. "And it's not the dog that is responsible."

Suget had ordered a second *ballon de rouge* to calm himself, and the effect had been the opposite. By now his faith in civility had been too sorely challenged. The letter he'd received had stoked his anger even before he'd become the primary victim of Emma's faux pas. His cheeks glowed as he finished yet a third glass of red wine.

124

"Exaggeration invokes exaggeration," he said.

"Unwrap the guillotine!" shouted Clément the unemployed computer programmer, as he kept on shaking the pinball machine.

"You say any old thing," said Ginette the waitress to Clément.

"Totally out of place," said Elodie Couteau, the retired chambermaid, who, having observed high society from her vantage at the Ritz, was the arbiter of etiquette at the Jean Valjean.

"Do you really think I meant it?" he answered testily. There was always a current of antagonism between Ginette and Clément. Perhaps because Ginette's husband was constantly fatigued by his long-haul truck job and Clément saw fit to do nothing but rack up colossal scores on the pinball machine by tilting it to the edge of what the machine tolerated. Clément was living mellowly on unemployment payments nearly as high as the salary he'd gotten from his defunct dot.com.

Thibault and Louis-Paul, the dapper real estate agents, simultaneously finished their coffee and as if on cue, simultaneously shrugged and walked out. Monsieur Strasbourg looked at his watch. His wife was at the hairdresser's and they'd agreed to meet at the entrance to the Espace Bonprix supermarket in five minutes. They had to shop for food and things, and Monsieur Strasbourg was already cross at the prospect of carrying a six-pack of liter-and-a-half bottles of mineral water all the way home.

"*Ecoutez! Monsieur Suget,*" he said, "we can't go on about this forever. Listen. It's simple. You put signs up: 'Curb your dog or you risk being fined.' You establish a reasonable fine. But your idea of taking people to the police station is an exaggeration. And as such, it is also impractical."

"There'd be lines blocks long outside the police stations," Ginette chimed in. "Monsieur Suget," she added, "everyone knows where I stand regarding dogs. As a dog lover I cannot help but take objection to the harshness of your solution."

"Whom do you fine?" Clément said with an edge of nastiness, happy to be about to shoot down what the others were saying. "Granted you don't fine the dog. You fine the owner? But in this *quartier* how many people do not even walk their own dogs?" Clément's recent unemployment had stirred class antagonisms in him, even though he, himself, had been classified as a middle-range manager.

"The one who walks is the one who pays!" insisted Suget. All his morning's distress was boiling up in him again. "In their countries, nobody dares disobey the law. They cut off their hands. They beat them. They stone them to death!"

Just then Fatima walked into the café.

Suget didn't see her. "They cut off their hands!" he shouted, beside himself. Now he saw her, and embarrassment surged over him, stronger than the buzz from the wine.

Fatima stared at him. She fixed him in her gaze until he lowered his eyes.

126

"Monsieur," she said, "I am sorry about the dog." Her emotions were a confusion of shame and anger. She went up to Madame Richard's cashier counter.

"Four euros twenty on the Lotto," she said.

Madame Richard handed her a paper on which to check off her numbers.

"Like the last time," said Fatima.

She looked over her shoulder. Suget had vanished.

"Say, look at that," she heard Monsieur Strasbourg tell Ginette as he gathered up his *Figaro* and paid. Monsieur Strasbourg had cocked his head toward the sidewalk, where Fatima now saw that Suget was petting the dog tied to the lamppost with a sheepish air.

"Then should I fill them out for you again?" asked Madame Richard, gently. Madame Richard was an embodiment of French reasonableness. She did not like high emotion or tension in her café. "The joker? The last time you didn't choose the joker. It's a euro and you win more."

Fatima handed her another euro.

Suget was slinking away down the street. Fatima realized the strangeness of a feeling that had come over her — of having been betrayed. And he was strange, too. He had been so gallant in the supermarket.

Madame Richard noticed her pensiveness. She coughed.

"Everything the same as the last time, please," Fatima said. She understood well that the chances of winning were nearly nil, but playing had now gained an added meaning that was part of her will to be a Parisian.

Her spirits lifted when she got home, with Emma barking and frisking at the door. The Countess was so thrilled to see Emma in that state that she took the dog in her arms and even did a hobbled little dance with her.

A rich odor of garlic frying in olive oil wafted Fatima's way as she emptied garbage near the cellar stairs of 34bis. Carmen had opened the door to the concierge's *loge* and now she was standing in the doorway making a conspiratorial hissing noise to get Fatima's attention. She beckoned Fatima into her *loge*.

It was a neat room with an imitation leather couch and an iron bed, a big wooden table, a plain wardrobe, and a large TV set. Here Carmen and Angel had been living for years, almost ever since they'd arrived in Paris from a village near Teruel, in the harsh, arid countryside of southern Aragon. They had been eating and sleeping in this room for thirty-five years. They had conceived and reared children here. And the children — three boys — had grown up, learned trades, married, and moved away. One had to conclude that this room, where life had been enriched by the purchase of a car and of tickets home in August, thanks to what Angel had earned as a street-paver, was better than whatever they'd known in Aragon. But times had changed. Franco was long gone, Spain had moved into the wide consumer society, and no one was emigrating from the plains of Aragon to France anymore. Carmen and Angel were anachronisms now, especially Carmen, a woman with almost no learning, vulnerable good intentions, and a fearful, feudal diffidence to superior people. A photo of King Juan Carlos hung above her plastic couch, and a crucifix over her bed.

A fat white cat named Nieve was sleeping on the bed, insensitive to the garlic in the air from where Carmen had just finished frying a potato omelet, which Angel would eat with her when he came back from what she always believed was his constitutional walk. Carmen put the tortilla on the table to cool. Olives, a baguette, slices of chorizo, nearly black wine in a plastic water bottle, which someone might have brought up from Spain. Floral oil cloth. Fatima felt she was not quite in France here, but somewhere sunnier, and the thought reassured her, as if the Mediterranean that had somehow seasoned both her blood and Carmen's bonded them. She remembered that Spain had once been part of the realm of her ancestors. But this good woman was all the same an agent of the system at 34bis, and Fatima still did not know whether she could be trusted.

"*Señora la Contessa*," Carmen said. "First she asked me for names."

Fatima looked at her curiously.

"There are always people who come to me, wanting to know if I know where they can clean."

Fatima understood.

"She intended to interview some women."

"You are nice to tell me."

"That's not what I mean to tell you. I'm telling you she said, 'Ask them to wait.'"

"You will be victorious," Carmen assured. "You will be victorious," and she winked. That old Spanish formality in her voice might just have been colored by a subversive echo of *La Passionaria*.

Carmen blushed, embarrassed but relieved. Fatima sensed that Carmen had been ashamed from the start at being drawn into the Countess's conspiracy, but too obedient in her old-fashioned Spanish servant's way to have refused. Carmen's piece of intelligence and her complicity comforted Fatima, but not enough to tell her she was home free.

"*Petit con!*" squawked Cacahouète.

Hippolyte Suget had looked into the mirror after he'd gotten up to go to work that evening, pointed a finger at his face covered with shaving cream, and called himself a *petit con*, a little jerk.

Now the parrot wouldn't stop echoing him.

"*Petit con!*"

Suget sat on the edge of the lower bunk of his bunk bed, close to his table, reached for the milk that had boiled on his hot plate and poured it into a bowl of Ricoré, a powder of chicory and chocolate that was his wake-up beverage. Coffee was too strong for him at breakfast time — and why had he gone beyond one glass of wine the morning before!

"*Petit con!*" cawed Cacahouète.

He'd made a scene.

He finished the buttered *biscotte*, the melba toast he'd soaked in the Ricoré, and stared, without thinking, at his empty bowl as he held it in both hands.

"Hippolyte" was written on it. He'd bought it in a souvenir shop near the Cathedral of Notre-Dame along with the other one that read "Jennifer" that stood on his dresser, which he kept for the little girl's visits. Probably, he thought now, it was silly for a father to have a bowl with his name on it, like a child's. He looked up beyond the bowl at his jockey shorts hanging to dry on the rope that was strung across his room and he said it again before the parrot could: "*Petit con.*"

Once again he told himself he might well be unworthy of being the parent of the child whose photograph he'd blown up into the poster that was tacked above the commode. She'd already shown signs of being more grown-up than he was.

As for the embarrassing event, first of all, it could have been an accident. *She* might well not have expected the dog to do it right then and there — and how could she have stopped it once it started?

Suget realized he was making excuses for the woman. As if he wanted to. While everyone knew that if you rationalized in that way, the whole city would be covered with the stuff. And yet . . . In any case, second, the business about Allah and chopping hands had sounded like he was a *Le Peniste*, a rotten fascist. Which he definitely was not. That was definitely what he'd done wrong. The wine had talked, not him. Truth to tell, all his sour frustration had seeped up and expressed itself. It was the letter of rejection that he'd found the night before that had talked, plain and simple. Plain and simple.

Suget had seen an ad for a receptionist in the hotel trade paper *L'Hospitalité*. A day receptionist in a three-star hotel on the Boulevard de Courcelles. Hope had flickered within him when he'd gotten up that evening, and he'd applied. He'd been rejected without even having been given an interview. For a moment, mailing his application, he'd conjured up a whole future, a rising career in the hospitality industry. But between the mention of the job he'd once had tending bar at a dubious nightclub off the Champs-Elysées and his current position at the Villa Saint Valentin, there was the gap. They might well have looked into it and found out what it represented without needing to ask him to explain.

He had no right to take out his frustration on others. And there was no point in pitying himself. So be it: He had a bird to keep him company and he was staying out of trouble. Asking for more might be asking for trouble.

He touched his underwear. It was dry. He looked at the weights below his window. He just didn't feel like doing his exercises this evening. He just wouldn't. That whole incident had thrown him off balance. A faint intuition came to him: The order he'd established in his life could all the same easily fall apart. Then where would he be? The street? *Do the exercises. Don't.*

Don't won. He took off his striped pajamas and folded them on the narrow bed he'd made as soon as he'd gotten up. *Don't let it all fall apart.* He got into the stall shower in the little bathroom that abutted his combination sink, refrigerator and hot plate, scrubbed himself in his usual pattern. As he tried to think of

132

nothing but the business of soaping and scrubbing, because otherwise his thoughts would lead him over and over to that moment of embarrassment, he heard his parrot squawking above the sound of the running water:

"*Petit con petit con!*"

"*Tais-toi!*" shouted Suget, shut up! But was the parrot wrong? He shut his eyes under the water, as if to close off all thought again. On the dark red screen of his eyelids, an image of the woman's face surprised him. She was saying, "Monsieur, I am sorry about the dog," in her sunny accent while her strange eyes welled with a gentleness. A gentleness like understanding.

"*Petit con* yourself!" he shouted at the parrot. He opened his shower door and splashed Cacahouète in his face, through his cage.

The linoleum floor was wet now. The order of his life was definitely falling apart. As for Cacahouète, he shook his feathers and shut up.

Fatima sat on her bed and wrote into a school notebook: "*Je, tu, il, nous, vous, ils,*" speaking out loud as she wrote. She compared what she'd written with her reading sampler. It was all right. She closed the book and closed her eyes and recited the alphabet, and then, opening to the front page of the sampler, she ran her fingers over the letters as she recited them again. She went over their sounds.

She wrote: *Jean va à l'ecole.* The accent was missing on the *e.* Straight up or straight down? Up. That was right, the way it was in the book. *Jean va à l'école.* She

133

compared that with the printed sentence, and it was perfect. Perfect!

"How long will it take?" she'd asked Hadley.

"No time."

"Please tell me."

"For you? No time. A few months."

"She will not wait that long."

"She needs you, dear! It's all about the dog. The dog is on your side and the dog is all she loves in life. She needs you, that's all you have to know." Hadley was such an optimist for a writer who'd never had a book published.

"Your words will be printed for me to read," she'd told Hadley.

"*Inshallah*," he'd answered. "I'll have to teach you to read English. Meantime, keep the dog alive."

"I know this will happen," she'd insisted.

"Funny how you know things," he'd said.

"You know, I love the dog, too," she'd said. It was true. A bond had formed between the animal and her. Was Emma all she had left to love in life?

Rachida's mirror gave Fatima back her face. It was round and unassertive but not really a servant's face. Its evenness spoke of a certain aplomb in her character. She knew that was how others saw her. The women on Djerba who came for her advice. Yes, Hadley had said she always looked "knowing." Ah, but she was no fortune-teller, and her own future was all in a mist. People in her situation, little poor people, are not supposed to think beyond one day to another, beyond holding the little they have together. They're not privileged with goals, but right now Fatima could not help but feel unbalanced and questioning.

Everyone, she thought, is alone in his own little boat. And no one really knows anything. All she had to go on was her intuition, and regarding herself, it was never very informative. No one truly knows anyone, and least of all himself. People are full of surprises. The way the Countess had danced with the dog. She loves Emma. She is capable of love. And yet there's a daughter she never sees. Thinking of the dog again brought to mind that slender man. What a surprise he turned out to be. All gallantry in the supermarket. The elegant wave from the bus. And then the horror that came out of his mouth in the café. Cutting off hands! Now she could not help but laugh at last. She saw herself laugh into her hand. A strange man. Her intuition told her he was not a happy man, that his life was full of wounds. All that birdseed in his shopping cart. He has a bird. Whom he no doubt cares for. And his gallantry, the gallantry of that little funny man, there was no denying it, had been nothing short of lovely.

And what were the stuffed toy and the lollipops all about? she wondered.

Her mood had shifted with her laughter, and as she looked at her face again, she had a peculiar thought: Would lipstick make a difference in her life?

"You can choose the main course, the rest will be a surprise," the Countess told Didi. It was his birthday and the call was about his birthday dinner. The Countess sounded radiant on the phone.

"Why are you so happy?" he asked. "At my age, one does not delight in birthdays."

"You're a spring chicken compared to me. I have one foot in the grave," she said with a chuckle that made him laugh, too.

"You sound radiant with joy."

"I have saved dear Emma."

"You saved Emma —"

"From a horrid butcher called Cheval. We need never see him again, neither Emma nor I."

"May I ask how you accomplished this miracle?"

"You may ask all you want, but I don't have to answer. There's more to your old auntie than you thought."

"I've always believed that there was a lot to you, *Tantine* Monique," he protested. "I know: You fed her something miraculous. You are, after all, a miraculous cook."

"What will it be?" she replied, evasively.

"Ortolans."

"Eating ortolans is against the law. Those poor little birds are a protected species now."

"But you can do anything! You always do anything you want. Do what I want, just for my birthday."

"I will not help destroy a species of bird, even if I had mysterious sources to obtain ortolans, like you with all your connections. Not so that you can pop little creatures in your mouth with a napkin covering your head."

136

The Countess was referring to the traditional French way to eat the little birds, so that none of their precious aroma was lost.

"Well then, sausage and lentils."

"Don't be cross, you can have something in between."

"I wish, I wish, I wish I could eat a coq au vin. Not a chicken, please, but a real rooster."

"That can be found. I'll send Fatima to the rue des Belles Feuilles."

"How is it going — with Rachida?"

"Fatima," the Countess corrected, but she ignored the question. "There'll be fresh noodles."

"I haven't had a coq au vin since you made it for me at Branchevieille." Branchevieille was the Countess's château in Auvergne, where she seldom went anymore.

"Don't mention Branchevieille."

"The plumbing again? *Again?*"

"The plumbing, everything."

"It was my feast for when I passed my Baccalauréate. I was eighteen."

"No!"

"Yes, and there were cocks' combs in the vol-au-vents to start with."

"Cocks' combs indeed! Those days are over, Didi, be happy if Fatima can get us a beheaded real rooster."

"All in all, we should be happy for what the good Lord has given us, should we not, *Tantine* Monique?"

"You sound," the Countess said with feigned ill-humor, "like you've been talking to my maid."

Two days later, Samuel pulled up in the avenue Victor-Hugo in his van, with Aboubakar Camarra singing "Alo . . . Alo" loudly on his cassette player. It was as if Samuel were proud to let people know that his truck had a cassette player. As for the rest, it was not quite something to boast about, but it ran, as it had for fifteen years, and by now it was an old friend. The van had taken more than a few dents in Paris traffic — Samuel was an impatient driver — and there was rust on the spots where the white paint had been chipped away. Fifteen years ago, before he was able to pay a sign painter, Samuel had written, on both sides, in his own hand SAMUEL DIOP, ELECTRICITÉ, COUVERTURE ET PLOMBERIE.

It was not the sort of van Monsieur Robert was accustomed to seeing in this neighborhood, and as he squinted at it from the doorway of 34bis, where once again he was off to give a piano lesson, he was not really astonished to see that new maid of the Countess's step out of such a truck.

She was holding a bag smeared with what looked very much like blood. But maybe he needed new glasses.

He stood there, astonished, or rather offended, as she began to enter the building.

"*Bonjour, Monsieur,*" she said.

He didn't answer. His eyes were still on that horrid truck as it pulled out into traffic, almost grazing Madame Marchand's Porsche as she stopped to back up into her usual parking space on the sidewalk while her cassette player played Céline Dion, accompanied by bagpipes, singing "My Heart Will Go On." Monsieur Robert was reminded of Madame Marchand's notorious trysts.

The black man at the wheel was smiling and waving goodbye to the Arab woman. She turned to wave back, and then, going into the building, Fatima accidentally grazed Monsieur Robert's leg with her bag. He hadn't been inclined to move aside for her. The bag felt oddly warm against his leg. God knows what could have been in there.

"Exquisite," said the Countess, staring at a rooster with its head on, on the table. "They had a rooster!"

Emma looked up at the dead bird with a puzzled air.

"They didn't, Madame. A friend helped me . . . to catch him."

"Ah yes, friends?"

"Yes, Madame."

"So soon? I wish I could make friends that easily. Who can catch me roosters!"

Fatima didn't know if she were being made fun of. She simply looked at her mistress serenely.

In the shop called Poulets de France in the rue des Belles Feuilles, the butcher had tried to pass a large headless chicken off on Fatima. But Fatima had seen enough poultry on Djerba to know just by the neck and feet that the bird was an imposter.

Fatima had heard a cock crowing in her recent memory. But now, because of the diplomatic negotiations of Samuel, there would be relative silence in the backyards behind the rue de la Goutte d'Or.

139

"I've bought some eggs as well, Madame," Fatima said, as she reached into the bag. "They were laid this morning."

"Laid this morning?"

The Countess wouldn't admit that she, herself, wouldn't know where to get fresh-laid eggs in Paris. She looked back at Fatima for a moment without saying anything else. Then she busied herself gutting the rooster, which had not been dressed, and she didn't ask why. Indeed, she loved cooking and preparing to cook. The thought crossed her mind that if she had close friends she would not have to wait for her nephew's birthday to cook up an impressive dinner. If she had close friends.

"Well, then, you and I could have an omelet for lunch," she finally said to Fatima.

Fatima looked at the kitchen clock, which read ten to one.

"I'll prepare it at once," she said.

"Of course not," the Countess said. "What do you know about omelets? I'll prepare it."

"As God will have it, Madame," Fatima said, and she smiled secretly into her hand.

"Well, if it's all right with Him," the Countess answered, "you can wash the lettuce for our salad."

Whereupon, as Emma snored on her Louis Seize armchair in the salon, the Countess and Fatima prepared their lunch.

"Sit down," the Countess said.

Fatima by then had understood something about the Countess that led her not to protest. And so, without

140

any further conversation, the two women sat down to lunch together at the kitchen table.

A while later, Monsieur Robert, back from giving his lesson, smelled a good winy-garlicky-herbal aroma in the hallway. The odor cheered him, gave him to believe that France still belonged to the French. And indeed, while the Countess stirred and skimmed, a genuine rooster of obscure origin was on its way to becoming naturalized as an authentic coq au vin.

The Countess had sent Didi into the cellar to get three bottles of wine. Fatima had given him a pair of disposable gloves from her supply in the kitchen and then he'd asked her to go down with him, first of all to hold the flashlight. (Years ago, Monsieur Robert had rallied the co-owners against the Count's motion to install electricity in the *caves*.) Fatima would also clean off the bottles. Didi didn't have a physical allergy to dust, but rather a more serious aversion toward touching dirt. Fatima would wipe the bottles, and since he had to fetch three of them, she'd help carry. They'd have to be carried very gently so as not to disturb the sediment.

"I'm not going to live forever, Didi, I don't care if we just drink a little from each bottle, but you will have three distinguished wines in proper order for your birthday. Three wines, the way good people used to and should have with an important meal."

He didn't object. There were enough good bottles down there to last for the important meals of several lifetimes. Didi remembered driving with the Countess's late husband, Geoffroy Poulais du Roc, to Château Ausone in Saint Emilion, to have the corks changed on the Count's two cases of Ausone '29. Uncle Geoff, who had lost his driving license after a number of accidents, fortunately damaging property alone, had revealed that his cataracts were inhibiting his ability to drive. Uncle Geoff had been a competition driver in the fifties, before sporting individuals came to have no chance against the big manufacturers. He'd once placed second with a cousin at Le Mans in an Alfa Romeo Giulietta, and he'd kept driving in road traffic with the same competitive zeal all his life, double-clutching loudly as he passed everyone, even though he was in the era of synchromeshed gears. By the time he lost his license, he had been like a bat flying by radar. A lucky bat. Aunt Monique, Didi mused, might have learned all her brio, close to arrogance but somehow more attractive, living with him. But it was more likely that those two had been born for each other, under the same star. She had been inconsolable after he'd died ten years ago — ten years next month, he remembered. She'd been unable to forgive him. One day Uncle Geoff had seen kids riding skateboards down the steps of the Palais de Chaillot, nearby, and he just had to try it. He did it — at seventy-five. That was all he had to do, prove he could do it. But Uncle Geoff enjoyed the experience. The second time he slipped on a McDonald's wrapper someone had left on a step, flipped, and broke his head.

Uncle Geoff had always loved danger, but it was a trivial way for him to go, after all he'd accomplished in the face of it. So the Countess believed. Small. He who not only had raced fast cars but had also flown a Martin Maryland with the *Forces Aériennes Françaises Libres*, attached to the RAF. Didi was comforted to remember now that the family — both his and his aunt's husband's — were on the right side of the war. Gaullist not Pétainist. Uncle Geoff's medals were still out there in glass on a table near where Emma liked to sleep. He'd done nothing else with his life except be a hero — had never worked. The Countess still didn't forgive him his tactless death.

In any case, drinking wine always brought him back to mind for her, and that could be a painful experience. Except when an occasion made wine the seemly thing to do, the Countess usually just drank the water from that well in the rue de la Pompe.

"You choose, and don't underestimate what you're worth," she'd told Didi.

Fatima unlocked the steel door of the *cave*. Her flashlight swept over hundreds of bottles, covered with dust and cobwebs. Didi's thoughts darkened as he looked at that accumulation that spoke so strongly of age. Today he was fifty-five.

He heard again in his mind, where it felt now as if cobwebs were gathering: "I'm not going to live forever." And today he was passing a watershed. The other side of fifty-five was old age. "Don't underestimate what you're worth." Aunt Monique esteemed him, with the esteem their class had been bred to have for traits unrelated to accomplishment. At the Quai d'Orsay he'd never pushed himself forward. Maybe if his generation had been Uncle Geoff's, he would have been a hero, and that would have made him sure of his own worth. Cobwebs — his thoughts seemed to be sticking, blurring. He burped, as if that would right his head.

In the close atmosphere of the chilly cellar, Fatima could smell alcohol on Didi's breath. In point of fact, he had begun steeling himself for his milestone dinner with a few scotches at the Travelers' Club.

Fatima could make out reverence in Didi's eyes as he scanned the shelves, a look to which she couldn't relate. At the Club Rêve the wine bottles were clean and new and a lot of them were kept in the refrigerator, which Ahmed filled every day. The holiday-makers, when they weren't drinking Coke, favored rosé. It had such a lovely pink-orange color. It glistened in the glass, alive. Why this communion with the aged? Everything that's out in the sunlight and alive, that's what counts. That simple presence of vitality was something she'd taken for granted on Djerba. She gave Didi a look of pity.

Didi reached for his first choice, the Sauternes to go with the foie gras. He chose a Château d'Yquem '47. Fatima started to wipe the bottle. The label meant nothing to her. She didn't know that on Djerba you could buy a sound used car for what that bottle was worth.

"It's the year I was born, my dear," Didi said. The whisky was creating an egalitarian familiarity in his voice. Fatima sensed the desolation that was driving it as well.

At that moment, while Fatima was still wiping, a rat crossed the *cave*, screeching, and liberated itself in the

144

hallway of the cellar. Fatima was startled and the bottle fell to the floor and smashed. She stood petrified while a rich odor like the most delicious of raisins rose from the broken glass and her splashed djellaba.

"Well, the forty-five was a whole lot better," he simply said. "Let's find us the forty-five."

"I'm very, very sorry," she said.

"Oh no," he said. "You accidentally did just the right thing. I would have had to stare at that year eating my dinner." His voice actually had a sincere cheerfulness to it now. That prompted her to add:

"You know, there are people who believe it brings good luck."

"Broken glass? Do you believe that?"

"Why not?" she said.

"What's there to lose?" he assented.

"Everything happens as it's supposed to."

"*Inshallah*," he said. "Anyway, Uncle Geoff would forgive us. He knew about accidents. It was he who laid all this down. You know? My aunt's husband.

"She never stops thinking of him."

Fatima recalled how much she would think of Mahmoud. She couldn't help it.

"They were a perfectly matched pair."

Even though she and Mahmoud were far from perfectly matched. What was it, then? We don't have the answer to so many things, including those about our own hearts.

"One brain," Didi was saying, "one heart in two bodies. The unique love, the grand love of her life."

He sighed. "'Love,'" he recited in English, "'is a durable fire, in the mind ever burning.'" He saw she didn't follow. "Have you been in love?" he and the whisky asked.

She didn't sense a patronizing note in his voice. She gave him an honest answer: "In a way."

"Married?"

"Yes."

"He, uh —"

"As God had it, we were divorced."

"Never been in love myself. I've had my flirts. It seems so damn hard to cross over into someone else's life. Worse than a country where you don't speak the language."

"It happens by itself, Monsieur," she said.

He didn't answer.

She felt a twinge of guilt again about the wine. "Thank you for your understanding," she said.

"Oh, you're the one who understands."

"Happy birthday, Monsieur," she said. "*M'brouk li-k*, may you be blessed. You will have a good year."

"*I'aych-k*," he answered. May He keep you alive.

She looked at him astonished.

"Well, you know, dear, I did a four-year tour at the consulate in Aleppo. I hate to be anywhere where you can't speak a little of the language. You feel like a child."

"Monsieur," she said, and the words came out of their own volition, "there are places you must go where you should not be afraid of feeling like a child."

146

He stared at her, and the buzz of alcohol seemed to fade for a moment. She put her right hand on her heart. After a second of hesitation, he did the same.

"Where exactly are you from?" he asked. "I don't remember your sister's having said."

"Batouine. Djerba. When I smelled the wine I dropped, I thought of how the air smells even better on my island, this time of year."

"You miss your island?" A wild thought raced into Didi's mind, an imaginary moment: himself, on a white beach, and Jocelyne Fontaine beside him. They were rushing into the waves, hand in hand, just like in the *métro* ads for all those holiday clubs.

Fatima gave him just a nod of assent. Yes, she missed Djerba, but missing Djerba wasn't a way of dealing with anything. With here. With the woman upstairs. With Sheboygan, Wisconsin. She waved her flashlight over the bins, to remind him of why they were where they were, exactly, that real moment.

"Ah yes," he said, home from the beach.

As she held the light for him, Didi fetched the Yquem '45, a '61 Haut-Brion, and a half-bottle of Chambertin '90, one of the last bottles that Uncle Geoff had laid down before he'd died — and one that, as burgundies must, should be drunk before it faded.

Carpe diem, Didi said in his mind. And he reminded himself again of Jocelyne Fontaine, that vivacious young person from the Ecole des Sciences Politiques who'd been his brilliant intern at the Foreign Ministry. They'd hit it off in a mental sort of way. She'd actually said she wanted to stay in touch with him when she left. She took his home telephone number. He'd heard she'd become a vice prefect now near Lille. Once he almost had the courage to ask her to dinner. Well then . . . she's a grown woman now. Lille . . .

Fatima was thinking it was getting late and that all this risked delaying her reading lesson.

Hadley had boiled water on his hot plate and was about to drop two Goutte d'Or eggs into it when he heard a knocking at his door. He opened the door to Fatima and wrinkled his nose at the incongruous smell of spilt wine that her djellaba was giving off. "Hello there. I was about to eat something quickly before the lesson," he said.

She held out a copper pot covered with an initialed linen cloth, triumphantly.

"What?"

She lifted the cloth and the dark odor of good sauce rose. "I didn't steal it!" she said, with a twinkle in her eye. "She made me take it before she began her own meal. They're serving themselves. They're having a lot of wine."

Hadley smelled the dish and imitated a swoon.

"Wine!" he said. He pushed a pile of books away from the door of a cupboard and reached for a bottle of "Vieux Papes."

He read the label to her in French as she looked around and found two unwashed dishes in the sink. The label guaranteed that connoisseurs would find this table beverage refined and well worthy of their

148

confidence. He laughed, fundamentally at himself, at his situation, but wine was wine. She shook her head, miming that she was impressed as she washed the dishes.

Hadley was inspired to unwrap an embroidered tablecloth he'd once bought in Portugal and had never used, and on it he placed the crisp baguette from Béchu, whose original purpose had been to relieve the boredom of eggs. The coq au vin was still hot, and they made short work of it before it got cold. Hadley swiped the last bit of sauce with his bread. He cracked the rooster's thighbone between his teeth and sucked the marrow.

"Hadj-li, Hadj," she joked. She started to clear their plates to wash them. "Tell me, how bad can a people be whose food can be so good?"

"Hadj-li says let's finish the wine," he said.

He proposed a silent toast with their last glassfuls. There was a little wine left afterward in the bottle, a tiny drop that Hadley poured into Fatima's glass.

"The one who gets the last drop will be married," he said. "That's what the French say. No use my having it."

She let the glass sit in front of her. He saw the weather change in her special eyes, from bright to cloudy.

"Rachida wants to go home," she said.

"What?"

"My people, wherever they die . . . they go home."

"God knows where we go when we die, Fatima."

"Shall we begin the lesson?" she asked. She looked at the drop in her glass, and without thinking, she finally drained it.

Below, the Countess and Didi had finished their dinner with a cake she'd baked him. An old-fashioned *genoise*, with pastry cream, not one of the cakes she deplored eating in restaurants these days, which were no more than puddings. As she tried to put a second slice onto his plate, her hand missed and the slice fell sideways onto the tablecloth.

"What does he say?" Didi asked.

"He say?"

"Doctor Bonheur. Professor Bonheur."

"It's the blood vessels. He spoke of the possibility of eventually becoming 'legally blind.' Can one be illegally blind? *Bonheur* indeed. Professor happiness. Where do these people get their names?"

"Not everyone has a family seat."

"You're talking to the wrong person about snobbery, nephew. I smell people out for what they are individually. Professor Bonheur is Doctor Badnews. Anyway, don't bring up Branchevieille. The repairs . . ."

"You shouldn't ever be there without heat."

"Nobody ever had heat at Branchevieille. It would ruin the furniture."

He was silent, chastened. Finally:

"And . . . Fatima?"

"And I can't abide having workmen around me. And you can't trust anyone unless you're there. Fatima wants to learn to read. Carmen told me this. Carmen is my eyes and ears in this building. There's this young blond Muslim on the sixth floor I have teaching her. He seems to have nothing else to do. You know how their men are."

"I think she's bright," he said. Finding the thread of reality in some of his aunt's stories always intrigued him. Somewhere in this tale of an idle Arab looking like Peter O'Toole there must be something that corresponded in some way to the truth. It was Carmen, no doubt, who had the straight story.

"She's definitely bright," he said.

"She better be. Emma gets along with her in any case."

"Emma is doing well?"

"I cured her."

"Yes, you'd said you cured her."

"My way. There's no need to go into it. Fatima was a great help to me with this."

"I think you get along with her as well."

"I was fond of her sister, Didi, and where did it get me?"

Didi didn't see fit to give an answer that might open a door onto his aunt's entire, very personal way of looking at the world.

In any case, days became weeks, and Fatima remained.

CHAPTER
TWO

During all that time Hippolyte Suget's presence at the Café Jean Valjean was much missed. It wasn't that he had greatly animated the life of the café. Chilling out over his morning wine, Suget had rarely contributed to the conversation. His eruption, on the last day he'd been present, was all the more shocking because of his usual reticence. It was just that *being there* at the Jean Valjean was more than a personal physical presence. It was belonging to something composed of living parts. One piece missing changed everything; it was a little like a balanced aquarium. Suget's absence made things organically different. The café was an asylum from a world of change. None of its regulars wanted *it* to change.

Clément went on tilting the pinball machine. Except for a brief sojourn in their condominium in Cannes, the Strasbourgs came faithfully for their morning *café allongé*, over which Maurice would expound to Vivianne in detail on the geopolitical implications of the *Figaro's* morning news. Ginette kept everyone abreast of her dog and her garden. Elodie Couteau told over and over again the stories no one tired of hearing about the quirky requirements of American millionaires who would stay at the Ritz. The dark intellectual whose name no one knew, whom the American Hadley had dubbed "Raskolnikov" one afternoon during his absence, kept on scribbling to himself. Louis-Paul and Thibault, the real estate men, looked ever more sprightly, with a healthy upturn in the market. But a faint malaise rode the air of the Café Jean Valjean. Suget's absence was subliminally perceived by all as a desertion. It challenged the stability of life in their aquarium. It raised a question about its very worth.

Pedro, the concierge of the building that housed L'Ecrivain directly across the avenue, had informed everyone that that was where Hippolyte could be seen these days.

Hippolyte was going there every morning for his glass of red wine. And in truth, Hippolyte felt his self-imposed exile from the Jean Valjean more painfully than any of the regulars there could.

Things were bad at L'Ecrivain from the start. He'd walked in asking for a "*coup de rouge*" and the woman behind the bar, with purple-tipped hair, in her black jeans that fit deeply into her crotch, had asked him: "A merlot? A cabernet?"

Suget did not want an oenological seminar. He depended on that "*coup de rouge*" hitting home with the first sip and washing away another night-through at the Villa Saint Valentin. The wine he was offered was expensive, and having experimented with the merlot and the cabernet from one day to the next, he concluded that neither tasted like wine as he knew it at all. More like juice spiked with sawdust and alcohol.

The bar, which had once had a zinc top, was now in funereal granite. The walls were chocolate brown and the chairs upholstered in pink plush. There was music all the time of a monotonous urgency. Men bitching in rhyme. Life, in short, was very different in the redecorated Ecrivain from what he'd been used to across the street. Maybe once, before the makeover, L'Ecrivain had had its micro-community, but that wasn't the case at all now. Well-dressed people with briefcases wolfed down croissants or what were called "muffins" and "brownies" at the bar, before the offices opened. Afterward, Hippolyte Suget often sat alone, assaulted by the music, while people came in alone or in pairs. They were always engrossed in their own business and rarely offered even a *"bonjour"* to the young help.

The only thing that made Hippolyte Suget bear all this was the conviction that he had earned it. It was the same feeling that had made prison bearable. Hippolyte Suget was not a fatalist. Having been born privileged, which is to say into a life of ample choices, he believed he was responsible for his life. When you make bad choices, you assume your guilt. He still blushed to feel how badly he'd disgraced himself with that blowup at the Jean Valjean. The question remained, how long should his sentence justly last? Any answer was beside the point, though, because what he felt now was that he hadn't the courage to try to go back.

And then it happened. He saw her tying up the dog as she was about to go into the Jean Valjean for that cup of take-out coffee. Something made her look up as if

154

she sensed she was being looked at. She saw him at the edge of the bar, near the window of the Ecrivain, and she fixed him in a gaze that somehow kept him from looking away. He couldn't see those strange eyes of hers, but he could make out . . . a smile.

That was it.

Her smile was in no way demeaning or ironic. For a moment he had the odd thought that she might cross the street and go up to him face-to-face. He turned away, as casually as he could make it seem, and ordered another juicy cabernet. When he looked up from the wine, she was already inside the other café.

And then the next odd thing happened: He gulped down the wine, paid, and got up . . .

Maurice Strasbourg's eye roamed toward the front window of the Jean Valjean as he was explaining the European Union's policy on genetically manipulated wheat to his wife. He broke off and exclaimed jubilantly to the entire room:

"*Regardez qui arrive!*" Look who's on his way.

Monsieur Strasbourg spoke so loudly that Nelson poked his head inquisitively out of the kitchen. He tugged at the napkin tied around his neck and broke out into a rare Portuguese smile, which said the world was rife with oddities.

By then Hippolyte Suget was unconsciously pushing open the door of the Jean Valjean where it said "pull." He went up to the bar. Madame Richard didn't know what to say. She felt tension, and that maybe another explosion was in the offing. She put a glass of red wine in front of Suget without his asking, as if to placate him.

Fatima was just coming away from the bar with her coffee cup covered with a saucer when she noticed him. It was an awkward moment for her. She had smiled at him, without thinking, from across the street. But here he was now beside her, and there was not the neutral, de-energizing distance of the width of the avenue to ensure a safe banality to things. He was close to her face now. He was holding out his hand.

Everyone was watching. The pinball machine was silent; Clément had let the ball go by without trying to shake out some more points. For the first time in a long time, Raskolnikov looked up from his notebook and seemed to realize that he wasn't alone.

"I'm sorry," Suget said to Fatima. "It was not my real intention to insult you."

She smiled again, and this time he was close enough to see her eyes smiling. She shook his hand.

And it was as if that smile had touched Suget somewhere where his courage lay — his courage, his imagination, and his ineffable hopes — and struck all of it, where it all lay obscured, with some kind of spark. He heard himself talking briskly.

"I see that you like animals," he said.

"Yes," she said.

"As I do very much," he said. "I happen to be very close with a bird."

"A bird," she said with an approving voice.

"Cacahouète."

"Cacahouète?"

156

"Who is a parrot."

Clément was smiling behind Suget's back, but it was not a mocking smile, as Suget took out his wallet and showed Fatima a colored photo of himself with Cacahouète on his shoulder. She could make out a pair of jockey shorts hanging in the background, but she pretended not to notice them. She also saw, blurred, a poster of a little girl with dark pigtails tied with red ribbon, but was too discreet to ask who she was. If he'd meant to point her out, he would have.

"He has beautiful feathers," was all she said.

"I have a timer on my camera," he said. "I can take my own picture." At this point he was not sure what he was saying or what he would say next.

"Do you like bears?" he blurted.

The mention of the bears caught everyone's attention. Though everyone in the café knew him for a good fellow, Suget had never seemed so interesting to anyone before.

"I can take you to see bears."

"I have never seen a bear," she said.

"That's excellent," he said. "Seeing something for the first time is like eating something for the first time, it counts as much. You can make a wish!"

By now everyone could hear Emma barking out on the sidewalk. Ginette was aware that the coffee in Fatima's cup must be cold. She took the cold coffee from Fatima's hand and put a hot cup in its place.

"Thank you," said Suget. He might have been thanking Ginette for her comprehension or he might have been so distracted that he could say thanks for someone else's coffee. One thing was for sure, he was aware that he had never spoken so boldly to a woman who was a stranger before and that in itself might entitle him to a wish.

As he watched Fatima untie the dog outside the café, he realized he was still holding his photograph. He saw the poster of Jennifer behind his bed.

"*Un coup de rouge*," said Hippolyte Suget out loud, blushing, to Madame Richard.

"Bears, Maurice?" said Madame Strasbourg. Her husband cleared his throat, shot his starched cuffs, and coughed into his hand. But Monsieur Strasbourg could not come up with any file in his head on bears.

Hoot! Hoot! went *le petit train* each time the young woman conductor in a jogging suit pulled on a cord, and each time the little boy of four or so, seated behind her with his father, screamed in terror. Behind them, a boy and a girl of eight and nine laughed cruelly in response, while their parents, a couple in their thirties, each looking out toward different sides of the train, ignored them. Soon their laughter made the little boy stop screaming. It readjusted his take on the world and he started to laugh, too. Then everyone on the train was laughing: the children, the single parents, the parents who were alone together. They were all delicately associated by their spontaneous, unreasoned laughter, including the odd childless couple in the rear car: a plump Arab woman in a djellaba and a compact Frenchman with pepper-and-salt hair poking from below a tweed cap.

158

Fatima didn't know why she was laughing, but it felt good.

Hippolyte Suget laughed because he was nervous, and fortunately it filled the time he would have spent searching for conversation with Fatima. He'd started the day determined to be relaxed and had put on his relaxed clothes — corduroys and a crew-neck sweater — but he still felt unconfident.

On the road left of the tracks, children peered at the train from passing cars. People were out in the park just for a Sunday drive. Bikers overtook joggers on the path alongside the road. The sun bathed everyone and everything in a soft light, giving the impression that all this banal little activity had been touched with a blessing. Springtime in Paris on Sunday. Suget could remember everything about Sundays like this, in this same place.

The toy train made its way along the edge of the Bois de Boulogne until it arrived at the toy wooden station in the Jardin d'Acclimatation. The families got off and headed for the amusement rides.

Fatima looked at Suget. Her look conveyed expectation that encouraged him to believe that he was wrong in fearing, that morning, that he'd made a mistake. But he still had to make the outing go right. His ploy in getting into this was bears, but warmly remembering the whole place now, as he stared at the entry gates that had been redone into great clowns' hats, he acknowledged to himself that he wanted to share more with her.

Near the gates, the same old wooden water mill was churning, supplying the swift current that propelled the light little boats of the Enchanted River. Suget saw that Fatima was intrigued by the water mill and the little boats with families in them that raced along their narrow channel until they disappeared into a grove of trees. He wondered if she thought the boats were really going somewhere.

Without saying a word, he bought tickets and helped her into a boat. The attendant released a lock and they were gliding along the channel. They passed into the grove, but only a few minutes later the channel made a bend and they were on their way back to the starting point. She looked disappointed.

He bought more tickets, while a father waiting to take their boat railed that two turns in a row were not allowed. The attendant said that there were no written rules on the question and whether someone could have two turns in a row was a matter for his own discretion. While they argued, Suget got back into the boat beside Fatima, who had not budged, and he waited defiantly, arms crossed, for the ride to begin again. The attendant sent them on their way while the complainer's son, who was as ugly as his father and already old-looking, waved his fist at them and screamed.

"People can be so rude," said Suget.

Fatima was embarrassed, but she could not suppress a tinge of delight that this man had engaged himself in a faint form of combat for her sake.

"Do you like to travel?" he asked, as the boat approached the grove again. The bottom of the boat was bare, except for some staves, and her feet, on one of the staves, were getting splashed. She hiked up her djellaba a little.

He looked at her wet feet and it struck him that he'd made his first mistake with this boat ride, but she just looked back at him and shrugged, shrugged the problem off. Still flustered, he accidentally put his own two feet down between the staves right into the water. He felt the cold water soak through his sneakers into his socks, but he put his feet back onto the staves, as if nothing had happened.

"I haven't traveled except to get to Paris," she said. She hesitated, wondering if she had to say more. "But I expect to go to America," she said. As she said it, she realized she'd said it to impress him rather than to insist to herself on her mission.

"To Wisconsin," she added, faintly guilty at not having already put that marker down. But that was all she wanted to say on the matter.

"I don't know about Wisconsin," he said. His feet were cold. "But I have seen New York. My father took us there one spring vacation. If you haven't seen New York, something big is missing in your knowledge of what the world is like."

"There are a lot of things I have yet to see," she said. She put her hand into the channel and let the water rush through her fingers.

The boat reached the bend again. There was a man standing beside the channel now with a Polaroid camera. He snapped them.

161

When they got back to the dock, the man with the camera was already there. He showed Suget the color photo he'd taken. Ten euros. A lot of money, thought Suget, but he peeled off the bill from a wad he'd counted out to arm himself with that morning, and gave the picture to Fatima. She looked at it and smiled and handed it back.

"It's yours," he said.

She blushed.

"It's just a souvenir. Everyone must have one."

The man took another picture for Suget while she hesitated before answering. Then, "The bears?" she asked, not knowing what else to say.

The mother bear, the father bear, and what looked like an adolescent bear were sitting in their cement cave overlooking their moat, each with its head leaning on the sill of a window. Their eyes were closed.

"They're napping," Suget said, with an authority in his voice that he'd assumed without any justification other than the need to be in charge of the outing.

She looked at him and nodded as if she had no reason to question his expertise on bear habits.

"We can have a coffee and come back," he said. On their way to the terrace of the café, Fatima pretended not to hear the squeak of Suget's wet sneakers. They paused at a waffle stand where Suget bought a little container of churros, and they dipped churros into chocolate syrup and ate them with their coffee at an outdoor table of the café.

"You know your way around. Did you work here?" she ventured, innocently.

162

"I was a spoiled child," he said. "I came here any time I wanted and went on all the rides."

"The bears —"

"Different ones. But they're all very much the same."

Nearby, what seemed like a spaceship ride was flashing lightbulbs of all colors as children piled into the pod-like seats on long metal arms. A great, expensive machine, Fatima thought, just to titillate children. Fatima was already doing cleaning at the Imperial Hotel when she was not much older than those childen.

Suget seemed to read her look.

"Money was not a problem to my parents.

"Until they lost it all," he added.

"You are someone who doesn't think about money," she told him.

"Oh it's been a while," he said. "I don't miss it."

"The photograph was too expensive," she said. "It was very thoughtful of you, but there was no need."

She reached into her djellaba and took out some bills she had in her handkerchief tied with a safety pin.

"Let me pay for the coffee."

And then he did it — he reached over and closed his hand over hers to make her stop getting out her money.

"Why are we talking about money?" he asked.

She drew back her hand and he felt he'd made his second mistake.

"Let's do a crazy ride," he blurted, "before the bears wake up."

They went on the Chinese Dragon Ride, a low roller coaster that moved through a little Chinese pagoda onto tracks that swept up and down and around a dragon flashing lights from its tongue and tail.

The speed and the sudden ups and downs made Suget's stomach churn just like they had when he was a child. Fatima tried to sit serene through all of it. Terrified, she told herself that her fatalism was just being subjected to yet another little test.

The bears were out romping on their cement cliff. The mother hugged the adolescent bear that licked her on the face. Suget believed it was an act for the people on the other side of the moat, in the hope of some peanuts in compensation. Fatima seemed ingenuously touched.

"What do you think?" he said. "You can make a wish."

Fatima had never seen a bear before, she had never gone on an amusement ride, but more important, she had never spent an afternoon with a man she barely knew. There'd been only Mahmoud and Hadley, her new confidant. By now her life had been so far tilted off balance in Paris that she was not sure what above all to wish for.

Suget reached for a piece of sugar he'd saved from his coffee, but Fatima stayed his hand with hers. As he felt its warmth, he heard her read the sign in a child's rhythm, moving the index finger of her other hand from word to word:

"For your own security and the health of the animals, it is strictly forbidden to feed the bears."

He was sensitive enough to perceive the note of pride she showed as she read. He knew it was something in her life not taken for granted. He was overwhelmed by that, yet another indication of her innocence, and somewhere, he knew, though he was far from innocent in the common meaning of the word, there was a place where their lives mirrored each other. It was hard to specify where, the differences between them being so enormous, but in some way each — he could say it objectively about himself — was still a child. Himself particularly. And if fate had it that they would always be that way, unable to grow up, then they might be able to protect each other from the adult world, if ever — for the first time it seemed to him conceivable — they became close. It made him feel good about himself to fantasize that he could somehow safeguard someone like her. At the same time, listening to her read, Suget had a strong inkling of how competent an innocent Fatima could really be, in dealing with the world. She had a certain power that he intuited as benevolent. And that was when he remembered that he was also a father. A child's father. Poor Jennifer. For her sake, was it not time he grew up as best he could?

He waited for Fatima to remove her hand before he popped the lump of sugar he'd intended for the bears into his own mouth. And the sweet taste filled his awareness, blotting out the discomfort of his wet feet, until they heard the train hooting at the station and she told him — with what he was buoyantly convinced was regret in her voice — that it was time for her to go back to the avenue Victor-Hugo.

165

The hooting stopped. The train was silent. Children were piling into the seats in front of them, with their parents.

"So you like bears," he was able to say.

She looked at him with a mischievous twinkle.

"Definitely," she said.

"And donkeys? Why not donkeys?"

"Why not?" She smiled. "There are many donkeys on the island I come from."

"So we can do another excursion. There are some very sympathetic donkeys in the Jardin du Ranelagh. It's not far from where you live. We could go on foot. A stroll, if the weather is good."

As she started to shake his hand good-bye, she smiled, as if to say that might be nice.

"I'll bring Jenny along." That was it, he'd said it.

"Jenny?" In an instant she put it all together. But she waited for him to say the rest, which came now more easily for him:

"Do you like children? If so, I want Jenny to meet you. She turned six last month."

Monsieur Robert was shocked to see a very black man seated in the Countess's kitchen. He stopped and stared through the open door on his way to the butler's pantry to look for some water for his dry cough, and when the man looked back at him with an amiability Monsieur Robert interpreted as insolence, Monsieur Robert thought for a second that that dark face looked familiar. Where?

166

Taking the risk of gulping down a glass of water from an unlabeled bottle before he hurried back to the meeting in the salon, Monsieur Robert still could not for the life of him imagine who that man was and what he was doing there, in front of a spread of cards, playing solitaire, in a light suit and tie.

"We were saying," said Madame Marchand to Monsieur Robert, as he sat down beside her, "that once again we are faced with . . . excuse me —"

She looked around at the room full of co-owners with a timid air, but Madame Marchand felt it had to be said. She was a woman with a big heart. She swallowed.

"With a matter that can be of life or death."

Monsieur Robert could smell Madame Marchand's floral perfume. Tuberoses. The air he inhaled tickled his stomach. It was a physical thing he couldn't control.

The Russian couple looked at each other as if to ask if the other understood. Monsieur Roumatov was a short dark man, with Georgian blood perhaps. His stout, purple-haired wife, wearing several gold necklaces, had the thin, even-featured face with upturned nose that had no doubt made her an attractive catch before she had put on weight. The Countess had held her breath watching the woman sit down on a fragile, gilded Régence chair. But that sort of risk couldn't be helped; it was the Countess's turn to open her apartment to the co-owners' meeting.

The Countess had baked a chocolate cake that morning, not so much in honor of her guests as for the pleasure of having a reason to be in the kitchen. Fatima

167

was passing the sliced cake now, which she had found too small for the assembly and which, without a veto from the Countess, she had supplemented with oriental pastries that she had Samuel bring with him from the Goutte d'Or.

The chairwoman of the meeting, Madame Hénault, who owned the *syndic*, the company charged with administering the building for the co-owners, licked syrup that had stuck to her fingers from a semolina cake, and studied Madame Marchand. She had known Madame Marchand as a person who became emotional about matters in former meetings, and she did not want to have the whole unfortunate incident of the fallen skylight, regarding which the *syndic* might have been found in some way responsible by a clever lawyer, to come up again. Madame Hénault, a plain-faced woman of forty who gave a lot of attention to her highlighted upswept hair and dressed authoritatively in her gabardine suit, was there to stand for moderation and logic. She said:

"There are three estimates I consider reasonable in the documentation you have all received. Our *syndic* has worked with each of these companies in the past."

Monsieur Robert said, "I have never had the slightest problem with my electricity. Obviously," he said, eyeing Madame Marchand, "if you plug in all sorts of gadgets at once —"

Fatima was offering him the platter of sweets. He paused in mid-sentence to look at them and then at her, and into his mind, uncontrollably, came an image

168

of her lovely sister. He turned his look toward the plate again.

"The rose *loukoum*, Monsieur," she whispered, "is very nice. With walnuts."

He didn't know whether to take a sweet or tell her to take them away. His mind wasn't on sweets, nor was it back on electricity, and during that muddle, Mathilde Paumier d'Aurange, wife of the retired Admiral Hubert Paumier d'Aurange, of the second floor, stood up and interjected:

"This is a communal issue, Monsieur Robert. Everyone here, except perhaps yourself, has changed his wiring in his apartment. But in the years I have been living here, I cannot remember the hallway wiring ever having been changed."

"A danger exists," insisted Madame Marchand. "There are sparks at the *minuterie* on my floor." She put her forefinger into her mouth. "I burned my finger."

"Monsieur Robert," began Jacques Finkiel, with a soothing voice, and he paused strategically and looked around the room before relighting his pipe. Monsieur Finkiel had been covering the National Assembly for *le Monde* since the Fourth Republic, and he had learned a thing or two about effective oratory. "Monsieur Robert, let me preface what I am about to say with a tribute to the great care you have taken to keep both our monthly and our exceptional operating costs very reasonable."

He looked at Madame Hénault. "Not that I have any reason, at the same time, to disparage our *syndic*. The

169

time comes, in the life of a building such as ours, if I may speak metaphorically of such things, when —"

Madame Finkiel, a prim gray-haired woman, was pulling on his sleeve.

"Briefly, Jacques," she whispered, and turned to see Fatima beside them with her tray.

Monsieur Finkiel reached impulsively for a slice of chocolate cake. He found himself speaking as he chewed:

"In brief, there are times when we must face the costs."

The room went silent.

Fatima went back into the kitchen and sat down opposite Samuel. He looked at the tray she put on the table and she nodded. He took a piece of chocolate cake.

"I have no appetite," he confessed, but he began to do honor to the Countess's cake.

"You'll see," she said, "they are people like anyone else."

He chuckled, and reached for a *loukoum*.

They could hear the Countess speaking in the salon, in a raised voice.

"I must agree, Madame Hénault, with Monsieur . . . Monsieur —"

"Robert," he interjected testily. The Countess, he believed, was not just hard of hearing; she was of the sort who didn't care what your name was, because if it didn't begin with a particle, you were nameless. Being a man of some erudition, a quality valued after all in what was after all a republic, he could remember what the tyrannical Prince Alfred zu Windischgrätz had said in 1848: "Humanity begins with the baron." And yet he was irrepressibly flattered to hear that the Countess was agreeing with him.

In point of fact, Monsieur Robert's class antagonism was misplaced. A sui generis quirk of the Countess's was what this was all about. There were people she responded to favorably or unfavorably, in a spontaneous way, and others who might as well have been invisible to her, as devoid of any attraction as a gray figure in a passing crowd. He tended to be of the latter classification, but not entirely, because the Countess could recall more important things about him than his name. The lovely face of his late wife. Deep down, it all had to do, après tout, with the various components of her definition of humanity.

"Monsieur . . . Robert has rightly pointed out that all three estimates are too high."

"Scandalously!" he was encouraged to say, looking Madame Hénault right in the eye. The rules of co-ownership gave her syndic a percentage of every contract she assigned, and everyone knew that unless the co-owners kept a sharp eye, they were not invulnerable to a lot of overexpensive contracts.

"I should like to propose an alternative solution," said the Countess.

In the kitchen, Fatima nudged Samuel, who straightened his tie.

He looked at her. Her two-colored eyes were shining. He saw that she was sharing that moment of emotion with him, and he rose and spontaneously kissed her on the cheek. She winked her green eye.

He might have said something to her that would have had all the Senegalese eloquence that she was used to hearing from Victorine, but the Countess was calling from the salon:

"Monsieur Diop, Monsieur Samuel Diop!"

Samuel entered the salon smiling.

"Good evening, *messieurs-'dames*," he said. "I am Samuel Diop, licensed electrician. I have been apprised of your problem and of your perplexity in the face of the level of bids that have been submitted for its resolution."

"In what country are you licensed, Monsieur?" asked Monsieur Denis-Rabotin, with an accent full of moist vowels and sharp consonants.

"Monsieur, I am now a citizen of France, and proudly so," he said, waving a document he had enclosed in plastic.

Fatima passed Samuel's license around the room. And then she passed another plastic-covered document. It was a certificate from the Ministry of Education of the Republic of Senegal attesting that Samuel Diop had graduated from the Technical Program in Electricity, with *mention très bien*, highest honors.

"I have been asked to respond to your problem by a friend, a fact that enables me to make an offer inspired by friendship."

"How much?" asked Monsieur Robert. Wherever he was from and however strangely it was being worded,

Samuel Diop was speaking Philippe Robert's language now.

"Twelve thousand euros, tax included, Monsieur."

A murmur went around the room. Samuel's bid was a little more than half the price of the other three bids, which had been within a few euros of each other.

Monsieur Robert turned to Madame Hénault.

"This is not serious," she said. "There is no written estimate."

At which point Fatima spoke up. "Permit me," she said, and she began to pass out photocopied sheets with Samuel's handwritten, detailed estimate.

The room went silent again.

"*Eh bien*, it's you who decide, *mesdames, messieurs*," said Madame Hénault. "I am here to execute your will."

"We are here to see that you don't execute us," dared Monsieur Robert.

The Countess stood up.

"We shall vote," she said.

And Samuel Diop was awarded the rewiring contract of 34bis avenue Victor-Hugo by unanimous vote.

After the meeting broke up, Monsieur Robert walked with Madame Marchand down the stairs to her door.

"Now I know that fellow," he said. "He has a very odd truck. But the estimate —"

"Unbeatable," she said. "I feel we can trust her."

"The Arab woman? She was in the truck."

"Yes. Well, good evening, Monsieur Robert."

"Good evening, Madame Marchand."

"Her name is Fatima," she said.

After she closed her door, and he began to walk down to his own apartment, he realized that he missed the smell of her floral perfume.

Back in the Countess's apartment, Samuel was helping Fatima return the chairs to their proper places. When they finished, Fatima went to deal with the dishes in the kitchen and found the Countess eating the last *loukoum*. As she looked up at Fatima with powdered sugar on her lips, Fatima saw a child's features on her face.

"It was a good thing that I insisted that you bring him," the Countess said.

Fatima did not remember any insistence, but she was pleased that things had worked out.

"He would like to say good-bye, Madame."

"Is he going?" The Countess sounded disappointed. "Of course."

Samuel was in the doorway of the kitchen. He noticed the powdered sugar and stole a smile in Fatima's direction.

"Monsieur Diop."

"You may call me Samuel as my friends do, *Madame*."

"Samuel. I should like you to come to Auvergne."

She turned to Fatima. "We'll all go."

At that moment, Fatima didn't know where Auvergne was. It could have been somewhere in the Pacific, where the French once liked to explode their atomic bombs. But she realized that her rapport with the Countess had become its own kind of journey, on which going somewhere physically seemed a natural part. As for Wisconsin . . .

"*Inshallah*," she said to herself.

CHAPTER
THREE

When Didi phoned to check on how his aunt was faring, he found her unusually chipper.

"I'm thinking of running against the Monsieur on the third floor when the presidency of the co-ownership comes up."

"It's an onerous responsibility, my dear aunt."

"Poor man, since his wife passed on, nothing else seems to give him pleasure. He doesn't even play his piano and gargle notes anymore. But I've caught him out. He's not so sharp as everyone thinks he is. I can do better."

"It will take up all your time." And all your strength, he thought.

"What else do I have to do?" The drop in her voice seemed an unfair accusation as she added, "Whom do I have?"

He didn't answer until the silence extinguished her sub-text. "You'll have to ride constantly on Madame Hénault's back."

"But the smile won't be on the face of the tiger," she snapped.

He caught the reference. Remembered with a tinge of melancholy that he, like her, was of a generation that

176

still had British nannies. His was the last. Sarah. Her nursery rhymes and her limericks. "There was a young lady from Niger . . ." What happened to lovely Sarah?

"Well, after all, I have allies," said the Countess with mystery and intrigue in her voice.

Whom do I have, Didi asked himself. In any case, he thought, with all this talk about running for the co-owners' chair and "allies," his aunt was either entering a troubling stage of senility or had sipped some strange elixir of youth.

"Jennifer," Suget said, swallowing, "this is Madame Monsour." His voice was hoarse from a cold coming on — from those wet shoes at the Jardin d'Acclimatation — and altogether, considering his nervousness, his introduction came out very bleak. Had he made a mistake?

The little girl poked her head from behind her father's back and offered a smile that spoke more of the care her grandmother had taken in bringing her up politely than of her emotions. Her smile revealed a front tooth that wobbled as she closed her mouth.

Fatima smiled back and held out both her hands. The girl hung back from an embrace, holding a Pokémon doll against her chest.

They were standing near the statue of Jean de la Fontaine at the edge of the Jardin du Ranelagh. From there they could see, at the far end of the park, children tied into saddles bouncing along in a troop of donkeys. A little man with a pink carnation in the band of his derby was trotting beside the lead animal.

Suget looked at the bronze figure in seventeenth-century attire. Below him, a bronze crow and a bronze fox. The fables penned by the foxy old writer himself had made him dear to all French schoolchildren ever after. And to scholarly grown-ups, who got their pleasure decoding figures of Louis XIV's court among his animals.

"Look, Jennifer, that's Monsieur La Fontaine."

Memory surged within him. He saw himself at this very spot, at the edge of the open green lawn, before the statue was installed, in short pants, holding his father's gentle hand. The unfortunate man's clothes smelled of the compulsive tobacco that would kill him so painfully, after his business had failed. Why had Hippolyte never taken his daughter here, among all the parks they'd been to together? His life, he realized, was divided into compartments, which might be because that was the only way he could keep it together. And now he was trying to bring together Jenny and this woman — was she already a compartment? Had he indeed made a mistake? Was it not better to leave things undisturbed where they lay?

Fatima, of a less complicated makeup, was simply happy. Happy to enjoy the presence of a child on a May day in Paris out in a lovely park. Of course the girl was shy, but Fatima read goodness in her right away. The little girl with neatly plaited pigtails seemed well brought up. And so it was Fatima who would make everything happen the way it did, although not even at the end of the outing could she bring herself to ask more about the two of them, where the child lived, for

178

instance. She could not even bring herself to ask him if he were married.

Jenny walked up to the bronze ensemble, where the old fabulator stood looking down on the fox about to finagle the crow into dropping the cheese it held in its beak.

"Master Crow," she said, deepening her little voice, "how pretty you are. How lovely you seem to me. Without lying, if your way of speaking resembles your feathers, you are the phoenix of all who dwell in these woods!"

Fatima was wide-eyed. The girl seemed as bright as she was pretty. Suget blushed with pride. She remembered everything. From those nights she came to visit and he read to her from his bunk, with her legs hanging from the bunk above. She remembered because listening to him read had given her pleasure.

The donkeys had arrived across the road. Mothers and fathers were unstrapping their children from the saddles. The man stepped away and lit a cigarette. Suget smelled his father again and drove that presence from his mind. He lifted Jenny and set her down into a saddle. The child grabbed the animal's coat for dear life. The donkey shuddered.

Fatima reached out and steadied Jenny in the saddle.

"Do you really want to try it?" she asked. Jenny looked at Suget. "Only if you really want to," Fatima said. Suget blushed. Was this another Hippolyte screw-up? he asked himself.

Jenny hung fire.

"He's a sweet donkey," said Fatima, stroking the animal on his muzzle. She called to the man who was crushing his cigarette on a tree and anxious now to get another round going. Other children, behind them, were fidgeting in their saddles. She asked the man: "What's his name?"

"Alphonse!"

He came up to Jenny.

"Does she want to ride or not?" the man said.

"I'll have a word with Alphonse," Fatima told Jenny. And she whispered something into the donkey's ear. At that point, the animal shook his head up and down, as if he'd concluded a deal.

"He says he has never hurt anyone in ten years as a donkey," Fatima said. "It's up to you, but as far as Alphonse is concerned, it will be a very gentle ride."

Jenny looked back at the other children, as if she'd regret letting them ride off on donkeys while she missed out on the experience.

"I'll walk right beside you," Fatima said.

Jenny flashed her hanging tooth again.

"Will you hold my Pokémon?"

"Of course."

The donkey man pulled on Alphonse's tack.

And they were off, all around the park and back. When they got back to Suget, Jenny was laughing. She threw her arms around her father, giving him an indulgent look that made him smile and recover from his embarrassment. Between the two of them, Fatima thought, it was hard to know who looked after whom.

180

"How can you talk to donkeys, Madame?" Jenny asked Fatima, as they sat now on a bench watching another round of children go by.

"You just say what you have to say."

The girl giggled.

"Would you like another ride?" Suget asked his daughter.

"It's too expensive," she replied, almost scolding.

"Jenny?" Fatima asked.

"Yes, Madame?"

"Can we do a trade? I'll give you something and you'll give me that tooth."

With that, Fatima took out a package of *loukoum* she'd bought at the Goutte d'Or. "Close your eyes, open your mouth," she said.

Jennifer wavered.

"It tastes like a rose," she told the child, holding out a sugar-dusted pink sweet. Jennifer's eyes were already closed. She opened her mouth, tasted a flower.

"You have to bite."

She bit. Fatima pulled the *loukoum* away.

"Open your eyes."

There in the sticky candy lay the tooth. Fatima took the tooth out of the *loukoum* and dropped the *loukoum* into the wastebasket beside the bench. A look crossed Jenny's face as if she'd been cheated, but in a moment Fatima was handing her the tooth wrapped in a tissue and the whole package of candy.

"Both for you. Put this under your pillow tonight."

Fatima still wondered where that pillow was.

Suddenly it began to rain. Suget grabbed his daughter in his arms and he and Fatima ran across the park toward a bus shelter. They were drenched by the time they arrived.

"Thank you," Jenny told Fatima. "Thank you very much, Madame," as they stood under the shelter waiting for the downpour to slacken.

Her politeness made Suget feel very proud. He was feeling good inside now, although his soaked jacket made him fear that his cold would get worse. Did it matter?

"Thank you," he murmured to Fatima.

She turned her head his way and smiled gently.

The day before the Countess decided to leave, she stopped eating and drinking. At her age, it was not a great hardship, and for her it was a necessity that had long existed. The Countess did not want to have to use the toilet on the train. Once when she was eight years old, she had walked into a first-class train toilet in a sordid state, and she'd never allow herself to be in that situation again.

Samuel had thought better of asking the Countess to drive down with him in his rattling truck with worn shock absorbers. The Countess gave him instructions on the route and established a rendezvous at the little train station where the *Micheline*, the local dink that connected with the swift TGV at Clermont-Ferrand, would deposit the two women. From there it was only twelve kilometers to Branchevieille.

Hadley was pleased for Fatima. He bought her a Green Guide to Auvergne.

"You'll love the country down there. It's like nothing you've seen, all those dead volcanos turned into soft green mountains. And a castle!"

"I can make a wish," she teased, as she pushed him gently into the hall while she swept the floor of his room. She was doing an especially good cleaning, not knowing when she'd be back. He seized a stray sock, guiltily.

She thanked him for the guide and flipped the pages.

"You know, I can really clean my own room," he said.

"We have an agreement." She flipped through the book again. "I can't understand all of this."

"I think you'll do better than you say. You really can read well, you know. You read so well you don't even think you've had to learn it."

She put the book down on his bed, turned her back and reached into her bra. She had a wad of euros in her hand when she looked at him again.

"What's that about?"

"Please, Hadley," she said. "I want you to keep this safe for me. I don't want to carry it on a voyage."

"I'm not so sure it would be safe here."

She looked at all the books and papers she had managed to keep clean and in something resembling order.

"Whatever you'd hide here," she said, smiling mischievously, "no one would ever find."

"Is that your . . . Wisconsin money?"

"Yes," she said.

Afterward she went down and packed the Countess's old Vuitton trunk for the railroad people to pick up.

Hippolyte Suget was having a hot wine on his repossessed barstool in the Café Jean Valjean when he saw Fatima just outside the door on the lottery ticket line. Suget had just about recovered from the case of flu that had kept him in bed, with a two-week *arrêt de travail*, a certificate from his doctor justifying his absence from the Villa Saint Valentin. The doctor had blamed the soaking his feet had gotten in the Jardin d'Acclimatation. But Suget felt that a general state of excitement had lowered his resistance. The fever was in its way an escape, a furlough from the new agitation in his life, having to do with the woman who was now on the line. Cacahouète had noticed the change in him and had become testy, intuitively jealous. He would scream to have his cage cleaned more often than it needed to be, and poor Suget, in the throes of fever, would have to get up from his bed and make the changes. Those two weeks were the one time Suget appreciated the tightness of his quarters, which enabled him to get back to bed in a hurry from whatever chore was necessary for his own or Cacahouète's sustenance. Cacahouète seemed to have acquired a permanent ill humor.

Suget was beside her now at the cash register, while she was paying Madame Richard. She spoke first.

"Monsieur Suget, I was worried."

He gazed at her.

184

"Whether you and Jenny were all right."

"Quite all right."

"Is there a new tooth?"

"Oh yes." Then, "Do you go to the movies?" he blurted.

She blushed. On Djerba once, someone from the government had put up a screen and a projector in a public building, and she had seen a film about modern agricultural methods. And twice at the Club Rêve, Monsieur Choukroun had invited her to sit in the rear during movie night. Both times, she saw Louis de Funès playing Rabbi Jacob. It was very funny.

"They're showing *Bambi* again," he said, "on the Champs-Elysées. I'm um? . . . I'm taking Jenny."

She didn't know who Bambi was.

"Considering your affection for animals . . ."

"I have to go away," she answered.

His heart sank.

"To Auvergne."

"There's nothing there but tall volcanic mountains," he said.

"I've never seen volcanic mountains."

He looked at her again with an air of having reconciled himself to his fate.

"Well then, have an excellent trip."

He held out his hand, and she took it, saying good-bye in that French manner.

"There are cows!" he said as she began to walk away. He was saying anything to prolong that moment. "You'll enjoy the beautiful cows."

She gave him back a smile. Her two-colored eyes were smiling as well.

"Cows," she thought to herself, as she untied Emma outside. "What a silly man." But Emma looked at her in a way that made her think, what's so silly about cows? Cows and dogs and people, all of us on this earth on flat islands and tall mountains, sharing a place in time as well. She thought of how he'd reached out his hand, awkward, silly, and endearing. She felt an odd tickle in her stomach remembering an undeniable charm in his gallantry.

Fatima told herself that when she got back to Paris she would find out about Bambi from Hadley.

CHAPTER
FOUR

Emma stared at the landscape going by in a frightening blur. She had never been on the autoroute before and it was the first time, as well, that she'd been separated from the Countess. The van had a funny smell. Though a dog, of course, couldn't identify it, it was a mixture of grease, plastic, wood, glue, and paint or whatever that Samuel would carry around on his jobs, a ripe industrial effluvium of human activity, thickened with diesel fumes seeping faintly through the floorboard. A particular acid smell detectable to a dog was coming from the pile of copper pipes filling the rear, alongside the gas heater still packed in a box and the boxes of radiators. Samuel looked at Emma and saw that she was nervous.

A sign indicating a roadside restaurant came into view.

Emma reached her paw over toward Samuel. He was all she had against the whooshing environment. He took it as he drove into the side lane leading to the restaurant. "*Allons, mon amie,*" Samuel said, "we'll get you something for lunch. What do you think about a steak tartare?"

Emma's paw stopped shaking, as Samuel laughed his generous laugh.

All this while, the TGV was drawing out of the Gare de Lyon with Fatima and Countess Poulais du Roc aboard. The Countess, flouting tradition for the sake of company and even perhaps, by now, out of a version of affection, had bought Fatima a first-class ticket. Fatima sat by the window of the carpeted car, in a plush chair, and watched France reel itself out, as if putting on a show for her, personally.

The jumbled urban landscape of the poor suburbs, the tall slabs of public housing and the low warehouses, gave way with surprising quickness to the green country of France in June. Pastures sliced with rivulets still flushed with spring, uplands with stone hamlets, each with a little church, here and there a manor or a castle. Sheep and cows.

Cows. Fatima chuckled, remembering . . .

The Countess leaned over her and peered out the window. "Something funny out there?"

Fatima was spared the need to answer. The conductor had come up, asking for their tickets. He was a tall, athletic man, and Fatima wondered why someone vigorous like him should have such a job as gathering tickets every day. He punched them and looked at Fatima in her djellaba and then at the Countess, as if there were something irregular here that the rules should but did not cover. He pushed the tickets back into the Countess's hand, brusquely.

"There is too much rudeness in the world," the Countess said, as he walked on. And suddenly Fatima saw herself in a little boat. She remembered Suget and the ugly man with the ugly child. "*People can be so rude.*" And that whole outing came back to her with a rush of pleasure.

A hostess was offering trays of food like the one she had had on the plane from Djerba.

"You must eat something if you can, Fatima," the Countess said. "Even if it's what it is."

"You haven't eaten since yesterday, Madame."

"No need to remind me. I'll survive. You eat."

It came out as an order.

It was food and Fatima ate it, even though it wasn't tasty. The hot chicken and rice under a piece of aluminum and all the wrapped-up little things. The thought crossed Fatima's mind that eating in this totally compartmentalized fashion, from the tray down to the butter in its foil, was a way of complementing the separation between people. Give everyone, wrapped-up, protected from the germs of others, his separate measure of things. The landscape of this country was lovely, inviting, but too many people on it were cold and distant. As for the proud old woman beside her, Fatima could sense that there were sparks and embers. In the face of all obvious appearance, she did not believe that the Countess was cold. What mischief she might be capable of was another matter.

"I don't envy you," the Countess said, looking over at the pile of wrappings that were what was left of the meal on Fatima's tray. "Which is the trash and which is the food?"

Fatima kept silent as she gave the Countess a polite smile. Should she have explained that where she was born people did not turn back an offer of food? But the chicken had nauseated her all the same.

The Countess got out her copy of the *Figaro*. As she started to read below the headlines, she became aware that the glasses she had had increased in strength only a month ago were unable to put ordinary-size type into focus. She flung the newspaper onto the seat opposite her and closed her eyes, as if trying to sleep.

Fatima looked at her stricken face for an instant and reached for the newspaper. She began to read it, moving her lips.

In a moment, the Countess opened one eye and stared at her. "Out loud," she said.

Fatima continued to read haltingly to her about an earthquake in Honduras that had killed forty-seven people. The Countess clucked and sighed over the grim details, but her pleasure in being read to seemed to surpass her empathetic sorrow, for she soon eased into sleep for real.

The landscape changed after they transferred to the *Micheline*, the old yellow diesel train from the fifties, with wooden seats. Now for the first time Fatima saw mountains. They took her breath away. The *Micheline* stopped and strained and started again, climbing, climbing. They reached a height where the train crossed between two mountains on a narrow bridge. Looking down, a little dizzy, Fatima saw a waterfall spraying from a cliff, and the sun was making a rainbow in its mist. So lovely. Allah, she thought, must have a reason to be so good to the French.

Samuel was already there at the little railway station of Branchevieille when they arrived. He was sitting behind the wheel of his van, with the door open to the sunny day, and Emma was snoring in the warmth of his lap and of the bright air. She jumped up sniffing the moment the train doors opened. She'd smelled her mistress in her sleep and bolted off to greet her.

Emma was all over the Countess, and the old woman loved it. It was as if they'd been separated for a long time. The Countess looked around, smelled the country air and beamed a smile.

"I could eat a cow," she said. "And down a whole bottle of Marcillac."

Achille Picard, the stout old stationmaster, had already alerted Madame Monjoux, the owner of the Hôtel des Voyageurs beside the station, that the Countess was arriving, a piece of news he'd immediately put together in spying the dog Emma with the *homme de couleur* in the van with Parisian plates. Samuel had hit it off with the stationmaster while he sat waiting for the train to arrive. Like many a tiny village in the heart of France, Branchevieille was losing people day by day to the cities. Raising cows on the rugged mountainsides was no longer a viable way of making a living in the face of the milk industry on the polders of Holland. The old people were holding out on their pensions, but the young had nearly all moved on. The village's one café, opposite the hotel and restaurant, had closed when the owners retired. Otherwise, Picard said, he would have treated Samuel to an aperitif. He did not explain that he did not feel comfortable going into Madame and Monsieur Monjoux's fine restaurant just to drink. Picard was delighted to encounter an entrepreneur. There was no one left for miles around who could fix anything. The news from Samuel that the Countess was doing repairs at the château heartened him. An obscure belief still prevailed in the village, rooted in illusory nostalgia, that the château was its protector, as it had been at the time it was built.

Monsieur Monjoux had set about preparing the lunch the Countess always ate on getting off the train. He was now beating an *aligot* with a big wooden spoon. *Aligot* was a dish of mashed potatoes with as much fresh local cheese forced into it as it could take. The *aligot* was coming off his spoon in long strips like taffy. It was ready, and he put it on the back of the stove to keep warm.

While the Countess was washing up from her voyage and Fatima and Samuel were outside seeing to the bags and feeding Emma some of Monsieur Monjoux's rabbit pâté, Madame Monjoux set down a place setting at one table of her dining room and another for two near the door.

The Countess stepped out of the bathroom and looked back and forth at the two set tables.

"Madame Monjoux," she asked, "where would my husband have sat?"

"At the best table, *Madame la Comtesse*, which I've set for you."

"With his fellow diners," said the Countess, and she walked to the table near the door and began removing the plates, a task Madame Monjoux relieved her of in an embarrassed hurry.

Out of reverence to the old woman and not willing to presume, Madame Monjoux had indeed committed a faux pas. No one in Branchevieille would have thought it odd for the Count to sit down to lunch at the Voyageurs with a maid and a workman. Count Geoffroy Poulais du Roc would eat or drink with anyone in town who wasn't boring. He had been the beloved mayor of the village for years, elected always without an opponent. His wife, though she may well have had numerous exigent and perhaps cruel criteria for ranking people individually, and though she loved to be served and was by nature bossy, never contradicted his antipathy to making a cut-and-dry matter such as station in life an issue for snobbery. Not at Branchevieille in any case. Which was partly why the villagers loved her as they'd loved her unfortunate husband. As for the Countess, she never felt better anywhere than in Branchevieille.

There was fresh white asparagus, the fat kind that swells in June, in Madame Monjoux's kitchen garden behind the hotel. To honor it there was butter from chez Florent, the village's surviving creamery, and fresh eggs from chickens running in the road to the train station. No virtuoso chef in Paris could have accomplished a better hollandaise sauce than Monsieur Monjoux had whisked together with those ingredients.

The three travelers dug into their lunch. After the asparagus there were sizzling mutton chops from sheep that had grazed on the surrounding mountains and Monsieur Monjoux's ultimate *aligot*. It stretched in ribbons from the plate as Samuel lifted it with his fork, but with a grace that was part of his manual deftness, he twirled it round his fork tines like spaghetti and gave no further sign of estrangement than a quirky smile. There was ripened hard local cheese with the salad. They finished the Marcillac and out came Madame Monjoux's fresh strawberry tart, which gave off an odor of buttery crust and warm berries the minute it was set down. The Countess took a big dollop of crème fraîche from the little pot Madame Monjoux set down and passed it to Fatima. When Samuel tasted it in his turn, he couldn't help but exclaim: "*Ma foi, Madame*, it tastes like a mouthful of flowers."

"The cows are on the mountainside, you see," the Countess explained. "Unfortunately, nobody has the courage anymore to mow the fodder up there with a hand scythe and no machine can work on those slopes. They just drive the cows up there to eat as much of it as they can and the mountainsides are covered with flowers. They eat the flowers, which is what you're eating now."

"Madame, I can eat flowers until the cows come home," laughed Samuel, while the Countess tried to pour wine from the empty bottle. She shrugged and winked, as if they'd been naughty.

Was it the wine or the combination of the wine and the heady, clear air that made Fatima so drowsy? Her eyes closed and she fell instantly into a dream. In her dream, she was in Wisconsin. In reality she had no idea what Wisconsin was like, except that Hadley had told her it was cold there and flat and there were many cows. She was on a train, not the TGV, nor the *Micheline* that had brought her to Branchevieille, but a miniature train like the one in the Jardin d'Acclimatation. She saw Mahmoud standing on the little wooden platform waiting for her train to pull in, but the train kept going, past the little station, on past blackberry bushes like those in the Jardin d'Acclimatation. Mahmoud looked hurt, but Fatima had barely time to wave to him before he was out of sight behind her.

She felt a foot on hers. Samuel stepped gently on her toe and she awoke, startled, then worried what the Countess would say about her falling asleep. But the Countess was herself snoring softly in her chair and must not have noticed. Samuel had helped himself to the rest of the cream. He looked at them both and chuckled. "What a pair you make, *ma soeur*," he said.

When the Countess awoke, Monsieur Monjoux had his son, Jean-Claude, start up their immaculate Citroën *Déesse* vintage 1969. Jean-Claude was a handsome, curly-haired young man in his thirties, who dressed impeccably in a crisp blazer but who had the misfortune of being what is sometimes called "simple." His good fortune was his parents, who treated him with great care and, equally important, with respect, even

195

though they knew he didn't seem to have the same grasp on reality that most people had. His stuttering seemed evidence of the extra time it took him to make all the connections in his mind that defined what was going on. He was all the same an accomplished driver. The family Citroën was his charge in life, and Jean-Claude had a responsible rapport with it resembling one between a man and his living ward in the animal world.

Monsieur Monjoux had bought the car to celebrate Jean-Claude's birth after he and Madame Monjoux had tried for years to have a child. At the time, though, Monsieur Monjoux had felt remorse over having to sell his previous car, a 1954 black Citroën *traction avant*. He'd be the last person to believe in obsolescence. Other than some periodic repainting, the Hôtel des Voyageurs had changed little since his late father had run it. The décor was pure thirties. What had changed was that there were very few voyagers passing through this old village since the autoroute had pierced the surrounding mountains. But Monsieur Monjoux had no debts, and his country cooking, albeit neglected by the guidebooks as old hat, had enough of a reputation among true trenchermen in the region to keep the three of them. What would happen to the hotel and to Jean-Claude after he and Madame Monjoux were gone was nonetheless a question that often kept both of them up at night.

Jean-Claude held the rear door open for the Countess. She was still a little groggy and the sunlight made her a bit dizzy. But suddenly, after he'd closed the door behind her, she cried, "Emma?"

Emma was bounding out of the hotel and frisking over the gravel of the driveway. She sniffed the whitewall tires of Monsieur's Monjoux's blue and white sedan. She looked up at her mistress and then she was drawn to the sound of Samuel starting up the van. The dog wheeled and jumped through the open door of the van.

Fatima was getting in after her. "Emma!" the Countess shouted, but by now Jean-Claude was rolling out of the driveway with the van following. Jealousy surged over the old woman for a moment. She comforted herself by believing that Emma had simply made a choice for novelty. But still another thought came over her, bittersweet. If I died, she thought, Emma might still have someone to love her.

Slowly, taking great care not to strain the car that was the love of *his* life and its one responsibility, Jean-Claude drove toward the château. Samuel clucked as he held back the van. But for Fatima the slow drive was a treat. The road followed a river with old farmhouses on the shore. There were hosts of flowers in the fields behind them and the mountains were blanketed with yellow gentiane. She could hear the echo of the cowbells up there.

Bicycle riders in tight shorts, bent over their bikes, passed the two slow vehicles. Jean-Claude honked his horn at them for no other reason, perhaps, than to let them know that his car was bigger than they were all the same.

Soon they came to the gates of the château, and when they turned into the long, unpaved allée, bordered by chestnuts, Fatima saw the castle that Geoffroy Poulais du Roc's ancestor had built in the seventeenth century. Long and low, with sharply peaked roofs at the end of each wing, and with a stone porch reached by a delicate stairway in an arc at each side. The Green Guide Hadley had given Fatima had pictures of stern, granite medieval fortresses, but Branchevieille seemed an image of lovely femininity to her. It was built in a moment of peace here, after the bloody wars between the nobles and the king that had ravaged the countryside, and it had fortunately survived the bloody revolution that followed a century later. Fatima rolled down the van window and thought, it's beautiful. And the mountains are beautiful and the lunch was lovely and the very air is a pleasure to breathe. In short, she was happy.

Sheep were grazing on the lawn in front of the château. Once the Poulais du Roc family had owned all the farmland surrounding the château, but Geoff had sold it off to his tenant farmer. The lawn didn't come with the farmland, but the farmer, old Ulysse, provided the château with vegetables in exchange for the grazing. Emma never understood this detail, so, as usual on arriving, as soon as the van stopped, she bounded out, and as best as the old dog could, she began chasing the sheep with a proprietary air. Samuel found this quite amusing and his rich laugh echoed against the mountains.

★   ★   ★

Fatima had removed the sheets from the furniture of the salon, folding them carefully against her chest as she revealed the timeworn needlepoint of the eighteenth-century chairs. Now she sat with the Countess beside a big wicker trunk full of objects wrapped in tissue paper, all the things that had to be set out again. The Countess unwrapped them and handed them to her one by one, revealing a little inventory of a life so different from Fatima's own. But all lives are fundamentally the same in their moments of happiness and sorrow, Fatima thought, and one by one, with each relic of some happy moment, Fatima could catch the thread that had run through the old woman's life.

"This is the Count in his RAF uniform," the Countess said. "He goes on the piano."

There were autographed pictures from President Giscard d'Estaing and from the young Prince Juan Carlos, who had come down to shoot boars at Branchevieille. There was another of the Countess and her husband with Pope John Paul I, with a seal below it. The date inscribed was September 1978, shortly before his mysterious death. There were ceramic Chinese animals and a nymph from the twenties in rock crystal, all sorts of similar bibelots . . .

Fatima carefully unwrapped a photograph and there was the Countess, a svelte, beautiful woman in a trailing wedding dress with a husband as handsome as a movie actor.

Fatima could not help but hold the picture and stare at it.

"It's my wedding picture, darling. Look at that dress."

"Beautiful. I've never seen cloth fall more beautifully on someone so beautiful, Madame," Fatima said.

"Eu-hem. Well, it's cut on a bias. Alix Grès. What do you think of Geoff, Fatima?"

"The way he looks at you, Madame . . ." Fatima sighed.

"We had a wonderful life together." The Countess sighed. "Fatima?"

"Yes, Madame?"

"You know, when Emma was sick, and I thought I would lose her, and we cured her together, right?"

"Yes, Madame."

"Well, I have thought a lot about it since. The Count would not want the heat. You know, it might crack the furniture that his family had for generations. But I've thought about it. I mean, if Emma had died. How everything is so fragile, and living creatures, well . . ."

Fatima felt she could finish the Countess's sentence: "Are more fragile, Madame, than things."

"Precisely. I love it here and we will spend more time here, and for that we'll need heat. My bones won't take the cold, you see? You understand?"

"Yes. Although where I come from it's never very cold."

"Well, that's lucky."

"Yet people are everywhere fragile all the same, Madame."

200

The Countess looked at her silently a moment. "Seize the day, right?" she said. "Tell me what you think, Fatima."

"I think do the right thing while you can, Madame. What you can."

The Countess was only half-listening. She had unwrapped a photo of a little girl in a white communion dress. She passed it to Fatima.

"That was my daughter."

Fatima gave her a pained look. She remembered Hadley's story about "Rockababy," the drugs and the music.

"She is still my daughter, but she doesn't like to think so. Do you have children?"

"I have not been so fortunate."

"Well, it's not only good fortune, you know."

Fatima went on unwrapping objects without replying.

"But you had a husband," the Countess said, "and you were in love?"

Fatima still didn't answer. Finally she shrugged.

"What does that mean?" asked the Countess.

"I married the man my widowed mother thought I could have. As God saw to it, I became fond of him."

"Well, that was fortunate."

"Mahmoud met someone else. They went to Morocco where he could send me a divorce in the mail . . . and then they went back to her country."

"Some horrible place, I hope."

"Wisconsin."

"Isn't that somewhere in America?"

Fatima took the photo of Rockababy as a child from the Countess's hand. "Where shall we put this, Madame?"

The Countess grabbed it back, roughly. She put it face-down into the wicker trunk. The gesture had the effect of a burial on Fatima. She sucked in her breath in shock. At that moment, it was as if the Countess and her daughter were from another planet. In Fatima's experience with human beings, mothers and daughters never reached that degree of estrangement.

The Countess seemed to sense Fatima's revulsion. She moved on:

"Help me up," she said, and Fatima eased the old woman out of her chair.

"Sitting here, over all this, you get stiff. No sense living in the past, darling, is there?"

The Countess went up to the uncovered baby grand piano, swept her skirt under her with a brisk gesture, and sat down to play. Her old hands moved over the keys slowly, but with certain phrasing, as she began to play a prelude by Chopin. Fatima stopped working and just stood there watching her, and the Countess didn't seem to mind. She cocked her head back and moved it to the music of her fingers, like a concert pianist.

The Countess played very well. Fatima realized that the Countess's daughter's association with music might have been inspired by her mother. The piano was out of tune, which gave a certain further pathos to Chopin's *Schadenfreude*, but the music filled the salon richly and echoed throughout the empty rooms of the ground floor of the château, until it was broken into by the sound of a drill.

"It's Samuel," Fatima said, as the Countess took her hands off the keys. "I'll get him to stop."

"Oh no, darling," the Countess replied, "he's working on our future."

With those words, a feeling of well-being came over Fatima. She sensed with her talented intuition that it was treacherous, but she could not help but let herself feel good. The drilling went on and then there was a clatter of hammering.

That night, Fatima slept in Rockababy's bed, the one she'd had until early adolescence, when she'd been given her own larger bedroom and boudoir at the other end of the long upstairs hallway of the château. The move was appropriate for her at her age, but that was perhaps, all the same, the first concretization of what would be a growing estrangement between mother and child. This room had been her nursery; a crib still stood in one corner opposite the bed, and a big dollhouse — a doll château — in another. It adjoined the Countess's own bedroom, just the other side of a connecting passage, with doors at either end. The reason — or excuse — the Countess gave for assigning Fatima this room, out of the numerous bedrooms that gave off the hall, was that she wanted Fatima to be close "for Emma." In case Emma "needed her in the night," whatever that could mean. Emma would sleep as usual at the foot of the Countess's bed. As for Samuel, he was granted the privacy of his own quarters in what had been a coachman's apartment above the garage, where he expected to speed his return to his own marital bed by working into the night.

The Countess had left the room exactly as her daughter had left it — the Rolling Stones and Bob Marley posters were still thumbtacked to the floral wallpaper. They were well faded but still seemed like ephemeral intrusions upon the 1920s wallpaper, the older ceiling moldings and the ancient bed. Fatima wondered just how old that high bed might be, as she tossed about, seeking the modus vivendi its previous user had found with the sagging mattress. Finally, with the open window sending her grass-scented fresh air and the open passage the sound of the Countess's soft snoring, she began an agitated dream of a turbulent ride in and around a steel dragon flashing lights from its tongue and tail, which only Hippolyte Suget's reassuring hand on hers kept from terrorizing her.

When she awoke, she recalled that it was just in the dream that he had taken her hand.

Jean-Claude arrived at breakfast time with his *Déesse*. The Countess had asked him to take Fatima and her on an excursion while Samuel hammered, sawed, and soldered away.

Fatima gave him coffee in the kitchen. And while she watched him drink like a youngster, bringing a bowl, in which he'd floated a slice of brioche, to his mouth with both hands, she did not quite know what to make of him. He'd begun to talk to her ebulliently, despite his stutter. As if he were excited to have instinctively found

204

an accomplice, like a child coming upon someone his own age in a party of adults.

He managed to make clear that he would show Fatima all the wonders of the region, as many as they could visit today and more on later days, and that what he wanted her to see most of all was his waterfall. What came out did not at all sound demented. Just full of enthusiasm that grown-ups would consider excessive.

The Countess said she was delighted to "get an airing" as she put it, with a grain of self-mockery about being an old woman. She knew the region well. She could remember racing around the hairpin turns of the mountains with Geoff, the rear wheels of his latest toy — she remembered especially the flat trajectory of a Morgan Plus Four — sliding until he flicked them back into traction with a nudge of his steering wheel, her Hermès head scarf blowing in the wind. He had taken her to every point of interest Michelin had starred, and many it had overlooked. A menhir up a cowpath, the ruins of a Romanesque chapel where there was no longer any road . . .

"Don't forget the dinosaur footprints!" she told Jean-Claude, as she stepped into the *Déesse*.

Her own memories made Fatima flush, as they entered a village called Saint Hippolyte. They went into the early Gothic church, where under a glass container and mercifully invisible in a wrapper of old silk were the finger bones of a saint. Near the church a shop window was full of wooden shoes, which she found equally fascinating. She'd seen old people in Branchevieille still wearing them. A thought came into her mind about Wisconsin. Farmers in Wisconsin in wooden shoes? Where had that association first begun in her mind? Sheboygan, in any case, was a city. As they left the village, she saw *his* name again on a road sign, with a bar across it. She closed her eyes, unconscious that her gesture meant to ward off an omen, and replaced the sign with the image of his face.

The dinosaur prints were in a farmyard. Chickens had splattered them — the territory was now theirs. The prints were clearly pressed into slabs of gray stone.

"Millions of years ago," sighed the Countess.

Fatima helped the old woman hurry back to the car. She felt that the Countess had come to believe that coming there wasn't such a good idea after all. By the time they got to Jean-Claude's waterfall, the Countess had fallen asleep, alone in the back of the car.

It was an undramatically low waterfall, only a few feet high, on a narrow stream. But Jean-Claude told Fatima that it was his special place. They let the Countess sleep while he took Fatima's hand and helped her over a path of rocks in the stream until they got to a pool, where the water tumbling off mossy boulders sprayed their faces. They sat on a dry boulder and he began to say things. And it was here, during the several excursions they would make in the days ahead, that they would always wind up, with the Countess asleep in the *Déesse*. Here, as if his secrets had been dammed up behind a wall of stuttering but were now pressing him to add to her tour of enlightenment, Jean-Claude would manage to reveal to Fatima the many objects of his

206

affection. He wasn't so simple after all, and not, in any case, so simple as not to know she was a rare listener.

Fatima had found an old bicycle in the former stable turned garage, where Samuel had set up his pipe-cutter. Samuel had pumped air into the tires with the little pump that was attached, and Fatima rode out toward the village square on the creaking bike. She had decided to dare to try to write another postcard, encouraged by her having been able to do one for Hadley. Emma followed her for just a few yards, as if out of obligatory politeness to an old friend, before she turned and headed back to the new role she must have imagined for herself as Samuel's apprentice. She hung at his heels wherever he turned as he cut pipe, whistling. Fatima had sensed that the dog had been particularly impressed by the presence of a man.

The way toward the village square was downhill, and Fatima coasted in the sunlight. It felt good to be back on a bicycle. She thought of the Hollywood bike and remembered Ahmed. She decided she would buy a third card in the village and send it to Ahmed.

Fatima had noticed the array of postcards at the desk of the Hôtel des Voyageurs the day she'd arrived with the Countess. Some depicted scenes of the mountain-ous landscape. There were also a few with a black-and-white photo of the entrance to the Grotto of Sainte Helvetia, a local adolescent who had retreated there, visited by the Virgin, until she was called to Her by a bout of pneumonia. The Countess had recounted the story over dessert during that splendid lunch. There were also some cards of women with naked breasts rowing a kayak on the Lot River. Fatima smiled to herself, thinking that that was the card Ahmed would appreciate the most, but she would never think of asking Madame Monjoux for it.

"I hear the Countess is well," said Madame Monjoux, wiping dirt from her garden off her hands before she lifted the two cards Fatima had selected from her rack.

"Very well," said Fatima.

"And the repairs are going well?"

"Very well."

"Well, *voilà*." She handed Fatima the card with a recipe and a picture of *aligot* on a checkered tablecloth and the other, a beautiful mountain scene with cows.

The *aligot* was for Ahmed, who loved to eat. Fatima sat down on a weathered bench beneath the statue of the World War I soldier in the town square and began to write on a piece of scrap paper. Ahmed would be surprised that she could write — and in French.

Dear Friend, How are you? I am well. Here they eat this like couscous. It is beautiful here. Regards to everyone at the Club Rêve. Monsour Fatima. It looked all right, but she still didn't trust herself with her spelling. *Inshallah*, if she kept it short it would not be too awful. As she started to transcribe the note onto the card, she realized that Monsieur Choukroun might be offended that he too had not received a card. Ahmed would surely show it around, but her mind was on the other card, the one she first thought of that would be harder to write, and she dispatched this one quickly.

208

She pondered the other for a long moment, but could come up with nothing better than:

As God saw to it, we arrived all right. The weather is beautiful. I hope you and the little Mademoiselle are well. Frustration came over her — there was so little she was confident in writing. And even if she could write better, she was not sure what would be appropriate to add. A mention about the cows?

With a feeling resembling defeat, she simply signed what she had written "Monsour Fatima." For the sake of discretion she had decided to put the card in an envelope. Madame Monjoux had given her an old one turning yellow, along with the card, whose own colors were already a little faded, evidence that too few tourists passed through Branchevieille for her to sell many cards. Fatima sealed the envelope and addressed it carefully:

Monsieur Suget Hippolyte
aux bons soins du Café Jean Valjean
34, avenue Victor-Hugo
75016 Paris.

She dropped the envelope and the card into the yellow mailbox on the wall of the Hôtel des Voyageurs and pedaled toward the bakery Leblanc for a big loaf of bread to eat with a picnic lunch.

The smell of yeast and burning wood was coming from the cellar window where Fatima leaned her bike against the stone bakery wall.

Downstairs, Monsieur Leblanc, sweating in short pants and an undershirt splattered with flour, was shoveling his second batch of the day into the oven. As he turned away from the heat to wipe his brow on an arm tattooed with a palm tree, he could make out the bottom of a bright djellaba flashing by the window.

"*Ah merde*," he muttered.

The bakery window was crowded with pies and cakes. Branchevieille, like many French villages, bereft of urban amusements, had a compensatory sweet tooth. A big glazed *fouasse*, the *auvergnate brioche*, dominated a marble and brass shelf. Around it were slabs of black cherry *millards* — something between pudding and pie. They looked worth tasting to Fatima, who was not an enemy of sweets, but her mission, she reminded herself, was bread, which the Countess never baked. That was another French quirk, she thought, no one ever baked bread at home. Whereas on Djerba . . .

She brought her mind back to France.

Madame Leblanc was in animated discussion with two gray-haired women when, with a chime of the bell over the doorway, Fatima walked in and said, "*Bonjour. S'il vous plaît* —" With that, the conversation stopped dead and the three women stared at her.

"— *un bâtard*," she said to Madame Leblanc, the baker's wife. The two others, Madame Caillot and Madame Pignon, simultaneously laughed into their hands.

"*En effet*," said Madame Caillot. Indeed.

"*En effet*," Madame Pignon repeated, almost at the same time. They tittered together, while Madame

Leblanc reached behind her for the bread Fatima had asked for, wearing a scowl.

Madame Caillot and Madame Pignon were twins. Very much so. They were both widowed in the same month — to two stonemasons who worked together. The former lost her husband to cirrhosis and the latter to lung cancer, so they were both the indirect victims of France's two premium vices — alcohol and tobacco — although neither smoked nor drank. They were prim, little women, whose obsessive piety might have driven their late spouses to the habits that did them in.

Fatima paid for the *bâtard*, a bread so-called because it was of a size too big to be considered an authentic baguette, and left, more perplexed than offended, not knowing that she'd interjected a *jeu de mots* into what was already a savory conversation.

When she'd shut the door behind her, Madame Leblanc wrinkled her nose as if she'd tasted something bitter. Monsieur and Madame Leblanc had had to abandon their prosperous bakery in the European quarter of Oran after the war that had separated Algeria from France. They had emigrated bearing Antoine, their newborn son, a couple of suitcases, and an indelible grudge against North Africans.

The reference to a "bastard" that had caused a titter in the bakery, however, had nothing to do with Fatima. It was about a literal one, who was soon to be baptized in the village church. And no one yet knew who was the father.

Fatima learned that much of the story from Samuel, a few minutes later, when she came to him in the garage with the chain of the old bike off its sprocket. He'd heard it from his new friend, Achille the stationmaster. He told it to her with a certain delectation — the two of them were after all outsiders looking at a world whose distance from their own created the objective quality of entertainment. Yet from her more personal stance, she didn't see the humor in it.

When Fatima went back into the château, the Countess looked up from her chair and rubbed her eyes, which were quite red. A book lay in her lap. "Fatima," she said, "I've been trying to read while you were away. Take the book, please."

Fatima picked up the book. It had been luxuriously bound in leather, many years ago. A gold Roman numeral two was stamped on the spine.

"Flaubert. Works. Two. Text established and ann . . . ann —"

"Annotated."

"Anno-tated."

It was the second volume of the definitive Pléiade edition of the works of Gustave Flaubert.

"— Wonderful. Well then, start on page seven hundred seventy-nine, where I left off, and read it to me. It doesn't matter if you make a mistake or two, darling, I know it practically by heart."

Fatima took a breath and started to read, pronouncing slowly but surely. The book was the author's last, unfinished novel about an eccentric couple of retired scriveners, *Bouvard et Pécuchet*.

She began where the two old fellows were staring at the night sky:

"... At length they wondered whether there were men among the stars. Why not? And since Creation was harmonious, the inhabitants of Sirius ought to be outsized, those of Mars of an average size, those of Venus very small. Unless things were the same all over. And up there, were shopkeepers, gendarmes; one finagled, fought and dethroned kings —"

The Countess responded to the author's cynicism with a concurrent "Humph!"

"A few shooting stars," Fatima continued, "suddenly slid across the sky, inscribing something like the parabola of a monstrous rocket —"

With that the front knocker sounded. A pause, a second knock, and then:

"Don't bother to get up, wherever you are, Monique," came a voice from someone already in the front hall.

"And if I happened to be somewhere stark naked?" called the Countess, as Pierre Beaulieu, the man who had succeeded Geoff as mayor of Branchevieille, walked into the salon.

"Ahh, Monique, if you were indeed naked." Beaulieu rolled his eyes.

He kissed her on both cheeks.

Fatima drew *Bouvard et Pécuchet* closer to her face. She was once again reminded that she was in another culture. Which led her to wonder whether *that* postcard had been appropriate. *Too late.*

Pierre Beaulieu gave her a nod. "*Bonjour*," he added, with automatic but sincere politeness. He was a tall, strapping gentleman of sixty, dressed in a French borrowing of Anglo-Saxon chic — chino pants and blazer. Monsieur Beaulieu, who kept horses on his restored farm, was still in excellent physical form. Riding was something that made him come as often as he could to Branchevieille. Alone. The job of mayor in a little French village was more or less an honorary post, and like Geoff, whose deputy he'd been, he didn't reside full-time in Branchevieille. He lived in Clermont-Ferrand, a few hours away, where he was an executive in the Michelin tire company, a family-run business that valued dependable and well-spoken men of his sort. Nobody in Branchevieille knew exactly what his function was for Michelin, since he never talked business. Geoff, of course, had liked him very much, which meant that his succession as mayor had been a foregone conclusion.

"I want to be sure, Monique," he said, in a serious voice now, "that you'll be at the ceremony."

"Why should I not?"

"We don't see you much in church."

"Do you think that I could fail to be there?"

There was a long moment of silence. The Countess didn't see this as a time to ask him how his poor wife was faring. Gwendolyne spent her life in and out of a mental clinic in Paris. She hated Branchevieille, having at one point concluded that the countryside, teeming with the inscrutable dumb life of nature, deeply depressed her.

214

Fatima didn't know whether to take it upon herself to leave the room. She placed the marker ribbon where she'd left off reading to the Countess and began reading further to herself, faintly moving her lips.

"I'm proud of her," Beaulieu finally said. "You understand that. Not of the whole event, but where she stands now. You can understand that?"

Through another moment of silence they could hear a car pulling up on the gravel outside.

"That must be Jean-Claude, who has come to take us for our airing," the Countess said.

She cast a glance toward Fatima, who was happy to leave to fetch their picnic from the butler's pantry. There was no more time left for reading now. The Countess was faintly annoyed that Pierre had barged in at a moment in the book that she liked very much, but the poor man needed a sympathetic ear.

"You and Hélène won't be alone there — the three of you," she said, assuring him again of her allegiance.

He shook his head and sighed.

"Oh no," he said, "there will certainly be quite a crowd."

Fatima stared out the pantry window at the shiny *Déesse* as she wrapped a linen napkin around a jar of Madame Monjoux's notable foie gras, *demi-cuit*, and tucked it in their picnic basket beside a slab of Cantal cheese and a bottle of mineral water and one of Marcillac. She was absorbed by Samuel's story.

The stationmaster had explained that Hélène was Pierre Beaulieu's youngest daughter. Until now, the only thing wrong about Hélène Beaulieu in the eyes of the villagers of Branchevieille had been her hair — or maybe her habit of chain-smoking as well. Truth to tell, her dyed blonde hair resembled the end of a frayed broom. She had been born quite plain, with a round face and features you could describe as "uneventful" in the sense that they seemed to inspire no one to give them a thought. Her hair might have been an event she created, in that sense. It gave her a definitely noticeable presence. Sometime after she'd let her hair grow out that way, while she was in nursing school in Clermont-Ferrand, she'd had a disastrous love affair with a married professor. It ended upon her graduation, and sick at heart, Hélène abandoned the city where she might have had to face him again and headed for the place she'd spent so many good summers and weekends amid pure air and simple people: Branchevieille. There was no doctor in the village; the nearest one was in Saint Jérôme, eight kilometers away. A nurse was more than welcome. Someone to give injections to the aged, to dress wounds, and bathe the bedridden living high up on obscure roads. Her hair notwithstanding, she became a greatly admired member of the village, and no one even dared to bring up the fact that whatever she did — even while giving an injection — she never removed a cigarette from her lips.

Hélène lived alone at her father's place, and when she wasn't driving to her patients in her 2CV, she groomed and rode his horses.

It wasn't until Hélène suddenly stopped smoking that people such as Madame Caillot and Madame Pignon saw fit to talk about that habit she'd had. When she gave up wearing tight jeans, there was more subject for conversation in the Leblanc bakery. Soon her new condition became apparent, even under her loose long skirts. One evening, after dusk, she drove off in her 2CV to Saint Jérôme and came back with an infant boy in a car cradle on the backseat. Whose was it?

There was of course immediate speculation about Dr. Dumas in Saint Jérôme, who had already sired a brood of six with his wife, also originally a nurse. In any case, Hélène categorically refused to name the father. She told Pierre Beaulieu that there would be no "blackmail," no shotgun held to anyone's head. "It is for him to say, and if we matter enough to him, he will."

There was something missing from the picnic basket, the madeleines the Countess had turned out in a jiffy while Fatima was away. They were particularly for Jean-Claude, spoiled by his mother's cakes since early childhood. He was in the kitchen when Fatima went to get them. His mouth was full. He might have already helped himself to one, as a child might. But his manners were otherwise quite grown-up, elegant, even.

He carried the basket to the car for Fatima and they set off. On their way out of town, they passed the church, where Le Père Benoît, all modesty, was sweeping the parvis with an old broom.

★   ★   ★

Le Père Benoît, a round little man in his seventies, remembered regretfully that it had been four years since he'd last performed a baptism. There were years without births in Branchevieille, while old people kept on dying. After sweeping, when he'd gone to get out the white brocaded cassock he kept especially for baptisms and weddings from the long wooden drawer in the sacristy, he found the folds had become creases. He'd gotten an ironing board and an iron from the sexton's closet and was ironing his white cassock when he heard footsteps in the nave.

Hélène Beaulieu came into the sacristy.

They just looked into each other's faces without speaking for a moment and then he said:

"You've come to confess."

"*Non, mon père,*" she answered, "just to be here."

She took the iron from his hand and began to iron out the creases in his robe.

He cleared his throat, but the words came out in a dry whisper all the same:

"Is it love?" Once, in seminary, on what seemed another planet now, he had fallen in love with someone.

She nodded.

"Is there someone else standing in between?"

"It's up to him," was all she'd say.

After she'd left, the priest downed a Suze, and as he inhaled the sweet herbal odor that was left in his glass, something inside him seemed to unbind, and he let himself remember looking at Hélène's firm backside in her stretchcloth beige riding pants when she walked

218

away through the nave. An absurd thought came to mind that matched his faint inebriation and his eccentricity. *If only she'd spent more of her free time with the horses.*

The Countess, Fatima, and Jean-Claude had their picnic at the waterfall. The sun, which made the spray off the boulders look like sequins, tired her eyes and caused the old woman to be drowsy. "I'm going to sit in the car," she said, "where there's a civilized place to put my backside." And where, of course, she fell asleep again. She awoke a good hour later, to see Jean-Claude and Fatima in animated conversation. They kept on chattering, oblivious of her, until she leaned over the front seat of the *Déesse* and petulantly blew the horn.

Pierre Beaulieu was not going to be intimidated by whatever anyone might be saying. The child was his daughter's son, his own blood, and Olivier would have a proper baptism and an appropriate baptism lunch as well, and because he was mayor there was no need for him to sort out an invitation list, he'd invite the entire village. He had the Monjoux prepare for a crowd. Whatever they were saying, they'd all be there for a good free lunch.

There was so much to do to prepare it that Madame and Monsieur Monjoux were both shelling the beans for the lamb on the day before.

"Do we have the *dragées*?" the mayor asked.

"They've been ordered," said Monsieur Monjoux. "Jean-Claude's gone to Saint Jérôme."

The *dragées* were the packages of candied almonds for each guest with the baby's name on it. Tradition requires them for every baptism party, and they'd been duly ordered at the Confiserie Maréchal in Saint Jérôme. Monsieur Maréchal had used up every almond in his stock for the *dragées* labeled "Olivier."

He was particularly disturbed when, by nightfall, no one had arrived to pick them up.

What with the baptism of Olivier Beaulieu, Branchevieille had little need of Jean-Claude's disappearance to enjoy its measure of the unwonted. The fear that something bad might have happened to him turned to dismay after the Leblancs' son, Antoine, the local real estate agent, reported having seen Jean-Claude sleeping in the *Déesse* that evening, opposite a pharmacy at the outskirts of Saint Jérôme. He'd driven past with a Dutch couple he was bringing back to his office, after having shown them a barn they could make into the kind of house the Dutch like to make out of barns. He might have stopped if he hadn't worried that it would get in the way of clinching his sale. Now the word from the pharmacist in Saint Jérôme was that the *Déesse* was gone.

That was how things stood when the sun came up over the day of the baptism, lighting Fatima's way, uphill on the rickety bicycle, all the distance to the waterfall.

★　★　★

The Countess was piqued by Fatima's absence. "Samuel," she sniffed, "Branchevieille has become the Bermuda Triangle."

Samuel believed that wherever Fatima had gone, she knew where was she going and why. "I understand that she's gone to Ulysse for some eggs," he lied, to allay the issue, just as Pierre Beaulieu drew up in his Mercedes. The Countess had no time to wait for Fatima to show up. She was determined to stand beside her friend and his daughter to greet, or to face down — however it would sort out in each case — the villagers arriving at church. She got into the car with Pierre and drove off calling a message to Samuel for Fatima:

"Tell her I'm displeased."

Emma began barking at the receding car, as if Pierre's necktie and dark suit told her that the Countess was up to something important, and the dog was slighted to have been left behind.

"Dismayed!" the Countess added through the barking. Emma seemed to think she heard a reprimand aimed at herself, and she ran and hid behind Samuel's legs.

"The Countess is dismayed," Samuel rehearsed to himself, with a chuckle that said that he was entertained. Samuel was the person with the greatest remove of all in the whole Branchevieille adventure he'd fallen into. He headed for the garage, crossing back into his own, separate territory, where he'd pinned a photo of his wife and children above the workbench. And where he'd been hurrying through his project without taking a day off.

* ★ ★

Sunlight from a cloudless sky bathed the little church square crowded with villagers, and for Pierre Beaulieu, as he stood near the door of the church, shaking hands, the weather felt like a benediction. He'd taken his stance regarding the event, and his constituents were responding with a *gentillesse* he had hoped for but in no way counted on. He was proud of them for the warmth so many of them showed him.

He was surprised when Antoinette, the wife of Antoine Leblanc, had kissed him on his cheeks, with a tear in her eye, as she took his hand in both of hers. She seemed so genuinely concerned. Was it something like the sympathy an outsider would bring to an outcast? She was not a native of Branchevieille. Antoine had met her in a discothèque when he was stationed in the navy at Brest. He was handsome, very handsome, with Alain Delon even looks marred only by a flashy self-awareness. But she had had, with her wiry sexiness, an allure to match his. Her self-consideration, however, had suffered from being someone from elsewhere in Branchevieille. She'd let her figure go and they'd become a testy couple.

Hélène stood near her father, holding little Olivier, in his baptismal gown and cap, crooked in her arm while the Countess held on to her other arm. Pierre saw his daughter accept Antoinette's kisses coldly. Once in a casual conversation Hélène had said that Antoinette was "of no interest" and "common." A surprisingly uncharitable comment from Hélène.

222

Something like a light flashed in his awareness and an apprehension close to dread came over Pierre as he glanced at Antoinette's husband. The dashing realtor and his parents had formed a little separate knot in the crowd with the sisters Caillot and Pignon. The Leblancs had exceptionally closed their bakery for the baptism, not so much to endorse it as to participate in a village event. Their business sense kept them from taking the risk of alienation in openly condemning it. Pierre had noted that this little group had been the coldest of all in greeting him. There were always five votes in Branchevieille for the ultra-right *Front National*, and everyone in the village knew who cast them. Antoine had turned their conversation toward something that concerned them more than this baptism and was of more interest even than his story of finding Jean-Claude Monjoux asleep in Saint Jérôme. He was urging the sisters to accept the offer his Dutch couple had made on the barn they'd inherited.

Just then the famous *Déesse* pulled up, with an old bike sticking out of its open trunk.

Everyone stared as Fatima got out. Then the car drove away, leaving her at the edge of the road. It stopped again a few yards away and backed into a parking place in the road. Jean-Claude stepped out from behind the wheel. He looked rumpled. He straightened his blazer and took a comb from his wallet pocket and combed his hair looking into the side-view mirror. He wiped each shoe on his trouser legs, buttoned his shirt collar and headed for the church. As he passed Fatima, their eyes crossed. His showed a flash of fright until she winked her green eye.

People got out of his way as he crossed the little square. He came to where Pierre was standing with the Countess and Hélène. His Adam's apple was pulsing as if he couldn't even get out a stutter.

Hélène looked up at him. If anyone there had the presence of mind to take a picture, they would have captured an illumination in her eyes that no classic Hollywood close-up could have matched. Jean-Claude made a movement of his left foot that suggested he might turn and bolt away.

Just then his son began to cry.

Hélène held the infant out to him and he took the boy and cradled him against his chest. The child kept crying, and now Jean-Claude had tears on his face, while Hélène's round face was one great smile.

From the crowd, Madame Monjoux let out a wail, but when everyone turned toward her, her face had already taken on an epiphanous glow. She had dragged herself to church, heavy with worry over her son's disappearance. And now he'd come back to her! And *miraculum miraculorum*, there in her boy's arms was an heir to the Hôtel des Voyageurs.

As Le Père Benoît stepped out of the church, he quickly realized that he had missed what could definitely qualify as an epiphany, perhaps even in a root, religious sense. He had steeled himself with a generous measure of Suze before he'd put on his white cassock, and he was still faintly red-faced but as if imbued, via the robe, with serene dignity. He tucked his

224

prayer book under his arm. It was his duty to bring this momentous event to a climax, and buoyed by that awareness, the good father made an elegant sweep of his arm that beckoned everyone into the house of the Great Parent of us all.

Fatima stood in the square with people stepping around her as they filed into the church. When the Countess had been swept in on the arm of Pierre Beaulieu, she'd cocked her head in Fatima's direction, but Fatima wondered whether, in something as solemnly religious as this, the best thing for an outsider such as herself to do would be to get back on her bike and head for the château. Now everyone was inside, except for the two generations of Leblancs and the barren sisters Caillot and Pignon. They were lingering near the church door as if they chose to be the last to give their assent. And now, as with a stroke of luck, their resentment found reason for enrichment. Their eyes fixed on the woman in the djellaba. Madame Leblanc, pulling her husband with her, stepped between Fatima and the open door.

"Excuse me. *Je suis désolée!*"

Fatima was ready to turn away. A vision of a human bone wrapped in decaying silk crossed her mind from her last visit to a church. Where she stood, she could smell the awesome church odor, the mix of damp stone, incense, and melted wax. The bike was still in the open trunk of the *Déesse*.

"Madame Monsour!"

It was the gravelly voice of the Countess. She was in the doorway, squinting at the sunlight.

"Good show. Jolly well done!

"Bloody sensational!" she added in Geoff's RAF English. And she raised her arm in a thumbs-up.

"But please don't bugger off on me again!"

It was as if she'd wanted to exclude the others there with her English, and now she reached her hand past Madame Leblanc and clasped her fingers around Fatima's forearm. Fatima got her drift from the English she'd heard at the Club Rêve. She felt a cold strength in the old woman's fingers as she let herself be drawn forward without saying a word. With her other arm the Countess simply brushed Madame Leblanc out of the way — no expression in her gesture, as if she were moving something inanimate with a stroke that required almost no effort. A taped choir was already singing as the two women entered the church on each other's arms. Backlit by the bright day, the rose window beyond the altar resembled an array of jewels. Pierre Beaulieu had had the altar covered with an abundance of white lilies. Fatima could smell the flowers now. Their heady odor seemed to blend with the children's voices on the recording to create a single, thrilling, immaterial presence. *All this for a child, and it was all rightly so.* The thought came to Fatima with a flash of irrepressible regret, as the Countess, still clutching her arm, led her all the way down the aisle to the front row and sat her down beside Pierre Beaulieu.

At the altar, the strapping Dr. Dumas and his athletic wife, Francine, who had come forward as godparents, were already into the ceremony with Father Benoît, renouncing Satan, his works and his temptations, while Jean-Claude Monjoux beamed angelically as he cradled his son against his chest. His eye caught Fatima's, and as if it were to please her, he straightened his posture and assumed an air of importance. Father Benoît, pouring his drop of holy water on Olivier, half-turned and caught the moment of complicity between the two of them. He saw Hélène squeeze Jean-Claude's arm possessively. The priest made her the gift of a reassuring nod, while Fatima closed her eyes, waiting for the pleasure of the music again.

Back in Paris, Hadley stood in his doorway with his head in his hands and kept repeating "God, God, God oh mighty!" His books were scattered all around him, some of them torn, bindings broken. The glass was shattered on the photo of his mother as a debutante at the Beaufort Bachelor's Cotillion that had sat on his night table. He stared at the telephone. He held back an impulse to sob, but he did not yet have the courage to pick up the receiver.

CHAPTER
FIVE

Fatima had found a great quantity of strawberries brimming in a wicker basket on the kitchen table the morning after the baptism. They were from the far end of the backyard vegetable garden that Ulysse, the former tenant farmer, was still maintaining, picking what was ripe for himself when the Countess was absent. He'd brought them in early that morning, when the Countess and he were both already stirring, two people of an age when one got by on little sleep. He'd brought a huge quantity, which was his way of saying, "The garden is still yours, after all." Ulysse appeared much older than he had when the Countess was last here, and looking at his already reddened face, as he'd headed out of the kitchen unsteadily, she knew what he relied on to wash down his breakfast sausage. She wondered who would care for the garden once Bacchus called him to wherever wine bibbers eventually go. But her thoughts had soon turned to the immediate question of all those berries.

Now they were bubbling in a great copper cauldron that Fatima had unearthed in the butler's pantry.

Fatima had also found a copper spatula to skim the jam, which she was doing, while it formed shining bubbles that gave off a rich fruity odor when they burst.

"So you were in on his secret?" the Countess asked. "Of course," she fibbed, "*I* sensed it all along."

"I didn't know until the last minute."

"Obviously he told you things." The Countess smiled wickedly. "That he was in love?"

"He told me, Madame, about a lot things he loved. Flowers. He said he was fond of lambs. And fish. Once, when you were . . . napping, he put his hand in the water and tickled a trout's belly —"

"Oh, he knew about tickling bellies."

"He said that he loved her, but the way he told it, it wasn't clear that he'd even dared to speak to her."

"The curious thing is, she actually fell in love with him. He's obviously —"

"Good, Madame. He's very good. And isn't he good-looking? But he was afraid to tell his parents. Wasn't that it?"

"He was afraid of growing up."

"But how could she keep loving him, if he didn't do something that *he* had to do and that she could admire?"

"Ah yes," the Countess said. "That's the difference between us — and trout. We are what we do."

For the Countess the matter was settled, and it was time to pour out the jam into the row of jars on the long kitchen table, on which the makings of so many delicacies and feasts had reposed. Fatima, though, was distracted. The Countess looked at her, a little awed by the distant expression on her face. There was a moment of silence.

Fatima had slept in fits, dreaming over and over again about water. Now the ceremony in the church had come back to her in a rush. The flowers and the music, the huge burning candle, the shining bowl of holy water, and the salver of oil. The priest was talking about the great Flood. "From the beginning of the world, Your spirit soared over the waters so that they might bear the seed of the power to sanctify." To her ears, it had sounded like *Bouvard et Pécuchet*. Unfamiliar rhetoric, all that about the universe, while it was just the child in the little white cap who had stirred *her* heart. Finally, all that discourse on God's prolific water of life had brought to mind what she'd kept behind a closed door inside her own small self.

The jam was bubbling too fast.

"Fatima!"

"Ah, Madame ... Madame, I'm an empty nut," Fatima blurted.

The Countess measured her sadness. She was tempted to warn, "Children can break your heart," but she knew that wasn't an answer that could bring solace. She turned off the gas. Finally she said: "Darling, you'll have to work on your social life. There are things one cannot accomplish on one's own."

Suddenly the Countess remembered: "Heavens! Fatima! A man called you! Indecently early! A man! He is going to call back."

The phone on the wall was already ringing again as she spoke.

★ ★ ★

There seemed an urgency in the very sound of the rings. The Countess simply handed Fatima the receiver and discreetly shuffled out of the kitchen.

"Hadley Hadley." Fatima's spirits lifted at the voice of her friend. "You are so good to telephone. I sent you a card."

"Hello, Fatima," he said sheepishly.

"We're making strawberry jam."

"Fatima, all is not well."

"You're not well? —"

"Not really. Fatima? —"

"What is it?"

"Are you sitting down? Your Wisconsin money . . ."

She could hear him swallow hard.

"Is all gone. Stolen. They broke into my room."

"Oh Hadley! Your room!"

"Are you listening, Fatima? They took your money I was responsible for. I'm going to pay you all of it back."

"And your precious books?"

"Fatima, never mind my books."

Fatima was silent for a moment.

"God wanted it," she said.

"Fatima, God is not a burglar. God did not send them up to the American's room on the sixth floor because there were all kinds of bells and whistles and armor on the doors below where the real money is. For once, never mind God, Fatima."

Fatima's eyes filled with tears, but she suppressed a sob lest Hadley hear her. She thought of the hours at the Club Rêve that had added up to create that

231

handkerchief full of cash and how she'd try to recalculate them into the time ahead before she could get to Wisconsin. God had to have wanted this. And God would want her to persevere all the same. Perhaps He had felt He needed more time for her to be ready to go. Perhaps, and perhaps again she was after all simply fated, for reasons known only to Him, to be misfortunate all through her life.

"Never mind the money, Hadley. You didn't steal it and I'll never take it from you. Never mention it. What about your books?"

"Well, let's say they need to be reclassified."

The thought of Hadley trying to put things in order made her smile increduously.

"And some backs are broken."

"Gather them in a pile, Hadley. And we'll put them back where they belong together, when I return."

"When will you be back?" His voice seemed to plead, even though he didn't want it to. "I'm glad you're happy down there, Fatima," he said, correcting himself.

"Oh, I am mostly happy, Hadley," she said.

There was a little click. Suddenly the Countess's voice came on the line.

"Monsieur," the old woman said, "may I now have my line and my maid back again?" If there were one word that could describe her voice as it sounded to Hadley then, it would, he thought, as he said good-bye to Fatima, be jealousy.

So there it was, the proof once again that she was born under an unlucky star. Well, Fatima told herself, she couldn't change that. She'd had to live the life that was hers to live, and accomplish what she could. She told herself that over and over, days later, while the countryside receded in the window of the TGV back to Paris. There might be hours of cleaning she could get, to make up for the lost Wisconsin money. Carmen could help her with that.

To cheer herself, she started to make a little ledger of accomplishments in her mind. Emma, on her way back to Paris with Samuel at that moment, was healthy again. The Countess had her heating system. Samuel had his contract for the electricity and Monsieur Robert had the contract at a good price. Hadley lived in a more clean and orderly way than before and, of course, there was Olivier, who had a father . . .

None of these achievements that came to mind had to do with her own trajectory in life. That was how Fatima tended to think. She had grown up in a village where women spent little time thinking about themselves. But she was no longer there. So she was able to add that she had learned to read, she had won the friendship of Victorine and Samuel and Hadley. And the affection of the Countess, grudgingly, as the old woman was wont to give it.

And the attention of a man? That was the kind of thought, being who she was from where she was, born under her particular star, she would never hear herself telling herself. But something obscure, an emotion rather than a thought, in this jumble of optimism that came to mind with his name, Hippolyte Suget, made her blush. She allowed herself to tell herself that she had found a friend in that man.

Such was Fatima's state of mind when, back in Paris, she walked into the Café Jean Valjean for the Countess's usual cup of coffee, and Madame Richard offered her the coffee for free. "Fatima," she said, "where have you been? You've won the lottery!"

She'd won ten thousand euros, or about as many dollars.

CHAPTER
SIX

July had come to Paris while Fatima had been away in the country. Hippolyte Suget felt a hot day coming on. The sun already glared on the sidewalk and glinted off the windows of the closed Café Jean Valjean next door, where Monsieur Richard's straw chairs were piled, waiting to be set out again next day, Monday. Suget saw his shadow grow shorter. He was waiting impatiently for Fatima to come down and he surmised that the old woman had collared her on her day off to get her to do something or other before she was free. He had on a tan gabardine summer suit and a necktie. He'd given a formality to this day, not for the sake of the impression he'd make at Fresnes, but for her. "Would you care to accompany me to the Vincennes Zoo?" he'd asked her. "I had hoped to take Jenny." Jenny, he'd explained, had gone to Brittany with her grandmother to visit her grand-uncle. When Fatima had explained the other excursion that she herself had to make that Sunday, he'd surprised himself by rising quickly to the occasion. "Well, I actually might also go somewhere on your way," he'd said. So here he was.

And so they would be together this morning. Perhaps for the last time. Madame Strasbourg had reported that

Fatima had once said something about having to go to America. And now she had the money. Cacahouète might have the last word after all: *"Petit con!"* It's a dead end.

There she was. Today she was not wearing a djellaba, but a long floral skirt with a white blouse flowing over it. Clothes a Frenchwoman might almost wear.

As Suget tucked Bobby's box of candy under his arm to shake her hand, the thought crossed his mind that perhaps he should have gotten her a gift, too. Flowers? That would have seemed very forward.

After the RER, the 396 bus drove quickly through the southern suburbs. Too quickly, Suget thought. Their time together was going too fast. There was no one waiting, bus stop after bus stop, and the driver accelerated each time instead of stopping. Sunday in these gray suburbs. Perhaps everyone, whether in the tall public housing or the little, cherished *pavillons*, was in front of his television, watching the Tour de France bike race. Those who had not taken July to go wherever they went, for the vacation to which the law entitled them. Fatima stared out the window, and he did not dare try to break her serious mood with small talk. So they rode together in silence. An empty day, he thought, was being lost forever. If only he had been able to detect Fatima's unconscious relief when she heard that his daughter was with a grandmother, not a mother. If only that, he would have been happier.

She pressed the buzzer. The bus stopped. They shook hands.

236

"Where exactly are you going?" she finally asked. She asked because she'd felt, since the day they'd shared a ride on this bus with Hadley, that he carried a heavy mystery with him on his itinerary. Perhaps they had reached a point in their acquaintance where she could comfortably ask, or just as likely, it was her empathetic nature coming out again, her nature to show concern, spontaneously — in the way she'd once put her hand on Dawn McConnor's shoulder. Or by now there was even more to her concern for him than she would give conscious thought to.

He didn't lie. "I have a friend in prison," he said. She didn't answer. There was no time to say anything more. She was on the sidewalk and the bus was moving away. From the window of the receding 396, he watched her determined gait as she headed toward those gritty, concrete walls and the dead behind them.

There was still no plaque on Rachida's grave. Just the little painted number on the side of the concrete slab, among those that stretched mostly nameless in each direction, a fleet of little stone barges on a concrete sea going nowhere. There was no point in complaining to the gatekeeper, the one with the story about waiting until there were enough new arrivals to order a group of plaques. He'd stick by his story. But that was irrelevant now anyway. She could not bear to think of Rachida lying here under a putty-colored French sky surrounded by strangers. She whispered something in Arabic. If there were someone there to hear it, it would have sounded like a resolution.

It was a long walk on the wide avenue of the cemetery back to the bus stop, past graves tended and those caved in or overgrown, with worn little stones or marble villas — the world of the dead as unegalitarian as that of the living, not to mention "*la fosse commune.*" Noon was gone and the day was in its dying half. All this filled Fatima's mind with an awareness of the passing of time, so that when she got to the bus stop, she remembered she had specific things to accomplish. With that thought, she did not hurry for the bus heading back to the RER, but stayed on the same side of the avenue and waited resolutely for the next bus going further out, toward Fresnes.

Suget's jaw dropped when he saw her reading the plaques to the martyred resistants at the main gate of the prison. He felt an impulse to skulk away along the side street, embarrassed to have told her where he'd gone, but she heard his footsteps and looked at him. His breeding saved the moment. "It's so hot," he simply said, "I do hope you have not been standing long in the heat."

She shook her head and gave him a polite smile.

"I wanted to be sure to see you again, before I went away," she said.

He heard himself mention a cold drink and in a minute he was holding her elbow, walking her up the hillside lined with neat little houses that led to the square where the Mairie de Fresnes stood, a little bourgeois square that seemed in another world from that of the fast highway and the great prison below.

There were tables set out in the café nearby, shaded by red and white Cinzano umbrellas.

She began to speak before the waiter even brought her iced tea and his *panaché* of beer and grenadine syrup.

"Did your friend like the candy?"

"Oh, yes. He always looks forward to it."

There was silence for a moment and then she said, "I'd like to know why you are always very sad."

"Why I'm such bad company."

"No, not gloomy. You don't make me sad. But underneath, it's there."

He stared at his *panaché* without drinking. The ruby color gave him an instant of pleasure. In some strange way, he felt a strong association between the beautiful liquid and the woman there at that same moment. He hadn't expected her to have said anything more than some guarded pleasantry. "You are very sensitive to have noticed," he said.

"I thought that if I didn't point it out to you, that I felt it, I would not be a true friend."

"You are a person of great feeling," he replied, and he took a long drink of his *panaché* as if he'd find the courage to continue in it.

Suget got two photos out of his wallet. He held them out to her. One was of him as a twelve-year-old in his ballet tights, and in the other he was wearing prison denims.

"So this is me," he said. He cocked his head back toward the street that led to the prison. Then he looked to see what those keen strange eyes would tell him. But she lowered her gaze.

"You did something very bad?"

"I broke into people's houses. Many times, with men who'd become my friends. Until they caught me once."

"You were a burglar," she said without any shock in her voice, as if she were beginning a list of information about him.

"That's it." He began to mock himself: "A dancer turned burglar."

"And Madame Suget?" As God would have it, that came out without her thinking.

"There is no Madame Suget. We never married."

The face of a little girl with dark pigtails came into Fatima's mind, but her intuition kept her from taking the conversation that far into his patently torn private life.

"A dancer." She looked at the photo of the boy.

"I was quite a dancer," he said, pointing to himself in ballet tights. "A *petit rat*. The Opéra school. And one day this foolish teacher — she believed I was very gifted — had me do a reverse pirouette from a *pont* while I had my legs crossed in *demi-pointe*, and then . . . And then I couldn't dance anymore. My back."

He looked away from her to signal to the waiter for another round of drinks. By now, he had to finish his story. She was comparing the two photos when he looked at her again. Bookends, the beginning and the ending of his youth, she thought. And now he was neither young nor old nor anywhere in his unfortunate life. What could she say to him? She didn't know what to say.

"I didn't know what to do with my life. I was very young and didn't know about anything except to dance. When I left the lycée for the dancers and went back to my neighborhood school, Janson, they all called me . . . effeminate. I felt I had to be very manly."

He swallowed and looked away toward the waiter again.

"Do bold things," he continued. "I found my level with some bad friends. Spoiled. Janson brats. With them I met some really 'bold' people. You know, it can be very stupidly exciting breaking into someone's apartment, thrusting yourself, dangerously, into a life other than your own. My parents died heartbroken, both of them. And unfortunately, with their money gone, too."

"And you paid what you owed in prison." That was what she knew he had to understand; for better or worse, he'd rounded out his past, there was no point carrying it around like an unpaid bill.

"How do you calculate that?" he asked.

"You should not try to change the past."

Silence. Maybe her words had made contact.

"Do you tell yourself that, too?" he finally asked. It was all he had the courage to say, although he had sensed from the start that she, too, was carrying around a regret, perhaps as heavy as his own remorse.

"You're going away," he said. "Madame Strasbourg told me you are going to America."

She gathered up his photos. "Let me have these," she said, "that way you will not always be looking at your past."

"You will come back?"

He spoke while she was reaching into her purse to get out a photo, and his words, which meant — she couldn't help but perceive — *I want you to come back*, made her flush, stirred her to the point where she could not even give him any answer.

The photo was the souvenir Polaroid of the two of them on the Enchanted River, in the Jardin d'Acclimatation.

"You should have this," she finally was able to say.

"I have one in my wallet. You will come back?"

"As God wishes it." Her voice was no more than a whisper.

Then she crossed another border: She took a paper from her purse and a ball pen and wrote an address. She pushed the paper across the table.

The waiter brought the fresh drinks. Coincidentally, both of them, unable to say anything more, nervously lifted their glasses and drank. To the waiter, it looked like a toast.

Fatima boarded her plane for her necessary journey feeling in several ways that a weight had been removed from her.

THREE

CHAPTER
ONE

Rachida lay in the little town plot near the palm grove fenced in with blooming red rose bushes. She was home, beside her parents. As she should be, according to the ways of her people.

Hadley had helped Fatima comb the Yellow Pages for a funeral director who handled exhumations and transfers. By the time she had bought her own ticket and paid the undertakers, she had three hundred fifty euros left from the ten thousand she had won. Rachida was home, although Fatima could not quite honestly say that about herself here, anymore.

Djerba was still lovely, despite the building that seemed never to stop in the hotel zones. Outside Batouine, the barley was high at the feet of the tall palm trees. Bougainvillea had grown all over Fatima's adobe house in the village. Inside, nothing had been touched. The rugs, the brass tea table that her mother had taught her to scrub regularly, now brown. The Formica kitchen set. Fatima sat down in the kitchen and drew a glass of cool water from the indoor sink that had been her mother's pride. She was a little tired by the heat. She was, she realized, no longer used to it.

Some twenty women were next door, in the courtyard of Leila and her husband, Anwar the barber. They were all wearing bright, festive djellabas that blazed in the sunlight as Fatima stepped out of the shade of her house. She looked at her plain long skirt and blouse and wondered if she, too, should have dressed for the occasion. Too late. They saw her and burst into a *zaratha*, ululating like an excited flock of birds. They'd come together in her honor. In all the years she'd been a friend to all of them, a solicited advisor, they'd never done that before. She blushed and smiled. And in a moment they were gathered about her taking turns kissing her cheeks.

Leila's bright brass table nearly overflowed with fruit and sweets. She poured potsful of mint tea. The women drank and licked their sticky fingers and splashed rose water on each other, and for a brief while they pressed Fatima about her life in Paris.

A description failed her. It was all so different. She voiced some banalities about the beauty of the monuments of Paris.

"I've learned to read," she finally said, shyly. But they all knew how to read and they all had seen pictures of the monuments of Paris, so their conversations quickly turned to their own lives: "Sem is cutting teeth." And "Kestel has gained a kilo" and so forth. Their talk about children excluded her; perhaps there was even a subtext there of matching their maternal achievements, of which she had none, with her exotic new life. Soon their village chatter about the latest visit of husbands, the price of couscous, and the quality of the year's crop

246

of barley and dates left her out entirely. Fatima could not help but realize that although her homecoming was the surface reason for their gathering together, the real purpose was to create a moment of amusement for themselves. Such moments, she remembered, did not come often.

At the Club Rêve, Monsieur Choukroun was waiting for her with a bouquet of jasmine.

"Fat'ma," he said. "You are radiant. Paris has been good to you?"

She nodded as she took his hand.

"Let me kiss you, finally," he bantered. "If you had not been married, and I were not married . . . and you were Jewish . . . I would have dared kiss you on the cheek long ago."

He took her two hands in his. Grazed her cheeks with his dry lips.

"France," he sighed, and as he looked into her eyes, Fatima could sense stress in his, despite his joking tone a moment earlier. His family had lived in the village of Hara Sghira for centuries. His grandfather had been a rabbi famous on the whole island for his wisdom. But nowadays it could not be easy to be a Jewish person in Tunisia. She could not help but think of the cosmopolitan city she inhabited now, where all sorts of people from all over, all the colors God had made, came together.

She asked about Ahmed. Monsieur Choukroun sighed again. "Ahmed is a big man now . . ."

★   ★   ★

247

The clean, bitter smell of the newly paved roads came up through the window of Fatima's taxi. Yards from the bright sea, houses were going up in a hurry, cement had oozed and dripped between their cinder blocks. Slapdash work, the kind Mahmoud would have said something about. Mahmoud . . . She had heard somewhere that houses in America were made of wood.

There was a stone gate and a man in uniform in a booth. A metal arm beyond the booth kept the taxi from passing through, but when Fatima rolled down the other window and said "Ahmed Brahem," it was as if the words were magic. The arm shot up.

Ahmed was wearing a green blazer with a crest on it. He looked very formal indeed, but the French couple standing there with their initialed luggage was astounded when he rushed out from behind his desk as soon as he spied Fatima.

"*Es salamou aleichum, Fat'ma!*"

"*Wa aleichum as salaam Ahmed!*"

"*Chnouw wa hwalk?*"

"*La bess. El hamdou'lah.*"

"*Fat'ma!*"

"Ahmed!" And she looked at his blazer and clucked.

He turned his desk over to a man in a brown blazer who appeared to be his assistant and took Fatima for a walk on the grounds.

"Monsieur Choukroun told you?"

She nodded.

"That I was kidnapped by the Lebanese. I am director of admissions," he said, with real pride leaking through the irony he put on for her.

248

"They saw me at the club. They said I had 'the human touch.'"

"The Lebanese?"

"Big money. A vast hotel group. This is their first center for thalassotherapy."

"Thallaso —?"

"Therapy. The sea cure! How do I look?"

He spun around and stood in front of her, pulling on his bow tie.

"You look like a rich man."

"*Inshallah*, perhaps someday I will be rich. In the group, there are people who go higher and higher."

"Ahmed, God has been good to you!"

"He has helped me to help myself. And you, Fat'ma, I have heard that you came into money. You are a rich lady."

"You heard? This is still such a small island," she said, smiling.

"But for people like you and me there is the big world."

They passed along the palm-lined path and came to the Olympic-size swimming pool. Two old tanned women with hair dyed jet black were wading at the shallow edge, with their breasts hanging out. Ahmed smiled sheepishly at Fatima, as if she might fault him for being part of this.

"I have spent my money, Ahmed. I am not rich at all."

"So you went to Wisconsin."

He gave her a deep look.

"No."

"Knowing you, you have spent all your money on the poor."

She was silent for a moment. "In a manner of speaking," she said.

The grounds of the center smelled heavenly. Their path led past rows of bougainvillea, roses, peonies, and jasmine, into a grove of palms, where an ornate green iron bench that might have come from France stood in front of a fountain. He gestured for her to sit down. The fountain gurgled. Cicadas buzzed somewhere in the palms.

"Fat'ma," he said, "there is something I am ashamed of."

She gave him a questioning look. She was reminded that she'd been everyone's confidante here on the island.

"You didn't ask . . ."

His voice became timid. "About the bicycle. The Hollywood bicycle. Fat'ma —"

He turned his head away. "It has been destroyed."

She didn't say anything. The bicycle. The Club Rêve. Dawn McConnor. All that seemed so distant, even here. But Ahmed looked deeply pained.

"I drove it very quickly. I didn't see this car with the English tourist. He was on the wrong side of the road, but it was my fault for going so fast and looking the other way."

"You were injured?"

"As God wished it, I was hardly scratched when I fell off. But the bicycle. It was totally smashed. I'm very sorry."

"Thank God you were not hurt, Ahmed. You have always had good fortune, and especially now. *Hamdou'lah*."

"*Hamdou'lah*, I have helped make my good fortune, Fat'ma. I work very hard."

"If the bicycle meant a lot to you, I am sorry, Ahmed. But do not feel bad for me about it. I was happy to hear from Monsieur Choukroun that you have a car now."

"Fat'ma, let me do something for you. Please."

"There is nothing I need. Thank you. Some day in Paris I will take driving lessons for a car."

"You definitely must, you must do everything to bring yourself up to date," he said and found his thread again: "Fat'ma. It is the off-season here at the center. We have very few clients at the moment. The people who come for the thalassotherapy are mostly of a class that doesn't want the summer heat. We get many people from the Emirates. But now we have nearly no one."

"I hope for you that that will change," she said.

"Fat'ma, Fat'ma," he blurted, taking her two hands in his. "Listen to me, you have never been pampered in your life."

No, she had not. And it was time, he'd insisted. He made it seem as if she'd make him deeply unhappy, forever guilty, if she refused. She perceived that with all his well-meaning generosity, he wanted very much to show her the power he'd acquired with his new station in life. She didn't mind that, because Ahmed was

251

holding it out as a power to do good. And that was how Fatima found herself in a tub of swirling water at the Vitalia International Thalassotherapy Institute. She had to admit that the bubbles bursting against her flesh made her feel good. The water churned all around her while her body floated in a rocking motion. She felt energized and relaxed at the same time. For a moment the churning water made an odd link in her mind: She saw the water wheel of the Enchanted River of the Jardin d'Acclimatation, and for that brief instant she felt what someone else might have identified as homesick. The churning stopped. The tiny woman in white, who'd left her to undress in the cabin and enter the tub on her own, stepped in without warning and Fatima rushed to cover her nakedness in the still, clear water. The woman turned her face away with a smile.

After the whirlpool saltwater bath came the dynamic shower, with saltwater-like needles from all sides. Next there was a fifteen-minute rest wrapped in towels on a lounge chair. Then the seaweed bath. When Fatima stepped out, she felt all her skin tightening. And then the woman burst into her privacy again.

"Time for me to hose you," she said.

"Like this?" Fatima had grabbed a towel and was holding it in front of her.

"Some people put on a towel, but it doesn't have the same effect."

"I'll keep the towel, I think."

Wrapped in her towel, Fatima stood against the wall of another shower room while the woman projected a harsh stream of salt water at her from a hose you could have used to put out fires. The pressure was so great that the little woman seemed to have to exert all her strength to hold on to the hose. She showed no emotion, though, as she worked it mechanically up and down, aiming at every part of Fatima's body. She was a bony little person, with gray hair. A European, with a clipped accent that betrayed the fact that French was not her native language. The hosing stopped. The woman left Fatima to gather a fresh dry plump towel from a pile on a stool. Next came an intimacy that Fatima could not mitigate. Neither did she have the courage to call it off. So Fatima had her first massage.

This next woman, also dressed like a nurse, was big and manly, a black woman who, by her accent, was a native of the island from the village of Arkou, whose recent ancestors had been slaves. Her people were known for mysterious rites, a talent for making touch with spirits. Here she was, though, at work as part of the Westernized future. Fatima felt positive about that. The woman had come up in the world, like Ahmed.

She had good, strong hands like Mahmoud's that pressed and kneaded. Fatima at first resisted, felt defensive, invaded upon, but the woman's hands had their way, squeezing out aches that Fatima had been unconscious of, buried deep somewhere.

In the afternoon, after Fatima's raw vegetable lunch with carrot juice, a young Tunisian who was actually a medical doctor put her on a bicycle that stood in one place and then a treadmill where she had to run and run. At the end of the day, splashed and sprayed and kneaded again, Fatima lay, deliciously tired and relaxed, wrapped in white towels in the solarium.

And this went on for days. She let it all happen, did whatever they told her, ate their rough salads and their steamed fish and brown rice. The carrot juice did not taste so bad, although she did not think it was worthy of making a wish over. The exercises began to seem easier. She looked forward to the hours spent in the solarium thinking of nothing in particular, feeling only the gentle fatigue, her energy drained in a way that seemed to drain her body of poisons. And after some time, she presented herself without a towel in the hosing room. It made her feel eerily free in a general way.

One morning, the boy in the brown blazer, who delivered her breakfast in bed of applesauce and herbal tea, left a letter on the tray that had been forwarded from Batouine. The handwriting on the envelope was particularly formal and elegant, but inside, on a piece of lined paper, was a note in a child's block letters.

Chère Madame,
Papa took me again to the donkeys. I rode on a donkey's back and I had a second ride on a cart with three other children. It was less expensive. My new tooth has grown in and I hope you are well.
Great Kisses,
Jennifer Suget

254

At the bottom of the letter, in the same hand as the envelope, was another note:

Chère Madame Monsour,

I too hope that you are well and are profiting from your stay. How agreeable it must be for you to encounter your old friends again. Except for your absence, we find Paris much the same. Jenny has asked me when you will return to our city, and since you did not volunteer that information at the time of your departure, I told her that it would be indiscreet of us to inquire too deeply into your affairs, and that it is possible that, had you reached a decision on that matter, you would have indeed informed us. I hope that it is not equally out of place for us to emphasize that, although the splendid weather would please you if you were here, Paris is certainly less agreeable to us than it was in your presence.

Please accept my sincere thoughts and well wishes,

Hippolyte Suget

It was the sort of note that the conventions of French letter-writing as they had survived into the twenty-first century could still allow as more refined than ridiculous.

Words like the handwriting, was what Fatima thought. But pleasure came over her at the simple fact that he'd written. Looking at the rhythm of his handwriting again, she thought she could make out something lyric enclosed in the old-fashioned formality, trying to rush out ahead of it. Her thoughts became a reverie of an afternoon at a café table, and that's where they were when the phone rang beside her bed.

The first thing Fatima heard when she picked up the receiver was the sound of a dog barking. And Fatima knew that bark. There was a loud throat-clearing and then:

"*Emma, tais-toi!*"

All at once Fatima was back in another, familiar place.

"Fatima," the Countess said, "you've given me a lot of trouble finding you."

In point of fact, before she'd left, Fatima had given the Countess the telephone number of the Club Rêve.

"That number was no goddamn good."

Fatima didn't answer.

"Luckily they were able to give me the right number. I spoke to a Monsieur Choucroute."

Fatima held her tongue.

"Listen, my darling, I know the Socialists declared everyone's divine right to five weeks' vacation, but . . ."

Emma began to howl now in the background.

"You hear that? Emma misses you. Emma, we — well, the dog has been worried whether you indeed planned to come home."

"How is Emma, Madame?"

"Well, she's as old as I am on the dogs' calendar, so how do you expect her to be? It's a precarious existence we have. We're hanging on. You can thank Hadj-li for assuming your responsibilities."

256

"Hadj-li?"

"The blue-eyed Turk or whatever. Your friend tells me he's a poet. Omar Khayyám. I give him four euros a day to take Emma out. He acts exceedingly grateful. He said to me, you know what he said? 'A thousand thanks, may Allah bless you, *Madame la Comtesse*, you who can understand the exigencies of *la vie de bohème.*' He kissed my hand."

"Four euros."

"He didn't ask for more. What in the name of Allah are you doing?"

"I . . . I am being pampered, *Madame la Comtesse.*"

"Well, I hope you're taking the proper precautions. Fatima, this is a long-distance call, and the second one I've had to make. I want to be certain, that's all."

"To be certain, Madame?"

"That you're coming home to us. Emma! Say hello to your Fatima."

Fatima could not see the Countess reach from her new wheelchair to pinch the dog gently, but the receiver filled once again with loud barking before the Countess simply hung up. In the doorway of the old woman's salon, the nurse shook her head and rolled her eyes.

The twenty-day cure came to an end. Fatima walked with a sprightly new step, and when she looked into the mirror in the salon of her suite, her skirt seemed like a tent. She went to her last facial and her makeup and hair sessions that afternoon, and then to the boutique of the Institute. She had passed it many times going back and forth for her sessions, seen the clothes changing in the window. Two-piece swimsuits, dresses with deep necklines and short hems . . . All those fashions had been no more than a display for her. Stepping over the threshold of that shop would have been a highly intimidating border crossing, but now, after standing for a moment gazing at a mauve knit suit, she pushed the door open. The bell that warned the salesgirl in the back room of her arrival made it impossible for her to change her mind and sneak away.

The girl could not be more than twenty years old. She was Tunisian, but made up and dressed like a *Parisienne*. Her blouse fell short of her navel, in which there was a rhinestone. Her stretch-cloth pants hugged her hips.

She eyed Fatima's floating skirt. Raised an eyebrow. But, as if she presumed that Fatima was an eccentric guest, she didn't dare to be snobbier than that.

"May I help you?" she said mechanically, keeping her distance, in French.

"The suit in the window," Fatima said.

The girl rustled through a rack of clothes and found a hanger with the suit in what she thought was Fatima's size.

Fatima took it from her hand, and as she looked at it for a long while, she held it gingerly, as if it were alive.

"Why don't you try it on?" The girl gestured magnanimously toward the curtain of the changing booth. "It goes with your eyes."

Fatima felt an innuendo in that about her two-colored eyes. She let it pass, and went into the changing room.

258

She came out and stared at the person in the mirror in the mauve suit with the lipstick and short hair. Somewhere in her mind she was not yet ready to assume that that person was her. Nonetheless, she bought the suit. The girl folded Fatima's skirt and blouse and stuffed them in a plastic bag.

There were three days left over in Fatima's holiday. Fatima was not officially employed by the Countess, but in fairness, the old woman gave her her rights according to the labor laws. Three days now, before she had to start working again. But, as she checked out of the Institute, Fatima had them reserve a seat on the very next day's plane to Paris. She did not want to go back to a farewell tea and pastry session with the ladies of Batouine.

Ahmed was gone. She could not thank him personally. The boy in the brown blazer who carried her bags told her that Ahmed had been sent to Switzerland for a hotel industry seminar.

During the morning she had left, she went to the great outdoor market in Houmt Souk and bought fresh spices, hot harissa, redolent curcuma, and grated rosebuds, as well as two *tajines* — clay roasting pots. One for Hadley and one for the Countess. At a stand selling music, she bought a cassette of Rai by Cheb Mami for Samuel to play in his van. She was also able to fit two bags of sweets into her valise, one for Victorine and the other, if the occasion arose, to give to Hippolyte Suget, along with a little wooden camel for Jennifer.

CHAPTER
TWO

The Paris sky already had an autumn hue, the putty color that would last, but for a few flashes of Indian summer, until the reprieve of April. The way from the airport to the city on the northern autoroute was gray, too. Past cement prefabricated warehouses and pale grass. But Samuel's van was rife with another climate: the odor of spices from plants ripened by a generous sun kept seeping up from Fatima's new blue canvas valises in the rear.

Fatima sat between Samuel and Victorine, who were both already gratefully consuming her gift of semolina cakes, stuffed dates, and rose-flavored almond paste. Samuel asked Fatima if she were happy to be home.

A long time ago she would not have thought that the pale limestone city they were approaching now on the *périphérique* would ever seem endearing to her. But she said, "Yes." To the left, the church of the Sacré-Coeur dominated the hills of Montmartre. Its spires and domes for some reason had been meant to capture an oriental feeling — the taste of the times? — but it was spiritless and clumsy. These are not a sensual people, Fatima told herself. There was none of the subtle languor of the Maghreb here, and yet, was she happy to be "home"? Yes. Her life had acquired a momentum in Paris that outmatched all of what had been home.

Samuel slipped the tape Fatima had given him into his cassette player and turned up the volume. Victorine passed the sweets. The music made it seem to Fatima as if they were not just coming home from the airport but rather off on a festive jaunt. Even the thought that she'd spent almost all her Lotto money and would have to begin saving all over again for Wisconsin did not mar Fatima's gaiety. All that seemed less real than the moment at hand.

His player still blaring "Meli, Meli," Samuel pulled up on the sidewalk, where Monsieur Robert was talking, with a certain affectation of gallantry in the way he stooped, to the Romantic Pharmacist at the wheel of her Porsche with the engine running. Madame Marchand's radio was lowly playing the plaintive love song of an Italian tenor, who had been the background voice for a recent French movie. Monsieur Robert bolted upright when he saw the new Fatima stepping out of the van.

The doors of 34bis opened while Samuel was putting Fatima's bags on the sidewalk. Out came Emma, with a slow, melancholy gait. Was the dog ill again? At that point, the nurse rolled out the Countess. The old woman spied Fatima and grabbed the brake of the wheelchair.

It was hard to tell who was more surprised when they first saw each other again, the Countess at the new

Fatima or Fatima at the sight of the Countess's wheelchair.

"Hold it!" The Countess looked at Fatima and Fatima looked at her, managing a faint smile.

"Get a look at you!" said the Countess. "You've lost weight and you've lost years and you're as alluring as a *louis d'or.*"

Fatima couldn't speak. The old woman looked so much older.

"Well, look at me," the Countess said. "I've had a little bit of a stroke, *c'est tout.* Nothing to put a long face on about." She craned her neck around while her body remained immobile. "You," she said to the nurse in English, "you've been making faces behind my back ever since you turned up. I've been paying for you by the hour, so I should like you to take off this instant. Fatima, *Prenez charge!*"

Emma was all over Fatima, jumping and prancing. The nurse, shocked, gripped the wheelchair. It was Samuel with his gift for diplomacy who broke the deadlock.

"*Permettez-moi, s'il vous plaît, madame,*" he said to the woman and gently wheeled the Countess away from her. The nurse stared at him, at Fatima, and now at the big black woman in her bright boubou with the face of an African president on it, who was stepping out of the van. Her own face pleaded for sympathy as she looked at Monsieur Robert and Madame Marchand, who were now pretending not to notice anyone else.

"Bloody bunch o' nuts!" she shouted in English with an Irish accent. She seemed paralyzed, a pillar of indignation for a moment, then she bolted and ran away.

Fatima brushed Emma off gently and took control of the wheelchair from Samuel. The Countess sat patiently, settled into her own thoughts, while Fatima bid good-bye and thanks to Victorine and Samuel with much kissing of cheeks. Carmen had come out by then and, with her usual self-abuse, began dragging Fatima's baggage inside. Samuel gallantly stopped her. When he came out again from bringing the valises inside and hopped behind the wheel of his van, the Countess suddenly shouted at him:

"Samuel, you've got powdered sugar on your lips!"

"*Merci, Madame la Comtesse!*"

He wiped his mouth on his sleeve with a theatrical gesture, laughed heartily, and in an instant he and Victorine were on their way to the Goutte d'Or, with the voice of Aboubakar Camarra singing "Alo . . . Alo" trailing after them. The Countess looked at the dented old van pulling away and did her best, suddenly, to make the hearty, deep, existential laugh of an African.

Fatima wheeled her toward the Bois de Boulogne. The Countess had told her Irish nurse that they would take the air at the lake and that was still her intention.

From the Café Jean Valjean, Madame Strasbourg had noticed the van pull away as she tuned out her husband's interpretation of the political intrigues behind the EC's ban on certain French cheeses. The Countess and Fatima were passing the café windows now. Just as Monsieur Strasbourg was saying something

263

unfavorable about Dutch dairymen, his wife broke into his monologue:

"She's back!" Madame Strasbourg announced.

Monsieur Strasbourg, offended by the interruption, looked at the woman in the mauve suit wheeling the old lady and said, petulantly, "That's not her." Then he realized that it *was* her.

Now Clément, the closest person to the window, stopped butting the pinball machine with his hip and stared open-mouthed.

Pedro muttered something that Spaniards mutter when a lovely woman goes by.

Everyone was looking out the window, even Raskolnikov, holding his fountain pen in the air. Then all the others turned to stare knowingly at Hippolyte Suget, who was staring at the new Fatima a little forlornly.

Suget's heart leapt to know that Fatima was back. But the change intimidated him. She might be so much a new woman, that slender figure in the stylish suit, that she'd never consent to go to the Vincennes Zoo or anywhere else with the likes of him again.

Soon Fatima and the Countess came into the avenue Foch. Between the cars speeding by, Fatima could make out Angel seated on a bench across the wide avenue. He was surrounded by prostitutes in short, tight skirts, and one of them had his/her arm around his neck. She made a right-angle turn with the wheelchair, hoping the Countess hadn't seen what she saw. Too late, the Countess tried out her African laugh

264

again. After a few minutes of dramatic silence, just as they were crossing toward the Bois, she said:

"Did you get a look at *Señor Corazon?*" She craned her head and winked at Fatima.

Fatima laughed into her hand. So Hadley had been sharing his lexicon of nicknames with the Countess. Since he'd been walking Emma, had they become friendly?

The Countess seemed to enjoy continuing the subject:

"With the gloo-gloo girls?" Her face turned sour. "That old Fascist is the bane of that poor woman's existence."

Later, while they watched a family of ducks glide along the lake, the Countess said, "My husband, bless his soul, never raised a gun toward a bird." Emma was dozing in the sun at the foot of her wheelchair as if she, too, had no taste for bird-hunting.

"But he killed Fascists, you see."

Fatima shook her head to say she understood. But by now her mind had begun to wander. The lake, the ducks on the water with their brood, reminded her that on the other side of the Bois was the Jardin d'Acclimatation with its farm and zoo and the Enchanted River. And that in her bags there was a package of halvah and a little camel to present to Monsieur Suget, if the occasion arose.

The Countess sat in her favorite armchair in the salon, awkwardly holding the floral-painted clay *tajine* with a tall, conical top that Fatima had brought her as a gift.

265

"It is a *tajine*, Madame. Because you love to cook."

"What's it for?"

"To make a *tajine*, Madame."

"It takes a *tajine* to make a *tajine*. I see . . ."

"Puff paste and stuffing and spices —"

"I tell you what." The Countess put the strange object down on the lamp table beside her.

"You show me the first time."

The Countess was reluctant to concede that being in a wheelchair had impeded her cooking, the activity that had been her greatest source of pleasure. In point of fact, it tired her to cook now. The Irish nurse had been preparing her meals according to her own culinary culture — one more reason the old woman had detested her.

"It would give me great pleasure to prepare you a *tajine*," Fatima said.

"A *tajine* in a *tajine*, splendid. I'm game. But not just for me, darling. Let's do a dinner party! We'll invite the American for a *tajine* in a *tajine*. We'll brighten up our life."

"The American?" Fatima feigned surprise.

"Well, he's not a Saudi terrorist after all, you know. You had it all wrong, Fatima."

"A *tajine* of mutton with turnips, Madame?"

"That sounds a little too Irish."

"Lamb, almonds, and prunes."

"That's the ticket! And there'll be spices I've never tasted before, I hope."

"Most certainly, Madame. And *Madame la Comtesse* can make a wish."

266

"Make a wish?"

"Because you've never tasted them before."

"Well, I wish you'll get right to it. And go and warn three-times Hadj or whatever his name is, Joe Smith."

The old woman clapped her hands. "And my nephew will come. He loves strange people. Why else would he put up with me?"

Didi did come, and what was more, he came with someone on his arm. He had rediscovered Jocelyne Fontaine. One morning, feeling his whole world was like an old vinyl record stuck in a groove, he picked up the phone and made a few inquiries among his old colleagues. No doubt they were buzzing about him now, smirking, giggling, whatever. The point was that he'd picked up the phone, and the needle had popped out of the groove. They'd given him her number and he'd called her and he and she had had dinner several times since. She was back from Lille, been divorced, and was doing something responsible on the African desk. Looking a bit older, he couldn't help but notice. But that also meant that a gap had shrunk between them. Her hair was a highlighted pale brown now. He rather liked it that color, even if it wasn't natural. We do what we can to help ourselves on this earth. For the rest, she really didn't need much helping. A lithe, saucy woman, oh yes, sexier maybe than when she'd been a gangling young girl focused on her ambition.

Fatima thought about her while she worked quickly at the kitchen table. She concluded by the way the woman kept Didi's hand in hers when she'd settled between him and Hadley in the salon that something might be happening in Didi's life. The woman gave off a candor that matched her bold perfume, and they'd both pleased Fatima. When she'd passed her the olives with the drinks, she'd casually gathered three at a time in her palm. She was hungry and she didn't mind showing it.

Fatima had buttered the bottom of the *tajine* and began laying down six leaves of the delicate filo pastry she'd made that morning with strong flour and good olive oil. Even in Batouine, there were women who bought their filo dough ready-made at the grocer's. She'd seen it on the shelves of the Espace Bonprix, but Fatima was certain that the Countess could tell the difference.

She dusted her cubes of lamb, her prunes and almonds and pine nuts with spices: grated rose hips, carvi, cardamom, cumin, curcuma, black pepper, ginger, cloves, coriander, and cinnamon. Just the right amount of each — no chemist would have shown keener calibration. The Countess, who had rolled in to watch, clucked, impressed.

Six more leaves of pastry on the top, and the *tajine* was ready to be fired. Fatima would remove the heavy cone to give the top a brown crust when the ingredients were bubbling under the pastry.

When the others had finished their *chakchouka* of sautéed vegetables, Fatima came in holding her big *tajine* aloft. She set it down in front of the Countess, whose first gesture was to point Fatima to a seat, with a look in her eye that both conveyed an order and contained a mischievous twinkle. Didi glanced at Jocelyne to get her reaction to this. Jocelyne gave him back a glance of complicity: They were in this odd dinner together and so far it looked like fun.

No one, though, can say how it might have turned out, what congeniality might have occurred, what enriching reflections and revelations might have been shared with the delicious food by these disparate people whom the Countess, with the flaunting of convention that was, ultimately, the affirmation to herself of her natural superiority, had put around the same table. Because before Fatima could take her seat, while the *tajine* was still bubbling under its crust, she froze at the sight of the Countess's eyebrow, twitching rapidly. The Countess was raising a glass of the Sidi Brahim that was Hadley's contribution to the feast and her hand began to shake, too. The wine spilt. The Countess cast a pleading glance at Fatima, still beside her, as if Fatima could save her, but Fatima could do no more than catch the old woman's head in her hands, before it fell into the plate in front of her.

That evening, a group of hungry American tourists were chattering gaily at a row of tables pushed together in the Café Jean Valjean, when the red fire department first aid truck came speeding into the avenue Victor-Hugo, blinking the blue light on its roof and honking urgently. Three of them ran to the window and saw the firemen in their tight blue uniforms and undersized caps get out a stretcher and an oxygen tank. A single woman among the tourists remarked that the well-built young firemen in their tight suits and little caps were cute.

Madame Richard, who was serving the Americans Nelson's *veau marengo*, stopped short and stared out the window when the firemen came back out of the building next door. An old woman lay covered by a blanket on the stretcher. A tall, distinguished-looking man got into the truck right after the stretcher, accompanied by Fatima the maid. The doors closed, the truck sped away honking and flashing. After a moment, an emerald-colored Jaguar hurried after it, with a pretty, young woman at the wheel and Hadley, the American next door, beside her. In the backseat, the dog that Fatima walked was barking in a frightened way. Carmen, the concierge, was on the sidewalk, wringing her hands and pulling on the cross around her neck. Madame Richard would have something to tell the morning regulars next day. Hippolyte Suget, she knew, would be particularly concerned.

Whether or not the old woman was alive by the time she reached the resuscitation ward of the Salpétrière Hospital at the other end of town was the unresolved topic of conversation that morning among the Jean Valjean regulars. Monsieur Strasbourg pointed out that, for political reasons, the Socialists had seen to it when they were in power that the state-of-the-art emergency hospital room of the city was located far from the wealthy quarters, which included the avenue Victor-Hugo. Indirectly, added Monsieur Strasbourg, the Socialists had been responsible for the death of

270

Princess Diana. Had the emergency room been closer to the Place de l'Alma, where she had the accident, she might be alive and carefree today. The mention of the glamorous princess set Ginette daydreaming, while Raskolnikov gave a cynical snort into his coffee and a giggle that brought Monsieur Richard close to asking him to pay and leave. Raskolnikov had lately begun to show signs of interest in the rest of life at the Jean Valjean, and Monsieur Richard wasn't sure that he welcomed that from so strange a person.

At that very moment, Hippolyte Suget spied Fatima and Hadley coming down the avenue Victor-Hugo with Emma, her tail drooping, snuggling Fatima's skirt. Fatima looked stricken. Suget gulped down his wine and stepped outside, but when he came up to them, he didn't know what to say. The calamity had happened so fast that they hadn't even had a chance to speak to each other since she'd come back to Paris. *To be together.* And now her grief had sidetracked them in where they'd gotten toward each other.

"Ginette told me of your misfortune," he finally managed. Fatima let out a long sigh as she heard that word once again in her life. Hadley looked at the two of them and sensed it would be a good idea if he took off. He squeezed Fatima's hand and murmured a word of parting.

"I can take Emma home," he added, "she's used to me now."

But Emma would not leave Fatima's side.

Suget cleared his throat. "If I may, I'll walk with you," he told her.

Hadley turned back to see the three of them heading toward the Bois de Boulogne. An odd thought leapt into his head: They had the air of a family.

"You must be extremely tired," Suget told Fatima.

"I have been sitting in a hospital hallway all night."

"Have you eaten?" he asked.

"Hadley and I had breakfast in a café near the hospital. He came to be with me."

"You and he —" Suget's heart sank for a moment. "Are very close?"

"Hadley is my good friend." Why did she feel moved to add: "Hadley is 'gay'"?

Suget cleared his throat again. "He is very lucky," he blurted.

Fatima looked at him curiously.

"To be your friend, I mean."

Her eyes softened as she began to understand his drift.

"I mean, to be your friend. He is privileged."

"Monsieur Suget?" She was helping him without even thinking about it: "I consider you my good friend as well."

"Well then, I'm lucky too!" With that his pluck was rising. He ventured: "Tomorrow you'll be hungry again." He realized that sounded totally absurd the moment he'd said it. He covered it with what he really meant. Here it came!

"I don't know what I can do for you, but I would like at least to give you dinner tomorrow."

Fatima could not suppress a contented smile.

272

"I have a week off from the Villa. It's my vacation. I have all the time in the world to make something nice."

"You mean you would make dinner?"

He blushed and nodded.

She lowered her eyes. "She needs me now, but if in the evening I'm free."

She held out her hand, and the two of them shook hands, while Emma, with the sense of discretion that perhaps an exceptional dog such as she might have, felt moved to slip behind a bush.

The building Hippolyte Suget lived in on the rue Viala in the clean-poor Fifteenth Arrondissement was very different from those on the avenue Victor-Hugo. It was a narrow six-story edifice whose unornamented façade was made of what is known as "*pierre de Paris*," which is actually just plaster. A small door led to a stairway that went to the quarters above the storefront restaurant that occupied the ground floor. Fatima noticed that it was an Indian restaurant called La Rose de Bombay.

The building was what is known as an "*immeuble de rapport*," built for the owner to make money on modest tenants. Hippolyte's floor, the sixth, was the most modest of all, and his room, too small even to be considered a studio, was what real estate agents call a "*studette*." Its door was wide open when Fatima finished climbing to the sixth floor. On her way, she had smelled the rich spiciness seeping up from the Rose de Bombay dissolve, floor by floor, into an increasingly heavy smell of burnt oil. As she walked into Suget's *studette*, the odor hit her in the face. There was smoke in the air. Suget's parrot paced his cage in a foul mood. Suget, whose eyes were red, might have been coughing, and now the bird was spitefully imitating a cough over and over. The minute Fatima crossed the threshold, Cacahouète dropped the fake cough and shrieked, "*Petit con! Hippolyte!*" Suget stood there, speechless, wishing he were dead.

"*Bonsoir, Monsieur*," she said, cheerfully, as if she'd noticed nothing but him. He looked at her in her new print dress, whose colors suited both colors of her eyes. At her eyes that shone now and at her svelte new figure, her short hair. His eyes fluttered.

Suget noticed the smell of her perfume in combat now with the reek of the burnt oil, and in his mind it oddly became the emanation of good taking on evil. Cacahouète looked at Fatima and raised his head, and it was as if this spoiled bird, who might have been an incarnation of old envies and jealousies, were about to utter something disobliging about her, too. Suget suddenly had the presence of mind to throw a dish towel over his cage.

"Excuse me, I ruined something. But don't worry."

Suget even forgot to say "*Bonsoir*." He had been in a panic. He'd bought some excellent milk-fed free-range veal from the *luxe* butcher in the rue Desaix and had attempted a Wiener schnitzel. He'd wanted to make a subtle suggestion, with the menu, of his worldliness. When the breaded meat was in the pan, he panicked to notice that he'd forgotten to shine his shoes. He'd gone into his little bathroom to shine them, and meanwhile the Wiener schnitzel had burnt to a crisp. All the more panicked, he'd managed to race out to the Picard frozen food store on the boulevard de Grenelle. He grabbed the first thing that came to hand, frozen lasagna. It was in his refrigerator now, and he wondered what suavity he could muster to produce it, put it in his little microwave and make it go over gallantly.

Fatima looked at the door, wondering whether the right thing would be for her to close it. She didn't fear anything unseemly on the part of Suget, alone with him in this little room with a narrow bunk bed, but she didn't want to seem forward, either. A bunk bed. She noticed the poster of the little girl and the bowl "Jennifer."

"You may leave it open to make yourself feel more comfortable," he said, realizing that his words expressed no charm at all. He blushed.

"There's a little smoke," she said, soothingly.

Suget whipped out a bottle labeled "*Ambassadeur*" from his mini-refrigerator. He had a bowl of ice inside, already prepared, and a bottle of Perrier. He made a little nervous laugh when the Perrier fizzed as he opened it. She watched him pour and remembered that when she was learning to read she kept trying herself out over and over on that long word "*Ambassadeur*" when she saw it on a billboard near the Goutte d'Or. There was a big picture of a lovely woman and a handsome man in evening clothes drinking "*Ambassadeur*." She sat down on a bridge chair beside the bunk bed and sipped. It was too sweet, but Suget's eyes were on her and so she smiled appreciatively.

"It's a little like red Martini vermouth," Suget said with the air of a connoisseur. "A notch above." She nodded in agreement. Suget opened a package of peanuts. Their smell immediately reached the parrot, whose name was not the French word for peanut for no reason, and he began to croak pleadingly for his favorite food under the dishcloth. Suget turned his back on the cage as he offered the nuts to Fatima.

"Monsieur Suget," she said, "perhaps you are being cruel."

He whipped the dishcloth off the cage and threw a few nuts at the bird. "We've got company!" he said, "Behave."

"*Ou quoi?*" the parrot seemed to croak from behind the cloth. "Or what?"

Hippolyte felt that his heart might not survive this evening.

By now Fatima had sat down at the table he'd carefully set and was feeling the handle of her bright fork appreciatively.

"The silver," Hippolyte said, "has been in my family for generations."

"It's very beautiful."

"It's all that's left." He shrugged.

He set out the avocado with packaged shrimps that had also been waiting in the fridge and sat down opposite her. Her appreciation of the silver had a surprisingly strong, good effect on him. Somewhere in his brain her presence now and his memories of his comfortable childhood touched base in no logical way,

276

but the result was reassurance. He was prompted to say, without sounding at all glum:

"It's something that I can leave my daughter. One thing, anyway."

"Monsieur Suget, you're far too young to be thinking of something like that."

"Do you think so?" Over her head, he caught his face in the mirror and in his mind he asked it if he were young.

"I mean, I didn't mean you should not think of your daughter."

"I think of her all the time. She has no mother, you know. I mean, she has a mother, but no one knows where she is."

Fatima kept silent.

"And she has me for a father, poor girl. Luckily her mother has a mother."

What should she say? One thing she could not do was ask.

They ate in silence for a while, and when he cleared their plates away, he slipped the frozen lasagna out of the mini-refrigerator almost furtively. He felt ashamed over the ruined veal, the smoke, the smell. But he had to go on.

Cacahouète began to whistle. Fatima laughed to hear him. Suget tried a laugh. The microwave pinged. He rushed out the lasagna and held his breath as he put it before her.

"Ahh!" she said. "Italian!"

"You know it?"

"The Countess made some once."

"I fear that mine will be nothing like hers."

Fatima, with the faculty of perceptiveness she could never turn off even if she wanted to, had been following all the acrobatics of Suget's nervous mood. She knew what was going on. Beyond being flattered, she was moved by his fear of not pleasing. Not pleasing her. Somewhere in her own mind, the depth of her perception of his timidity had become a form of intimacy in itself. Beyond empathy. Certainly not pity.

Now it was as if it were he who had read her mind: "Madame Monsour, may I say that I am very fond of . . . of my friendship with you."

He reached for the dresser near the table and found an envelope.

"Take this home with you, please," he said.

For some reason, perhaps because she was nervous, the envelope slipped through her hand and fell onto the table. He lunged for it to hand it to her again, a gesture that said how much he wanted her to have it. She reached for it as well, and that was when their hands touched. And then her hand seemed to think for her! And overrule any censorship by her mind. She let her hand lie on his a moment.

Suget's hand trembled. But then something within him rose to the power of the moment and told him to forget who he thought he was, because at any moment, because of the nature of time, everything can be new. He put his other hand on top of hers and held her there, so that she could not pull away and erase that moment.

278

She was not moved to do so. Instead, gently but surely, she squeezed the hand she was covering, in a gesture she felt now was protective.

Cacahouète, in his covered cage, could see nothing, but he might have felt strong vibrations, for he began to whistle pleasantly while Fatima looked into Suget's eyes over the light of the candle he'd set between them.

That moment seemed to her just like the one in the picture on the billboard near the Goutte d'Or.

A neighbor on the landing, Madame Lefranc, a widow of sixty who taught mathematics at the Lycée Louis le Grand, passed the open door and saw the couple holding hands in the candlelight. "*Bonsoir*," she said, as she always did when she passed Suget. Which would have been more polite? — to say good evening or pretend not to have seen them? Her sense of tact came down on the side of "*bonsoir*." She felt cheated when Suget, whose eyes were fixed on the woman in front of him, didn't even give her back her good evening.

By the time Fatima was helping Suget clean up, to anyone passing that door again the two would have had the air of complicity of an established couple.

At the end of the evening it was Fatima who'd lost her cool presence of mind. As she panicked over something so small as finding the right words to say thank you and good night, she was faintly conscious of a feeling like that of the loss of virginity.

As the elevated line 6 of the *métro* bore Fatima home, it was to her as if she were traveling weightlessly through the air. The irregular facades of the Fifteenth

Arrondissement sped behind her, then the Seine lay below, with barges passing in the darkness. To her right, the illuminated Eiffel Tower was a golden skeleton. This was her world, she told herself. Now she felt rooted here, but rooted was an inaccurate term for someone who felt so light just then. A moment of the dinner came back to her. The moment. When she'd left behind what were really centuries of history, and, as if she'd plunged into dark water, she, Fatima Monsour of Batouine, Djerba, Tunisia, had reached across a table and held a man's hand.

What did she see in him? It wasn't what she saw, which was what everyone saw, a slight person with bushy hair who spoke with great awkwardness but moved with a surprising grace, as if Hippolyte Suget, though he was a night clerk in a demi-bordel, still unconsciously remembered himself as a dancer. It was what she perceived. And no one could perceive better than Fatima. Because he was now poor, because life had humbled him, his awkward but certain delicacy seemed all the more genuine, unaffected. She perceived a good person, an intelligent person, too sensitive maybe ever to have become completely adult, a vulnerable man who was all the same not lacking in will — in his endearing way, he'd made his move. A good man whom life had dealt a bad card or two.

She remembered the envelope in her purse. And when she opened it now she saw a child's drawing of a donkey, and beside it a man, a woman and a child.

Fatima got off at the Boissière station, where once not so long ago she'd arrived, green from Djerba, in the

280

fortunate company of Victorine. Not so long ago, but in another era of her life. She paused on the platform to watch the train recede toward the Etoile, as if the movement of the train were an enactment intended for her. Watching its red tail-lights disappear in the tunnel, she was aware of her life as a journey. And at that moment the thought that it would take her to Wisconsin did not even enter her mind. She caught an image of her slim self in the mirror of a Coke machine. She liked it. If she were a different person with the same emotion at that moment, she might have blown a kiss to the mirror.

At that point, though, the Countess entered her mind, and the face in the mirror turned bleak.

CHAPTER
THREE

It was Samuel who accompanied Fatima to the American Hospital in Neuilly, where the Countess had been transferred from La Salpêtrière. Since their trip together to Branchevieille, Samuel believed that the Countess was his friend, and she might well have said the same thing about him, but the Countess was not able now to say anything.

Samuel whistled in awe as he parked his van among the Mercedes and BMWs in the lot of the hospital, which stood on a little hill in the green, expensive residential suburb.

He hurried inside with Fatima. The American Hospital had the reputation of being the solemn place rich Parisians came to die, but both of them felt cheered to see that the old woman had a room as pleasant as a good hotel room.

When Samuel came back from the nurses' station with a vase for the late roses he'd cut from his garden in the Goutte d'Or, Fatima was seated beside the bed where the Countess lay immobile. Fatima was reading a text she had read to the Countess before. He heard:

"All the waters enveloped the globe; they withdrew into caverns; then the continents separated themselves, animals and men appeared."

Bouvard et Pécuchet. Her favorite book. Samuel heard echoes of Branchevieille and his eyes went moist. The Countess's eyes, meanwhile, went back and forth from Samuel to the flowers. Fatima thought she could see pleasure in them.

"The majesty of creation," she read, "created an astonishment within them as infinite as creation itself. Their heads swelled. They were proud to reflect on such great matters."

The door opened without a knock. A woman of fifty came in. Her hair was orange. She had squeezed her body, which was neither fat nor thin but simply flabby, into a pair of black leather pants, which she wore over stiletto boots.

"Well, let me guess," was the first thing she said, addressing herself to the black man in the room. "You're the van out there."

She said "*tu*" for you, using the familiar form the way many white Parisians still do when they talk to a black person. Samuel let it go by.

"And you're the famous genius maid," she said to Fatima, keeping the familiar form.

Fatima didn't answer, but turned instead to look at the Countess, whose eyes glared now. The old Countess tried to mumble something but couldn't form a word.

The woman came up to where the Countess lay and stared at her face. She waved her hand in front of the Countess's eyes and made her blink. Fatima saw that her hand was yellowed with nicotine stains. The Countess tried to say something again. A few short sounds that were all the same able to express something: anger.

It didn't take long for Fatima to realize that the child from hell had just walked in.

If she had grown up in Paris or New York, Fatima might have aired all the possible speculations that would have come into her head about why this grown woman, Séverine Poulais du Roc, seemed to show not a grain of compassion for her mother, who had suffered a serious stroke. She might have thought about "issues" while Séverine was growing up, about how the Countess might have wronged the growing girl. But in the world that had formed Fatima during her own poor childhood, the personal "issues" were framed in conventions so binding that they obliterated all resentment and gave an objective, solid matrix to relations between a mother and a child. A mother, by unquestionable convention, owed her child, the gift from God, total care as convention defined care. The child owed total respect. Looked at from that perspective, "Rockababy" — Hadley's nickname came back to Fatima — was nothing other than a calamity as grave as a baby born deformed. The angry child from hell.

Rockababy lost no time.

"Leave me alone with her," she ordered.

Fatima stood her ground for an instant. It seemed to her that it was just possible that Rockababy would put a pillow on her mother's face the moment she and Samuel left them alone. But Samuel's hand was on her shoulder. It was *her* mother. Even if Fatima made a scene, the nurses would ask them to leave. No one can say what Rockababy wanted to communicate to her mother while they were alone, for Fatima and Samuel had barely stepped into the hallway when the woman rushed out, hysterically crying "Nurse!" She stopped running and began to wheeze, struggling to catch her breath. Fatima was suddenly aware that Séverine was not in good health — that she had abused her health.

"She doesn't need a maid anymore," she managed to say to Fatima, who noticed that there was at last a tear in the woman's eye.

CHAPTER
FOUR

Fatima packed her things quickly, while Hadley looked on from the doorway feeling more forlorn even than she did. They'd become something like roommates.

"You do have somewhere to go," he said.

"Someplace very nice, don't you worry. I'll still be in the neighborhood, Hadley."

"What will you *do*?"

She shrugged.

"How was the reception?" he asked.

"You should have been there. She often mentioned you. The 'blond Sheik.'" Fatima chuckled.

"*You* should have been at Père-Lachaise."

"*M'alesh.*" It doesn't matter. "I was with her in my heart."

Fatima had indeed not been invited to see the Countess laid to rest beside Geoffroy Poulais du Roc, in his crypt at the Père-Lachaise Cemetery, even though Séverine had put a notice in the *Figaro* inviting all those who'd known her mother to attend. Séverine had ordered her to stay home and prepare the reception that came afterward. So Fatima had served the old woman one last time, passing little sandwiches and drinks, with Victorine having volunteered to help her.

286

The Countess's peer group was large; there were even young people among them, although Fatima could remember the visit of very few friends. After they were all gone, while Fatima and Victorine were washing the glasses in the kitchen, Séverine had come in and fired Fatima.

At that moment, Fatima had felt no reaction. She was thinking about Didi, who had gotten quite drunk and had thrown up in the WC and then pathetically insisted, as the two of them whispered together in the hallway, that he would clean up the splashes himself. Of course she didn't let him. Poor Didi, she was thinking, all his diplomatic aplomb had abandoned him as he'd surrendered to grief. He took it harder than anyone. Fatima was thinking that, thanks to God, he had that young woman to go home with on his arm. She was thinking all this when Séverine came in and just said:

"Fatima, when you're finished in here you can go and pack. When you come down we'll settle what's owed you."

Victorine huffed.

Finally, Fatima had dried her hands and went into the living room where Séverine was already wrapping objects. She nearly dropped a Meissen shepherdess when Fatima stood in front of her and said:

"Listen to me."

"What?"

"There is something I want."

"You'll get everything due you."

"Not so much for myself." Fatima could not bring herself to call this woman "Madame." Her tone seemed to intimidate Rockababy.

"Tell me what it is," she said, backing down cautiously. "I'll do what I can. Is there some little object she meant for you?"

"Emma."

"Who?" Séverine didn't seem to even know the name of her mother's dog.

"Emma, the Labrador."

"Good God, the dog! I forgot. We'll have to put down the dog! Well, it's old enough, God knows."

"With God's help, I should like to look after her."

Rockababy's nervousness exploded into a shrill laugh.

"Well, of course, by all means! By all means!"

That was why Emma, in Fatima's personal quarters on the sixth floor for the first and last time, was now sniffing under the sink while Fatima packed her clothes with Hadley looking on, wistful.

Victorine leaned against her dresser, looked at Fatima and chuckled. Her eyes went up and down Fatima's new figure.

"Well, you're the lithe one," she laughed, "you'll take the top."

Fatima climbed the ladder of the double-decker Ikea bed Samuel had assembled. She stretched out on the top mattress and bounced. It felt good to behave like a child.

Emma was already installed on a soft chair.

288

"A château!" Fatima exclaimed.

Victorine covered her mouth and laughed into her hand.

For a maid's quarters, Victorine's room was indeed the equivalent of a château. Odile Benamou-Kahn, the celebrated lawyer who was Victorine's *madame*, was a leading member of more than one NGO in favor of human rights and brotherhood, and was president emeritus of the Muslim-Israelite Friendship Society. Victorine had been Maître Benamou-Kahn's *bonne à tout faire* for years, indispensable for cleaning up after her in many senses of the term. Combing hair, pressing jackets, answering the phone, knowing whose calls to take and whose not, polishing the floor, keeping an agenda, filling out tax forms to be signed, shopping, doing the household accounts, all this was Victorine's province, and Victorine had seen her conditions improve constantly over the years. Maître Benamou-Kahn had bought the maid's room adjoining hers and broken through a wall, so that Victorine now lived in a moderate-size studio, with its own shower and toilet, as well as what is known as an "American kitchen" — a wall lined with appliances, including a dishwasher. Madame Benamou-Kahn had given Victorine a G3 Macintosh when she'd bought herself a G4, and now with a cable installation, Victorine was regularly communicating with her children by e-mail through the headman of her village in Senegal. All in all, with the bunk bed, Victorine's quarters were enough for two.

Fatima climbed down and took Victorine's hands in hers.

"As soon as I have a new job, I'll be paying you. I promise."

"Good God! I live here free!" Victorine said. "*Ma soeur*, do you think I'm going to make money on you? Do you take me for a capitalist?" And she burst out laughing again.

Emma, who had not heard that kind of rich laughter since her last trip to Branchevieille with her friend Samuel, jumped off her chair as if she were frightened, which made Victorine grab the dog in her arms and kiss her on her wet nose.

Across from the Tuileries gardens, the line of people waiting for tables at the Angelina Tea Room overflowed into the arcade of the rue de Rivoli. Hippolyte Suget hadn't expected to see all those tourists there. He'd ordered an *orange pressée* immediately to be sure to keep his table, and he felt doubly good now that he had come early and gotten a place to sit near the window. This would be his last Sunday off for he didn't know how long. Monsieur Cartier, the owner of the Villa Saint Valentin, had told him that he'd have to work weekends from now on. He was going to have Tuesday and Wednesday off instead.

"Wednesday there's no school," Monsieur Cartier had said cheerfully. "You can be with your daughter." Of course, but there was no school on Sunday, either.

Monsieur Cartier — a sweet-talking old man whose sincerity seemed compromised by his dyed yellow hair — had told Suget that the change in schedule was a tribute to Suget's competence. Weekends brought couples less furtive, less pressed for time, more bent on a thorough good time and more exigent with the staff. Often businessmen, in town with a weekend between appointments, came with women they'd picked up in bars and whom they were anxious to impress with their importance. "Suget," Cartier had said, giving off a smell of mint from his gum, "you know how to make the good times happen." Truth to tell, Suget simply answered the phone promptly and got the champagne out quickly. The old man might have just been flattering him into accepting the weekend work. Suget felt he had no choice. He needed the job. He wondered what Cartier did to "let the good times happen" for himself on weekends. He was on his third wife, who had yet to set foot in the Villa Saint Valentin, although Agnieszka, the night maid, had reason to believe he'd met her in a bar. Agnieszka, an expert in her way on the perplexities of Eastern Europe, had sussed out that the new Madame Cartier was a Ukrainian teenager claiming to be Croatian. All this Suget put into the back of his mind. The point was he was here to seize the day, the day off. To be with her.

"I'm expecting someone," Hippolyte said, when the waitress took away his empty juice glass.

Hippolyte had set out by *métro* from across the river a good hour before the time of the appointment. He feared that either of two things would have caused him to miss the meeting. The *métro*, these days, was regularly plagued by what would be announced as "a technical incident" or a "social movement." A technical incident meant that either a piece of machinery had broken down or some tortured soul had jumped on the tracks. Suget thought it peculiar that the term covered both events, although they were very different. People's hopeless desperation reduced to "a technical incident" — the thought made Suget somewhat angry. As for the social movement, it was a strike that they meant to announce through the loudspeakers, a strike of people unhappy with their lot. The world was not such a sunny planet, Suget concluded, but it was on his own place on it that he focused now, and he had reason to be happy. Some time soon, the woman would walk through the door and spy him sitting there, waiting for her. In his mind, he saw her smile. And just then, Fatima came in, threaded her way through the tourists, and looked around anxiously. She seemed as worried that he would not be there as he had been that he might come too late. She saw him. She smiled.

He recommended the hot chocolate.

"The best in Paris," he said, with his air of a man of the world. "Thick and rich."

So it was. Fatima scooped the whipped cream that came with it and was about to put it into her cup when she remembered all the weight she had lost. She put the whipped cream back into the dish as casually as she could.

"You're comfortably settled, I trust," he said, making it sound like a line by a sophisticated person in a thirties movie that concerned the rich.

"I'm not settled at all, Monsieur. Oh, Victorine is very hospitable. But . . . I must earn my living."

"I am sure your qualifications are impeccable," Hippolyte went on, in that formal voice again. He realized he was taking a kind of refuge in the pose, and that he should have the courage to be more natural.

"I don't have any papers," she blurted.

"The Countess —?"

"She sent for me, she paid me well —"

"You said she was fond of you and you were —"

"I was fond of her. The papers just didn't matter to her. She couldn't get her mind into my life and know how important they were to me. You'd have to say she was very wound up in herself. She was fond of me, she was fond of my sister. She loved Emma."

"She knew everyone she had to know to get you your papers."

"For a computer scientist, it is easy to get papers. The law doesn't favor maids. The Countess would not have wanted to ask a favor of the people she had to ask. She was proud. If you like, you could say she was —"

"Arrogant," Suget said.

Fatima sighed. "She was good. But we should not expect more good of a person than of a fish," she said.

"A fish?"

"Do you ever buy fish, Monsieur Suget?"

Suget blushed. He admitted that he often bought frozen fish sticks that he prepared in his microwave.

"When you buy a real fish," she said, "you have to judge. When you get home and cook your fish and you start to filet it, you must not be disappointed that you'll not be left with the big fish you bought. There are all the little bones on top, and the bones on the bottom,

293

and the bone that runs through the middle. The good part is not nearly as big as the fish you bought, with all the rest, with all those bones. And even in the good part, the filet, you can find bones.

"People are like that," she went on. "There's all the rest. But I think there's always a good part. People are as good as they can be."

Suget winced and couldn't keep himself from squirming in his seat for an instant. Truth to tell, it was not the pain of her revelation about human nature but pressure in his bladder that caused his look. She recognized it, being her perceptive self, for what it was.

"So I have to go back to Djerba. I am an illegal immigrant, Monsieur Suget. You are drinking hot chocolate with a criminal." She smiled.

Hippolyte shifted in his seat.

"Meanwhile," she said, daring to tease him, with another smile, "if you want to go upstairs for a minute, I'll still be here when you get back. God willing."

Suget looked at himself in the men's room mirror as he washed his hands. "People are as good as they can be," he heard again in his mind. He heard another echo: "*Petit con!*" All his life unreeled in his mind. Was there hope for him to be better in some way than he'd been? He was a man so full of disappointment and shame, with so little faith in himself that every move he made that drew him closer to the rest of the human race required him to screw up his courage like a beggar trying to crash a cocktail party. And yet, he could do it. He would show her how good he could be. Or what? Or jump in front of the *métro* car? "*Petit con!*" he heard

294

again. Or go home and strangle his judgmental parrot and live minute by minute, one foot in front of the other, a totally banal, calm life. He hit the hand dryer and the roar it gave off seemed an admonition. Do what you have to do, he told himself. He walked back down an elegant staircase in the Belle Epoque tearoom, giving his way of walking a certain sophisticated *démarche* — something a born dancer knew how to do — as she watched him come down. He now said what he had to say, but because he was still too timid even to admit the real meaning of his own thoughts, he did not say it right:

"I have the answer," he said, as he sat down across from her.

She looked at him curiously.

He screwed up his courage as hard as he could, but all he could say was:

"*Un mariage . . . blanc.*"

"What?"

His temples were pounding, his face was red. He managed:

"A formality. If you were to marry a Frenchman, you would become French."

Her two-colored eyes swam before him.

"I would be very pleased," he said, "to do that. For you . . ."

His eyes went wet as a sense of disaster came over him, but he kept on blurting:

"It would just be a formality. I read that people do it all the time. It could just be on paper —"

She had stood up by then.

Before he could say anything more, she reached in her bag and drew out a package of halvah and a little wooden camel.

"Monsieur Suget, I forgot to give you these the other evening."

She was out the door. And he realized that for all his bravura in the mirror and his Cary Grant *démarche* on the stairway, he'd missed the chance to dare let his true self speak for him.

As the autumn sunlight began to recede over the Tuileries gardens, it was painting an insistent note of cheer on the golden chariot atop the little Arc de Triomphe of the Carousel. The day was disappearing, but Paris would still be Paris tomorrow. There was the lively sound of excited children running among the boxwood-lined lanes. The gardens were beautiful, in any case, in any light. As Fatima walked aimlessly, she realized once again how much she had come to love Paris, but the sinking day matched a sinking feeling in her heart.

The point was, she told herself, she knew what he meant and that what he meant he had not said because he couldn't say it. She knew his shyness. How could it all have played itself out differently? Say that she hadn't told him to go up to the toilet, so that he didn't have the moment, alone, to try to screw up his courage and fail at it. They would have drunk their chocolate and looked at each other. Maybe she would have even taken a bit of whipped cream, in a sociable way. They would have prolonged an instance of pleasantness together.

296

She could have told him how lovely his new silk tie with little rabbits on it looked with his dark blue shirt. They might have — well, she'd seen him, with his red face and his stammer, heading for a wall, and she'd let him go on.

She couldn't remember ever having gotten so angry in her life. And, oddly enough, she perceived that it was he who had given her that capacity, and oddly enough as well, she saw it as something that enriched her being, ultimately a gift. Or rather a right to which she'd long been entitled.

In any case, she'd been hit in the face with ugly words. *Un mariage blanc.* It was as if, at that instant, hearing that, she'd felt something being taken back and had relapsed into believing that that was all she was worth. So she ran. She realized again that for her to react this way, without the sage serenity with which people had always credited her, was definitely new. New and unsettling. Hippolyte Suget had unsettled her, thrown her off balance, and it was not because of him — that would be unfair to say — but because of knowing him that her stomach was churning now. A black Labrador that had been chasing a ball a boy was throwing spat the ball out and ran up to her and sniffed at her leg. The dog smelled Emma. The snuggling of the dog made her feel better suddenly, and she was reminded that Emma needed to be taken out for her late-afternoon walk. Do what you have to do and don't think about anything else, Fatima advised herself. What she definitely had to do was to go home soon, to Djerba, and she hoped that without her papers she could somehow manage some odd work, to get enough money together for an air ticket.

Suget climbed the stairs toward his *studette* as if his feet were weighted with irons. His tie hung from the pocket of the raincoat that hung from his hand and grazed the steps. He had thought that this existence would do. He had thought that after prison, a clean little life was all he needed. And once in a while to be with the daughter for whom he had no daily responsibility. And that hoping for anything else would be too treacherous. And look now at how, in trying to step out of that life in one way, he'd screwed it up entirely. A memory came back to him as a metaphor for his state: He was in a room thrown into hideous disorder, chairs broken, drawers thrown open, where one of his fellow burglars had flipped out. He felt exhausted, as if he'd physically done something like that.

Cacahouète looked at him in strange silence when he walked in.

"Don't say it!" Suget shouted at the bird. "Or I'll filet you like a fish."

Cacahouète kept mum and turned his back and let go a bit of bird-do. Suget took it as an insult and threw his raincoat over the cage. Perhaps, to be fair, the bird had merely shown that it was terrified, and perhaps, on the other hand, if someone who knew bird expressions were looking at Cacahouète full in the face from the other side of the cage, he would have seen a look of sympathy. This from Cacahouète for the first time.

Perhaps, with a glance at the face that came through the door, Cacahouète had at last perceived the gravity of his human companion's situation in life. Animals perceive our emotions more than we think they do, even if in their own lives they don't go through all the bizarre twists and turns that cause them.

And then, because the power of human souls to decide is as much with us as the need to breathe — and this, above all, makes us different from animals — a voice from wherever souls are installed told Hippolyte Suget: "If this is all you have to lose, let it go. Try something else. Try and try again."

"Victorine!" Madame Benamou-Kahn called from her bedroom, all in a tither over static electricity, "Come comb my hair!"

"In a moment, Odile."

Victorine was ironing a Christian Lacroix print jacket in the dressing room next door. Victorine did not call her mistress Madame. She called the great lawyer Odile. In this little setup, it was as if they were bound together by blood. As if, although Odile was ten years older than Victorine, Victorine were the proud mother of this woman who was one of the most brilliant — although in all else harebrained — courtroom figures in Paris.

How different this household seemed to Fatima, who was now in the butler's pantry polishing Odile Benamou-Kahn's Puiforcat silver, realizing and appreciating the fact that the woman had actually given her makework. The silverware lay already bright in its new chest, all of it newer than the pieces she'd cared for when she was with the Countess. Another household with another feeling to it, but people, Fatima believed, were never that much different. It was all about tugs at the heart. About wanting and longing, most of all. Odile was getting ready to have dinner with a widower she'd met on a music cruise named Alfred Weill.

Odile Benamou-Kahn's heart had gone out a little to Fatima, and Fatima was grateful for that measure of kindness. She was giving her "hours," paid in cash. Fatima glanced through the butler's pantry toward the living room, where Emma lay faintly snoring on a *design* chair in red plastic. It seemed comfortable enough for her, and Emma had shown no indication that she preferred chairs signed by Jacob, who worked for Louis Seize, to those that bore a new label under their seats that said Szekely. Odile Benamou-Kahn was being indulgent to Emma as well as to Fatima, and it eased Fatima's heart to know that when she would have to leave for Djerba, Emma would have a comfortable home. There was no question of bringing that poor old dog over locked in a box in some cold, noisy freight compartment of a plane. She would not survive that. Fatima blessed that harebrained courtroom performer, who was talking loudly to Victorine now about her next week's agenda. Just as earlier, still in her loud courtroom voice, she'd confided in her about the apparent virtues of Monsieur Weill.

Would Odile Benamou-Kahn and Alfred Weill's hearts beat, eventually, in harmony? Fatima would not be around the household long enough to know, because just then the telephone rang.

"It's for you?" Victorine said, handing Fatima the phone, in a hurry to go back and finish Odile's hair, which she'd indeed managed, nearly, to tame.

It was Carmen on the phone.

When Hippolyte Suget arrived at the mews in the suburb of Montreuil, where his daughter lived with her grandmother, Marthe Carton, there was a sign posted on the gate. It read PERMIS DE DÉMOLIR. Permission to demolish. So there it was, official, what Marthe had told him was imminent.

Permission to demolish had been granted all over Montreuil. High-rise housing already overshadowed the Cité Voltaire, the mews where Marthe had brought her own daughter up, at the time not long ago when Montreuil was a village of little brick houses, three-story apartment buildings and the single-floor workshops of all sorts of artisans. Now half the neighborhood was a building site.

"When must you leave?" Suget asked.

"We have nine months. Like a birth," she said. Marthe often liked to make what she said reverberate with suggestions of meaning. Marthe was what the French call a "*Soixante-huitarde*," a Sixty-eighter. She had believed at that heady moment in French history that it was forbidden to forbid. After the barricades of the streets of the Latin Quarter, Marthe had gravitated to the New Age. Jenny was being brought up as a vegetarian. But also, Hippolyte believed, with a lot of love.

"Does Jenny know?" he asked.

Jenny was in school as they spoke.

"I'll tell her when we have another place to settle."

"Ahh . . ."

Her tea was drawn. She poured some into the ceramic mugs she'd set out for both of them. He sniffed the potpourri of flavors as he lifted his mug. He would have liked a coffee, but the inscription on the tea package beside the spice bread told him that he would be rewarded with a sense of calm and well-being for drinking Morning Mist.

Perhaps the tea indeed helped him to say: "I am thinking of asking you for Jenny, Marthe."

She was calm. Marthe was always "cool" as the French say. She earned her living as a "relaxologist," teaching women with more knotted lives than hers how to breathe so as to become "cool." Marthe's life had followed conventions of nonconformism and been straightforward. Daughter of a notary in Rennes, she'd come to Paris to study anthropology, gotten caught up in the Situationist movement, a variant of Anarchism, and had a child by a fellow distributor of pamphlets who was now an organic artichoke grower in Brittany. That daughter, in her teens, had run away from what she, her even more radical self, had perceived as bourgeois habits, and had a child, in turn, by a burglar in the rough nightclub crowd she hung out in. That child was Jenny. Jenny's mother had never been heard

302

from since she had headed for Nice, with a more dedicated criminal than Hippolyte Suget.

Marthe lit a cigarette. Despite her New Age diet, Marthe had never given up smoking. Suget noticed the nicotine stains on her fingers and reminded himself that he had let his daughter be brought up by a woman who was a heavy smoker. For all her cool. It was not a detail in life. It was indicative. You don't bring up a child you truly love by smoking them up. You control yourself. And he had let this happen. Had ignored it. Yes, she did love Jenny, but just loving isn't enough. If she had brought up her own daughter, Suget thought, with the right sort of love, we would not be sitting here, the two of us, now.

Now of course the moment came for Hippolyte to blame his own careless life, and his decision to change it seemed much more urgent.

She said: "The two of you in your *studette*, and you working all night?"

"I will ask you for her when I'm settled otherwise. God willing" — he heard himself use that expression! — "it will be before you have to move."

"You're the father," Marthe said. "It was time you realized." She shrugged. Then she gave him a look that made her seem wise. He felt he had not made his decision a moment too soon.

Carmen was bending over a hole in the garden with tears in her eyes when Fatima arrived.

She turned to Fatima and was too upset even to say hello.

"*Oh là, là,* she ripped them out!" she said.

"What?"

"I raised them from stones!"

Fatima looked at her with curiosity.

"Madame Denis-Rabotin."

"She —?"

"She ripped out my avocado trees. They were that high!" Carmen raised her palm above her head. "I raised them from stones."

Fatima was shocked. "What could have made her do that?"

"Her light. They blocked the light in her bathroom. In her bathroom." She shook her head in anger. "*Oh là, là,* what good is it to be a concierge when they treat you like a dog?"

In the world Fatima wished to exist at that moment, Carmen was a landscape gardener with a retinue of laborers, one of whom was Angel, bending over weeds.

"You've come for the slip?" Carmen asked.

"Yes." Fatima felt a tinge of fearful anticipation.

"It's on my dresser."

The line at the post office was moving fast. Fatima stood nervously at the end of it when the dour young man, who was part of the flood of Romanians into Paris and who had appointed himself doorman for tips, allowed Madame Marchand to enter. He looked at the half-euro piece she'd just placed in his hand and then at her shapely rear in jeans, and the look on his face said his day had been made. Madame Marchand's expression, when she spied Fatima, was almost as joyful.

"Where have you been?"

Fatima thought that everyone in 34bis surely was aware that Rockababy had thrown her out.

"I'm still in the neighborhood, Madame."

"Well, that's wonderful! Listen —"

"Next, please," called one of the postal clerks. And then another. "Next, please." Fatima's turn at the desk was coming up soon.

The line indeed was advancing quickly ahead of them, and Madame Marchand felt she had no time for preambles. She whispered into Fatima's ear:

"A love potion."

Fatima's look said, "What?"

It showed impatience. She was nervous about what the slip waiting for her might forebode.

"I know what wonders you did for the dog."

Fatima could not help but laugh inside. She smiled at Madame Marchand. "Well, it's not quite the same thing."

Madame Marchand wrinkled her nose. "Maybe your friends up there —"

"My friends?"

"In the Goutte d'Or."

Fatima was noncommittal.

"I'm like you, Fatima," Madame Marchand insisted patronizingly, "I believe in magic. I believe that if you try at it, you can put magic into your life. I mean good magic."

"Next," the clerk called out from one of the counters.

"You'll do something? I can make it worth your while."

"It is not a thing that will work with money. I can make an inquiry."

"Next!" Madame Marchand kissed Fatima on the cheek and then she said, "Do you mind if I go ahead of you, I'm parked on the sidewalk."

But just then a second clerk called "Next!" and which of the two women would go first became a moot question.

The clerk who asked Fatima to produce a "piece of identity" when Fatima handed her the slip that said she'd received a registered letter made it sound like a challenge. She was a stern, snub-nosed Frenchwoman who seemed to know instinctively that the Arab in front of her was another of the many illegal immigrants. Fatima had come with her passport. The woman looked at it suspiciously, but the young man in a T-shirt at the counter beside her, who seemed far more pleasant, leaned over and insisted that it was a genuine "piece of identity."

Fatima walked away with her letter, and when the Romanian dramatically swept open the door for her, she handed him a twenty-cent coin, in the hope against hope that it would have a good effect — that in her other hand was not another piece of bad luck.

★ ★ ★

306

Victorine and Samuel went with Fatima to the office on the Quai de la Tournelle to give her moral support. They waited in the van while she stepped through the archway of a seventeenth-century building into the cobbled courtyard that led to the *"Etude de Maître Grégoire Larbresec."* Samuel had assured her that nothing bad could be waiting for her in the office of a *notaire*, but Fatima knew that *notaires* were officials, even though the law granted them their substantial private fees for legalizing real estate sales, marriage contracts, wills and the like, and for investing people's money. And she knew that her own situation was very unofficial.

Odile had lent her a business suit in flannel for the appointment. It itched, and the smell in it of Odile's heavy Guerlain perfume, redolent of tuberoses, which Fatima normally would have found delicious, was making her dizzy. The strains of Cheb Mami from the van died suddenly as the heavy oak door of the office closed behind her. Maître Larbresec, a little round man, too bald, too heavy for his age, which the skin of his pink face revealed to be surprisingly young — perhaps thirty-six — removed his wire-rimmed glasses with one hand and gave her a limp handshake with the other. He was so short that his suit jacket had the length almost of a topcoat, and its startlingly wide shoulders vastly exaggerated his own.

She saw Didi in the next room, smoking a cigarette and staring out the window. And now Rockababy passed in front of her with no greeting, her head down, as she entered the room with the desk, where Didi finally turned to notice Fatima with a smile. Larbresec put his hand on Fatima's back to coax her into the study with the others. He shot a glance at his Cartier watch. She sensed he was chary with his time. As he drew close, Fatima was now grateful for the perfume on the jacket she was wearing; it mitigated the man's sour breath.

The study was paneled in wood from floor to ceiling. There were drawers with handwritten yellow labels with letters of the alphabet on them and dates that went back to the 1920s. Obviously, Larbresec hadn't been here then. He'd inherited the *étude*, was guardian of pieces of life stories that he, too, would pass on someday to another person officially anointed for the role. Fatima read — glad once again that she could read now — a label that said "*affaire Poulais du Roc.*" It was on an oaktag file bound with a canvas belt on the table in the middle of the room. The belt was undone. Larbresec invited his three guests to sit down at the table, and with no further ado, he began to read from the file.

"I, Monique Poulais du Roc, *née* Belfroi de Murailles, on July 20, 1917, in Paris, daughter of Roger Belfroi de Murailles and his wife Mathilde, *née* Fitzgerald, and wife of the late Geoffroy Poulais du Roc, do hereby bequeath . . ."

The inventory of the Countess's fortune was complicated and long. Each corresponding paragraph of the will began, "in conformity with my obligation by law I —" and went on to spell out the particular form

308

of treasure that would now belong to Rockababy, who sat flushed with pleasure.

There was Branchevieille, the family castle. There were shares in a dozen blue-chip companies. There were acres and acres of forest in Alsace. There was a printing plant in the Jura, and a villa in Saint-Jean-Cap-Ferrat that hadn't been opened since Geoffroy Poulais du Roc had died.

After all this was enumerated, a new paragraph began:

"Having fulfilled my obligation by law regarding the portion of my fortune I must leave to my issue, and taking account, beyond that, what would have been the wishes of my late husband, I hereby detach my daughter from any interest in what remains. Namely: my wine cellar, which I bequeath with all its contents to my nephew, Didier Belfroi de Murailles, and from my remaining cash assets I also bequeath to Didier Belfroi de Murailles, a trust with a monthly income of four thousand euros, for life, which sum shall be doubled upon his marriage, which it is my sincere hope that he will enter into at last."

At that point, Rockababy frowned at Didi with one side of her mouth. Didi looked impassive, as a diplomat should under these circumstances. Fatima could not help but wave away the smoke from Séverine's cigarette that was reaching her from across the wide, polished table. At the head of the table, Larbresec mentally counted the cigarette butts in the ashtray in front of Rockababy and made a mental note to talk to her about her will.

309

At last Rockababy said something. "The jewelry?"

Larbresec handed her a key to a safe-deposit box. "It's simpler this way." He was helping her to beat some of the estate taxes and she gave him a smile of gratitude. He rubbed his hands with what seemed to her a note of finality.

"Well, what if anything did mother expect me to do for *her*?" she asked, as she looked disdainfully at Fatima and put her pack of cigarettes into her purse.

Larbresec started reading again. "And to my faithful employee Fatima Monsour, I bequeath a monthly income of ten thousand euros, which should serve in part for the care of my dog, Emma, and on the latter's decease, shall continue to be paid to Fatima, as she sees fit to dispose of it. And to house the said canine and herself, my apartment of 283 square meters, at 34bis avenue Victor-Hugo, fifth floor, right, Paris 75016, and all the furniture existing therein is hereby designated the property of Fatima Monsour, to be kept unsold for the life of the animal and to be disposed of freely thereafter as Fatima Monsour sees fit . . ."

"My God," Rockababy cried out, "she left the apartment to the stinky dog!"

"That's not how it reads, Madame," corrected Maître Larbresec. He sniffed and that made him catch Fatima's expensive Guerlain odor, and he gave Fatima, who had a tear in her green eye, a look of appreciation. Perhaps, he thought, once she got over her emotion, he should talk to her about her will.

"We have come to the conclusion," he said.

Larbresec poured himself a glass of water from the bottle of Vittel that had been set out on the table with glasses. His brow wrinkled at what remained of the text, which did not suit the language of a normal will.

"Dearest Fatima," he read, "thank you! It is because of your friendship that I came close to becoming a human being before I died."

At that point Didi's long years of diplomatic training abandoned him. He burst into laughter, ran around the table, grabbed Fatima out of her chair and hugged her.

"*Mazel Tov!*" he cried, too excited to know that he had gotten his languages mixed up, confusing what he'd learned during a brief appointment in Tel Aviv with the tongue he'd partly mastered in Aleppo.

Maître Larbresec concluded from this bizarre and apparently addled show of emotion that Didi might be older than he looked, and wondered whether he had drawn up a testament with anyone.

Outside, Samuel and Victorine heard a heavy door slam and suddenly spied Rockababy racing through the archway of the old building with her face red with rage. She slammed on her helmet, lit a cigarette, kick-started her motorcycle, and sped off across the sidewalk with a loud blare, nearly knocking over a father on rollerblades pushing a stroller. In a moment, Fatima came out with tears on her face. Her two friends looked at each other with expressions of dread. Neither could muster the courage to ask her what once again had gone wrong in her life, as she stepped mutely into the van. Samuel did not dare turn on his cassette player.

They drove in a silence that made Victorine fidget until, as the van rounded the Arc de Triomphe, Fatima at last felt moved to speak. Wiping away the tears that still flowed over the memory of her late friend, she explained that she at last had a reason to be happy in her life.

Samuel popped Cheb Mami into his player, and by the time they arrived at 34bis, they were all three singing "Meli, Meli."

CHAPTER
FIVE

A month had passed when, on a Saturday evening, Angel was distracted from the Paris–Saint Germain vs Saint Etienne soccer match on the TV by a series of visitors buzzing their way into the building. He'd closed his curtains and taken the second half of the day off from his duties as concierge, as was his right on Saturday, but curiosity finally prodded him to draw back the curtains.

First he saw the Africans, the handyman who'd worked on the electricity, wearing a suit and tie, a woman, apparently his wife, in a brilliantly colored boubou, with an infant strapped on her back and four little neatly dressed children in tow. With them was the big laughing woman, the African who had helped the Arab woman from upstairs serve at the Countess's wake. She had on another bright dress of their sort, with a picture of a black statesman on her stomach. Afterward there arrived a Frenchwoman with bad posture but plainly bourgeois in a knit suit, her hair meticulously swept up and lacquered. She was a stranger in the building. Angel had the right to ask her who she was, although his Saturday time of repose relieved him of the duty. He turned the matter over in his head and let Madame Benamou-Kahn go by without his asking, intimidated by her obvious class. Soon there was a veritable flood of strangers. There were the impeccable Strasbourgs accompanied by Ginette and her husband, Maxime, the long-haul truck driver, both dressed as if for church. Monsieur and Madame Richard appeared soon afterward, and Clément the pinball aficionado, who came accompanied by Elodie Couteau, the retired chambermaid at the Ritz. She carried a big bouquet of gladioli. Everyone else was carrying a package that obviously was a gift.

Angel was piqued to see Pedro, the concierge of the building of L'Ecrivain across the street, step through the doorway with his wife, Consuelo, both in their Sunday best. Angel and Pedro, having opposing interpretations of the Spanish Civil War, did not speak. Angel felt an impulse to confront the old Anarchist and ask his business on Angel's turf, but by then things seemed to be getting even further away from the natural order in 34bis, for, lo, the whole sixth floor — including the Filipinos, the German girl, the African student, and the artistic American — had poured down the back stairway and was crossing the garden and boarding the elevator that would take them into the co-owners' quarters.

"Carmen!" Angel shouted to his wife, who had been fussing behind the curtain that defined their sleeping quarters, "*C'est la pagaille!*" Which meant that, in Angel's scheme of things, total disorder had erupted at 34bis avenue Victor-Hugo. His wife stepped out from behind the curtain in her best dress. She had on

314

lipstick. He made a move to bar the door. Her dark eyes flashed. He inhaled a free sample of scent he'd got at the Espace Bonprix and had given her, years ago. She had one hand behind her back, and for an instant Angel, looking into her eyes, thought she might have picked up the knife they used to cut chorizo.

"You can stay if you like," she said. "I'm going."

What had happened to his wife? He hadn't seen her put on a new kind of courage — beyond endurance — in the mirror, together with the scent and the lipstick. Carmen walked past her husband out into the hall toward the elevator. He pretended not to notice the lovely potted orchid in her hand behind her back as he slumped into his lounge chair and turned up the volume on the game. After a moment, the buzzer of the door to the building sounded again. Too much! Angel raced out, ready finally to confront the latest intruder.

It was Didi, with a gift-wrapped box under one arm and Jocelyne Fontaine on the other. Angel bowed faintly and slinked back into the *loge*.

He knew where this great jumble of people was going and there was nothing he could do about it. The world was in disorder. It had lost all sense of rank and decorum, ever since global decadence had begun with the excruciating death throes of *el Caudillo*, the last great leader of the civilized world. As he reentered his *loge*, he caught the mouthwatering odor of spicy food and the languorous chanting of Oum Kalsoum, the legendary Arab Barbara Streisand, reaching him all the way from the fifth floor. His senses were sorely

315

tempted, as they often were in a different way on other occasions on the avenue Foch. He sank into his chair and saw a band of white and brown athletes in short pants hug and kiss each other on his TV screen. With all else, Angel had missed the last portion of the match.

By the time Carmen arrived at Fatima's apartment, all the co-owners were there as well. Victorine was greeting everyone, distributing her welcoming chuckles without regard to rank or degree of intimacy. Where, though, was Fatima, our hostess?

She was in her bedroom, which had been the Countess's, consoling Emma, who had squeezed herself under an old armoire, hoping she would be invisible. The murmur of so many human voices intimidated the venerable dog.

"Come out and I'll give you a brochette." Under the armoire, Emma, having been spoiled more than once by Fatima's lamb kebobs, pricked up her ears at the word "brochette."

"They're just people," Fatima said. The dog hesitated.

"A big brochette," insisted Fatima.

Emma stirred. She scrambled out. And now Fatima had no excuse of her own not to be out there with the people. Truth to tell, she, too, was intimidated. Would her party go over? It was an event that seemed necessary to her by the rules of civilization, as she knew them. No one she'd grown up among would think of taking over a new place to live without opening it to everyone around her for a feast. But she was a long way from Batouine, among people whose minds and hearts were conditioned by different histories from hers.

There was a knock on the bedroom door. She heard Hadley:

"Fatima, for God's sake."

She looked at herself in the long mirror, at her once-foreign knit suit. Well, that's me, the mirror told her. Pounds lighter than she once was, younger-looking. The mirror doesn't lie, whatever fears you may have, and if God may be responsible for our fortune, he's left us the chance, nonetheless, to assume it and help it along. Hadn't she told so many people that? "They're only people," she heard herself saying, in her head. She stepped out into the living room, with Emma nuzzling her leg. And everyone looked her way.

Hadley surveyed the array of guests and, already a little tipsy, raised his glass first to her and then to the entire crowd, delighted, in the way that people who are a little high can overflow with sentiment toward the human race in general. For, revolving and coalescing in the buzz of this room were spheres of Paris life that almost never come together. His eyes fell upon the two little Filipino girls, Maria Luisa and Imelda, talking with glasses in their hands to the overdressed Madame Roumatova and Clément, and he knew that the sixth floor is as far away as another planet from the five floors below it in a Sixteenth Arrondissement apartment building, as are the socially peripheral figures of the Café Jean Valjean from the established inhabitants of the address next door. But he realized that much of what he loved about Paris, that made it a great, vibrant city, was that life here was always an adventure, always in flux, and that someone with the force of Fatima could draw the currents together. A more prosaic conclusion came to him with a chuckle: All his experience told him that this was also a city of *pique-assiettes*, which translates to mean that a Parisian of any stripe will go anywhere there's good free food.

The guests had nonetheless come with gifts. The Denis-Rabotins had found a silver-plated ice bucket at a greatly reduced price in the Pier Import store of the Gallery Saint Didier nearby. Admiral Paumier d'Aurange and his wife came with a hand-painted copy of Vermeer's *Girl with a Pearl Earring*, which they'd bought across from the Louvre. "It's your portrait, Madame," said the admiral, gallantly, while his wife threw him a glance that said, "Don't get carried away." The entire sixth floor had chipped in to buy Fatima a television set. (The Countess had never wanted one.) Didi brought a book of nineteenth-century illuminations of the Koran. The Russians from the third floor brought vodka and a kilo can of osetra caviar, which Victorine immediately set out in the buffet of delicacies and which was nearly as quickly devoured.

They drank vodka and champagne, ate caviar and pigeon pie, couscous and sweet cakes, and soon, with the rugs rolled up in the living room, people were dancing while Samuel, with a panoply of CDs from all over the planet, played at being a disc jockey.

Fatima stood flushed, as people danced by her. She saw Madame Marchand, the Romantic Pharmacist, nod at her from the buffet as she entwined her arm on the arm of the tall dark man she'd brought with her. The potion from the Goutte d'Or seemed to have worked. Another set of lives in orbit.

The music stopped. Samuel took a break and a glass of vodka. At that moment Monsieur Robert, visibly under the domination of champagne, was chatting up Maître Odile Benamou-Kahn. It seemed that he had once had her daughter as a student for his piano lessons. Time had flown, they agreed. After that, they got on to the subject of music, and discovered they shared a passion for the Romantics. Odile found a pencil and paper in her purse and wrote down the name of the travel agent who specialized in music cruises. Monsieur Robert tucked the paper in his wallet. His face had taken on a glow.

A glass of champagne later, Monsieur Robert came up to Fatima and seized her hand with an urgency that took her aback. He murmured something. It sounded like, "I am sorry. Forgive me. The roof . . ." But Fatima did not understand him. She let him hold her hand a moment and he bowed his head as if he'd been shrived, as if exculpation had passed through his fingers. Suddenly, he squared his shoulders and walked to the piano, unsteadily, still holding a glass of champagne. He sat down and he played. He began to play a lied by Schubert, and then he gargled a few notes, gulped his champagne with a gesture that made Monsieur Roumatova of the third floor respond immediately in the same way. Madame Roumatova caught his hand just as her husband seemed about to dash his glass, Russian-style, onto the parquet floor. Others emptied their glasses, too, more timidly, but with an air of consecration. It was a moment, Carmen perceived, of *duende*. The arid Monsieur Robert, sodden now with champagne, had passed — as he began to sing Théophile Gautier's words for Berlioz — beyond inebriation to a solemn realm where he was inhabited by fire.

Monsieur Robert was singing while Victorine tiptoed about the room, topping up everyone's glass. The Admiral's dignified wife, who felt she'd had too much already, wasn't quick enough to cover her glass with her hand, so that Victorine poured through her fingers. When Victorine moved on, she shrugged and licked the champagne off her hand. And drank again.

Fatima went back into the kitchen where Samuel was popping another cork and Emma was gnawing a lamb bone, having had her ration of brochettes. As she arranged another tray of sweets, Fatima could hear Monsieur Robert's *haute-contre* voice soaring:

> Comme une fleur, loin du soleil,
> La fleur de ma vie est fermée
> Loin de ton sourire vermeil . . .

Coming out into the living room again, Fatima saw Madame the Admiral sighing. Fatima was fearful that she was unwell, but as she came up to her, Madame Paumier d'Aurange explained through tears that no one had heard Monsieur Robert's soft voice echoing through 34bis since the week he buried his poor wife, Céleste. Looking into the woman's swimming eyes,

320

Fatima decided it was definitely time to bring out the mint tea.

Fatima's presents lay now in a pile near the piano. She had opened all of them when Hadley came up to her with the box he'd hidden in the kitchen. She unwrapped it and threw her arms around him.

"Hadley, this is too much," she insisted, "you need this for yourself, not for me!"

"I'm of the old southern school of literature," he said, "I write with a pen."

She lifted the lid of the laptop computer.

"You're what's new, Fatima. You'll show me how to do the Internet, once in a while. But don't get me hooked on it."

She grabbed him and kissed his cheek.

"You'll write a book. About everyone here," he said. His eyes swept the room, where the conversation had reached the sensual purr you hear in a good Paris restaurant when people have eaten and drunk well. "You've got everyone's number, Fatima dear."

"I can't write a book, Hadley, but I'm happy that I'll be able to read yours."

He put his hand on his heart. "*Inshallah*," he said.

He frowned now as his eyes made an inventory of the salon. "It's all quite lovely," he said.

She flushed.

"Fatima?"

He saw her look go distant.

"Fatima, are we both thinking about what's missing?"

She lowered her eyes.

"A parrot, for God's sake."

Now she looked up. One of those moments now occurred, when all of a life seems to hang in the balance. Would she come to a decision? She knew and he knew what was missing. And after a long moment, she placed the computer in his hands, kissed him again on the cheek.

Hadley was suddenly overcome by the awareness that a great piece was missing in his own life and he swallowed hard. And that moment of thinking about himself, on whom he had not yet given up, when it came to the matter of fulfillment, kept him from turning to see that Fatima had stepped into the kitchen and slipped out the back door.

The lobby of the Villa Saint Valentin was like no place Fatima had ever seen before. Everything was red. The embossed fabric on the walls, the plush sofas and chairs, the carpeting even. In the middle of all this — which made Fatima think that like the man in the Bible, she'd entered the entrails of some mythic monster — an elaborate chandelier hung from the ceiling, with lightbulbs mounted on it in the shape of flames. But the bulbs had not been turned on. The room was quite dark. Fatima lowered her eyes when she spotted the long painting above the reception desk. It was of a nude woman lying on a couch, with her rear facing the observer.

Music rustled gently. The low strains of a tango. And then, as she stood there not knowing if she could take a step further into this room, Frank Sinatra began to sing:

"Strangers in the night . . ."

She hadn't counted so much on his need to be rescued, but there it was. From this place. She advanced, her determination enriched by that sense of mission.

She made out a figure sitting at the reception desk in the dim light with his back turned, typing into a computer. His rounded back seemed pathetic. His back was still turned, when he heard her moving over the thick red carpet.

"You're expecting someone? You're the sweetpea room?"

"Monsieur Suget?" Her eyes swam. She was too nervous even to hear that it wasn't his voice.

He wheeled around in his chair and saw her. A man of no more than twenty-five with a plump smooth face.

"Suget's gone," he said.

The natural, outdoor darkness of night felt like a relief as she hurried into the street. She breathed hard. She breathed even harder, a short while later, as she hurried up the six flights of stairs to his *studette*. She held her breath as she knocked.

There was a long moment of silence until she heard him opening his lock.

"You asked me something," she said.

His room was full of cartons. He had been packing, and he stood there with his "Hippolyte" and "Jennifer" bowls in his hands.

"I didn't mean to offend you," he finally said. "Could you ever forget what I said?"

"Ask me again."

They say that when people are drowning, their whole lives reel before them in their mind. This moment seemed to Hippolyte like that, a moment as crucial as dying, when he might just expire right there of grief, if what came next made grief happen. And so he saw a little boy in dancing tights doing a backward pirouette, felt a pain race through his back again as his spine twisted; he saw himself in a hospital bed and then in a prison cell. He saw himself in an elegant strange apartment with a lamp in his hand and men in blue rushing into the room. It all came back in a jumble. He swallowed and could not say anything, not the words that could create what would be next in his life. The possibility of disappointment frightened him so much.

The bridge that joined the two of them at that moment was that same phenomenon of recall, which at the same time placed them far apart. Fatima saw, in the silence, a ferry pulling away, Mahmoud smoking a cigarette on the deck, his head already elsewhere, no longer looking her way. She saw mounds of used sheets at the Club Rêve, and for an instant she was at Branchevieille reading Flaubert, a foreign story to a foreign woman. But reading! And what would all this itinerary of her life mean at present, all her good fortune, to be shared with just a dog and not the person who mattered, whose heavy, distressed breathing she could hear now.

She reached out and touched his hand lightly. *Stop. Stop and listen*. He looked, awkward, at his bowls, and set them down on his dresser.

"Why," she dared, "why can't you?"

"Because it's better not to know."

"What?"

"It's better not to know it is impossible."

All the same he couldn't accept despair. *Maybe if she gave him time. He was trying now. Trying to be new.* "The thing is: I don't know if I ever could be worthy," he said.

"Ah, Hippolyte," she said. "Ask me, please, now."

He still wanted to plead for time, but she'd pinned him down, and the risk was that he might never see her again if he did not take his step now. For a moment, time seemed to stand still once more and neither said anything.

Finally she said, "You asked me to marry you. I will."

Just like that, she saved him.

Stunned, he blurted: "Fatima, I promise. I will make myself worthy."

"And I want Jenny," she was about to say, but by then she had taken another step, and across the gap of centuries, of conventions that had become oceans of separation, or whatever, she'd thrown her arms around his neck and planted a kiss on his mouth — while the wraiths of all the women who'd died obscure and meek, subjugated and veiled in this world might have been applauding from wherever angels get together.

They stood there, kissing hard, for what seemed longer than the time it takes to drown, until Madame

Lefranc passed the open door and coughed. Then Suget, without removing his lips from Fatima's, reached out and shut the door.

As Madame Lefranc continued on the way to her own *studette*, from behind her back, she heard a parrot whistle.

Epilogue

Time flows, and some things stand and some get swept away, but no story ever ends. If, a few months ago, you'd passed the Café Jean Valjean on the avenue Victor-Hugo at about eleven at night, you would have seen Monsieur and Madame Richard sitting down, alone, with most of the lights off and the chairs piled on the tables, to the well-earned dinner that Nelson had left them to heat. As you would have seen them, night after night, doing the same thing after closing, for years on end. But after that evening, you would have seen them no more. Monsieur and Madame Richard were tired — no one had ever seen either of them sit down while the café was open, and Madame Richard had never stopped pining for their village of Bonval-en-Saire in the soft hills of the Aveyron. It was time for them to go home. Nelson was relieved that he would not have to tell them he was quitting. Béatrice was pregnant, and while having their own restaurant was still his important goal, what they needed now was more money. Nelson had been approached through a countryman about a job assisting a major culinary star at the Hôtel Plaza-Athénée.

By then, the life of the Café Jean Valjean had begun to dissolve. The change began one day when Elodie Couteau passed the real estate office of Thibault and Louis-Paul and saw a sign on the door of the emptied boutique that said that Elite Placements had moved to the rue de l'Université in the Seventh Arrondissement. Clément complained out loud about what the others had all taken silently to heart: The two had never even come into the Jean Valjean to say good-bye. And that abrupt departure was felt like a betrayal, or rather it cast doubt on the worth of their little community. Elodie Couteau pointed out that Thibault and Louis-Paul, whose last names no one knew, had never quite been part of the group. They drank their coffee quickly at the bar before hurrying to the rest of their lives. Her years at the Ritz had made her very sensitive to class distinctions, but she did not see fit to shake anyone's esteem for the Jean Valjean further by suggesting that the pair had always been present from on high. In any case, the change wrought by their absence drew attention to the place in everyone's minds. It made them think consciously of where and who they were.

One morning, soon afterward, Madame Strasbourg returned from Jacky Internationale with her silver-gray hair turned blonde. Elodie Couteau overheard her telling Monsieur Strasbourg, "Maurice, we need a new life." On her instructions, Maurice, who could deny his wife nothing, sold the cabin cruiser he kept near their apartment in Cannes and bought a Beneteau 411 Ocean Clipper. A month later, the Richards got a postcard from the Strasbourgs on the Turkish coast. "We have a new life," they wrote. That week, Clément had to make the grave decision of giving up his unemployment checks and his ambition to set pinball records because he had been offered a job with an engineering consulting firm. He went to work in the maze of high-rises at La Défense and was not seen again in the neighborhood. When Ginette, suffering from varicose veins, took retirement shortly afterward, the Richards knew the clock was ticking loudly.

That same week Elodie Couteau had passed the window of a bookshop and discovered the picture of the chicken-chested, silent, and dour young man, "Raskolnikov," on the back page of a book. The rave review from Le Figaro Littéraire in the window described a comic novel about a serial killer who spent his free time in an old-fashioned café very much like the Jean Valjean. The book, published by the blockbuster house Laffont, turned out to be a best-seller. Raskolnikov, better known now by his real name, Xavier Coutume, stopped coming to the Jean Valjean, but he has been seen regularly autographing copies of his book over lunch across the street at L'Ecrivain.

At about the same time that Raskolnikov's CRIME WITHOUT PUNISHMENT hit the best-seller list, the American who had given him his nickname, who sometimes liked to come to the Jean Valjean for a five-o'clock pick-me-up, inherited a considerable fortune on the death of a distant spinster cousin in Mississippi. Hadley then founded a literary magazine to promote the work of a new breed of American writers in Paris, and he now spends his days at his office near the Gare du Nord.

Of course, Fatima had stopped coming for the morning cup of take-out espresso. And she had not had much time to stop in socially. She had her duties as the new chairman of the co-owners' association of 34bis avenue Victor-Hugo to attend to. She was regularly seen with her dog, however, taking her daughter, Jennifer, back and forth to the private school Les Oiseaux on the avenue Raymond Poincaré, attended by all the privileged children of the neighborhood. Her husband, Hippolyte Suget, had also stopped coming to the Jean Valjean since he'd left his job at the Villa Saint Valentin. Suget had been hired to manage a new boutique hotel, designed by Philippe Schwach. The owner is a young Englishwoman who'd cashed in her fashion site at the height of the nineties Internet craze and gone into trendy little hotels. Noted for her intuition, she no more than looked at Hippolyte Suget before she said: "He's right. He's both romantic and edgy." Suget was since photographed at his desk by *Condé Nast Traveler*, which classed his new place of employment among the world's "hot hotels" of the year. The caption mentions a bar where guests feed peanuts to the resident parrot.

Suget hired Elodie Couteau, who was bored with retirement, to oversee the chambermaids. So soon she, too, was gone from the charmed circle of the Café Jean Valjean.

330

And now the Jean Valjean exists no more. The young new owners closed it for three months, during which it was totally *"relooké"* in brown leather and black wood and stylishly renamed "Paragraf." There is a corner with bookshelves, among which you will find the complete works of Victor Hugo, and overstuffed leather club chairs. It is really quite a comfortable place to enjoy an excellent Italian coffee, or some sushi for lunch.

We are having a very hot, dry summer in Paris. The Parisians have been warned to save water, as a drought is quite possible, but Parisians are not notably disciplined, and if, for example, you were to pass 34bis avenue Victor-Hugo at any time of night or day, you would see the automatic sprinkling system of the micro-jungle of ferns and flowers that crowds Madame Marchand's balcony sending liters of water down into the street. The street sweepers, despite orders to the contrary, still open the taps every morning that create streams along the curbs, where they swish away the refuse with their long brooms topped with green plastic imitation twigs.

But the Seine doesn't look distressed. Even though it seems to flow more slowly than usual as it makes its way, flashing streaks of light, in a great loop through the city. Past the stone Zouave, whose feet are now quite dry, past the little Statue of Liberty on its tiny island, on out toward the white cliffs at the beginning of Normandy. And from there into its estuary at Tancarville, which leads into the English Channel. At

331

the île de Ouessant across from Land's End, the Channel joins the Atlantic Ocean, which churns across a good portion of the earth, invisibly in tow with swirling celestial bodies, on whose surface, as Flaubert's two odd gentlemen speculated, there are no doubt creatures such as on earth, who finagle and fight and depose kings, and who, we might add, are probably quite lonely together, until some of them, with luck, fall happily in love.